T0012478

The Sirens
of Soleil City

THE Sirens
of Soleil City

A NOVEL

Sarah C. Johns

RANDOM HOUSE
NEW YORK

The Sirens of Soleil City is a work of fiction. Names, characters, places, and incidents are the products of the author's imagination or are used fictitiously. Any resemblance to actual events, locales, or persons, living or dead, is entirely coincidental.

A Random House Trade Paperback Original

Copyright © 2024 by Sarah C. Johns

All rights reserved.

Published in the United States by Random House, an imprint and division of Penguin Random House LLC, New York.

RANDOM HOUSE and the HOUSE colophon are registered trademarks of Penguin Random House LLC.

LIBRARY OF CONGRESS CATALOGING-IN-PUBLICATION DATA
Names: Johns, Sarah (Sarah C.), author.
Title: The sirens of Soleil City : a novel / Sarah Johns.
Description: First edition. | New York : Random House, 2024.
Identifiers: LCCN 2023036313 (print) | LCCN 2023036314 (ebook) |
ISBN 9780593730485 (trade paperback; acid-free paper) |
ISBN 9780593730492 (ebook)
Subjects: LCGFT: Novels.
Classification: LCC PS3610.O297 S57 2024 (print) |
LCC PS3610.O297 (ebook) | DDC 813/.6—dc23/eng/20231106
LC record available at https://lccn.loc.gov/2023036313
LC ebook record available at https://lccn.loc.gov/2023036314

Printed in the United States of America on acid-free paper

randomhousebooks.com

2 4 6 8 9 7 5 3 1

FIRST EDITION

Book design by Ralph Fowler
Illustration by shopplaywood, stock.adobe.com

For my mom

West Palm Beach, Florida

FEBRUARY 17, 1999

CHAPTER I

24 Days

CHERIE

Seventeen hours after arriving in West Palm Beach, Cherie was already wondering how soon she could leave.

She pressed the piece of concrete that she held into her hand, having picked it up from the ground after it fell from the building and hit her on the head as she left her mother's apartment to go to the pool. Cherie looked at the balcony railing on an apartment across from where she sat, dangling her legs in the water. Two potted plants blocked the gaping hole left by missing balusters; duct tape held the remaining six in place.

Oh, Florida, Cherie thought. So slapdash and sketchy and yet also so *sunny.* Cherie turned her face toward the sky to feel the warmth. This might keep her in West Palm Beach a few extra days, away from the frozen tundra of Minnesota in February. She splashed her feet in the pool, the gorgeous pool. The four aging concrete buildings of Cherie's mother's senior apartment complex looked like they might be pushed over by a light breeze, but the pool at its center looked like it had been dropped into place straight from a Florida tourism ad—an ad that showed a Florida that could exist only in the minds of people who had never actually been to Florida before.

How had a pool like that—Olympic-sized and sparkling clean, surrounded by tropical flowers, pristine lounge chairs, and unblemished tile—ended up in a place like this? It should have been in the fancy new senior complex down the street with its terrazzo tile and grass cloth–covered walls, not in this place filled with residents surviving on Social Security and the occasional largesse of family.

"Our landlord forgets to fix the broken laundry-room window and doesn't repaint the lines in the parking lot, leading to absolute chaos, but we do get this gorgeous hole to splash around in," a small woman with bleached blond hair and overplucked eyebrows said to Cherie as she sat down beside her, letting her own veined legs fall into the water. "Welcome to Soleil City. I'm Evelyn," the woman said, offering her hand. Cherie took it. "You're Dale's kid."

Cherie nodded. Dale was her mother, even if Cherie wasn't entirely sure how to tell anyone what that actually meant. At Cherie's daughter's spring wedding almost three years ago, the wedding that had supplied enough monogrammed cocktail napkins to last a lifetime, Dale had introduced herself to one of Cherie's friends as the secondary mother. *Secondary mother.* Was this the term Cherie had been trying to find to describe Dale for the last five decades of her life?

"Marlys is Cherie's primary mother," Dale said, grabbing a mini crab cake off a silver tray as it passed during the wedding's cocktail hour. "Marlys took Ed, Cherie's dad and my first husband, from me—they're not here because Ed is busy dying—but I guess it worked out because Marlys and Ed have been married nearly fifty years and I had five more husbands. Anyway, Marlys got the husband and the child and did a much better job with both of them than I ever could, and not just because I was a goddamned teenager when Cherie was born. So, she's Mom. I'm Dale. My place is more around the edges. Just to be clear."

It wasn't clear to Cherie's friend, of course. It still wasn't entirely clear to Tom, Cherie's husband of thirty years, who flinched each time he heard Cherie refer to the woman who gave birth to her by her first name. But it was clear to Cherie. Dale's husband left her for Marlys, then Dale left them all and ran away to Mexico, not seeing her daughter for almost five years, and only briefly when she finally did. Marlys stayed. Marlys was her mom.

Marlys had been the one to tell Cherie that there was a threat to tear down Dale's apartment complex and throw all the residents to the wind. It's how it had always been. Dale would tell Cherie all the good things and tell Marlys all the real things. Cherie would hear about how Dale had seen Audrey Hepburn walking down Fifth Avenue in the summer of 1956 and then Marlys would hear about how Dale had left her fourth husband after only twenty-five days of marriage.

In the nearly two years since Dale had moved less than three miles away from Marlys in West Palm Beach, a fact that still surprised and confused Cherie, the updates had come more frequently and become less newsworthy. Dale wouldn't eat the crusts on her chicken salad sandwiches. Dale liked to sing "Fever" by Peggy Lee, complete with hip thrusts, when she went out to karaoke with her friends from Soleil City—the friends that seemed to take up most of her time. Last month, Dale had negotiated a better contract with the ice vendor as part of her role on the complex's leadership council, which was important because that lot could *drink*.

For both Marlys and Cherie, Dale remained something of an enigma that fascinated and repelled them. A mother and a mother-maker. She lived a life in cities they had only visited, had marriages to men they had never known. Dale told them a little and let them imagine twice as much.

Now, according to Marlys, Dale was in trouble. What did that mean? When Cherie's dad was dying, her mom would say things like "he had a rough night," which Cherie would later find out meant that he had "coded"—his heart had stopped beating—before he was successfully revived. Was there something she wasn't being told? A secondary mother is still a mother. Cherie called her travel agency the moment it opened the next morning and bought a one-way ticket to find out for herself.

It was Tom, Cherie's lawyer husband, who Marlys had initially requested. "Dale needs Tom's help. She might lose her apartment. She doesn't really have anywhere else to go." Cherie remembers her anger at the suggestion. Sure, Tom could handle whatever legal thing they needed. But Cherie could solve problems. Cherie solved problems all the damn time. How hard could this be? Dale needed a new apartment; Cherie could spend a few days in Florida finding her a new apartment. Maybe Dale wouldn't be able to lounge by the pool with the same group of women every day, but was that such a big deal? She just needed a place to live.

Cherie's first surprise upon arriving in West Palm Beach was that Marlys had been right. Dale really didn't have anywhere else to go. Dale was broke. Her apartment was practically bare. She didn't have a coffee table in front of her couch. She had an old, folding TV table that had clearly been a garage sale special. She had borrowed a camp bed for Cherie to use from her neighbor, covering it with a jumble of old sheets from different, incomplete sets. She was watering down her shampoo to make it last longer. True, Dale was a child of the Depression, but she had never before acted like one. This wasn't habit born of early childhood trauma. This was poverty.

"So you've heard about how the Jackass—"

"The Jackass being your landlord," Cherie interrupted to clarify.

Evelyn nodded. "The guy who wants to tear this place down and start all over again," Evelyn said. "Little pipsqueak. The man can't be more than thirty-five. But he's seen the high-rises they've built in Miami and that goddamned fancy Hawthorne Haven complex down the street."

"Oh, I'm familiar with Hawthorne Haven. Quite a security apparatus they've got over there. Very . . . active," Cherie said, rubbing the ankle she had twisted the night before.

After unpacking her toiletries in the small bathroom she and her mother would share—"That's a hell of a lot of moisturizing you're doing there, Cher," Dale said, as Cherie lined up all six bottles on the back of the toilet for lack of space—her mother offered to provide dinner. *Provide.* That word alone should have served as something of a warning as to what was to come.

After eating criminally under-seasoned grilled chicken breasts in Hawthorne's dining room—there was an unused grand piano in the corner—Dale shoved the check in her purse with a wink and pulled Cherie through the kitchen into a long dark hall. As Cherie realized she had just participated in petty theft, a large security guard suddenly appeared, yelling at them to stop as Dale broke into a sprint, Cherie following closely behind.

Evelyn smiled. "Dale used the magic exit, right? She parked on the far-right side and pulled away before they even realized you were both out the door?"

"We stole our dinner correctly, yes."

Once in the car, Cherie rubbed the ankle she had slightly twisted—Dale could have at least warned her not to wear heels—then rolled down the window for fresh air before turning to her mother.

"Did we have to do that, Dale?"

Dale laughed. "Oh, darling. Things aren't that bleak. We did that because we could do it. And because we should. Before Hawthorne came in, Soleil City was fine. Now, we aren't enough. So screw 'em. Plus, wasn't it just a little bit fun?"

Evelyn waved away Cherie's concerns about the theft. "A victimless crime. Those rich bastards over there will never miss it. Do you know what they charge for a simple one-bedroom?"

"No, what?"

"I don't know, actually. But a hell of a lot. Way too much. So we take a free meal every now and then. Nobody's getting hurt."

Cherie kept her hand on her ankle, then remembered the small gash on her head from the concrete that had hit her moments before and checked to make sure it wasn't bleeding. "Sure."

"My point is that this place isn't Hawthorne. Not even close. But the Jackass thinks it should be. Then what the hell are we supposed to do? None of us is made of money. We don't need lifeguards and bartenders and waitstaff and programming and *amenities*. Well, I'd take a few strapping lifeguards. But otherwise, I don't want all that. I want this. I want to be left alone to do whatever the hell I want to do all day. I don't want some program director who speaks to me like I'm a child telling me to keep active. Fuck off and let me read my gossip rag in the sun," Evelyn said with satisfaction. "Pardon my language."

"Oh," Cherie said, and waved away the suggestion that she might take offense at a four-letter word. She dipped her hand in the pool and put the cold water against the back of her neck. If Cherie's arthritic fingers were to be believed, the morning's light humidity was nothing compared to the fug that would soon envelop them. She had left Minneapolis in a snowstorm after a blast of arctic air had kept her inside for the last few days, a brief hibernation she had quietly welcomed.

"If it weren't two degrees here, would you still be going?" her husband asked, uncomfortable with the one-way ticket his wife held.

"Tom, honestly. I'll only be gone a few days."

Cherie had to give her mothers a few days. For two years, since her dad had died, she'd had a break. Cherie had done only light daughtering, calling Marlys nearly every day, providing some financial help. Dale, as usual, didn't ask for a thing.

Since her elder daughter, Laura, got married and her younger daughter Jessica's band had gotten increasingly successful, Cherie had only done light mothering. They were living their own lives, Laura asking for a little bit more, Jessica asking for nothing at all. For the first time almost since their births, Cherie could go hours without thinking of either girl until she'd pass Laura's old bedroom or see the small crack in the vase that Jessica had once knocked over, and she'd chide herself for pushing them too far off to the side.

This was just a lull. Cherie knew the stillness would end. Laura was pregnant; in less than three months Cherie would be a grandmother whose level of involvement in her grandchild's life, her daughter had already made clear, would be high. Her mothers, who spent decades smoking like chimneys and drinking like fish, were bound to need more care. The call was always going to come. Now, it had.

Dale took care of herself. She had always taken care of herself. When Dale picked Cherie up at the airport, Cherie saw that her mother had barely changed, even though almost three years had passed since they had last seen each other at Laura's wedding. Dale, a woman who had been generously described as handsome and practically described as distinctive, wore a heavy cotton caftan-style dress with contrasting thread, designed and sewn by Dale herself. Around her neck was a chunky amber necklace, and she wore coordinating amber earrings that pulled just slightly on her earlobes. On her feet were a pair of ancient leather Mexican sandals. Her short hair had been colored blond and she wore a new shade of foundation that was thick but blended well. Her rose-pink lipstick—not nearly as bold as the red that had been her signature for decades—was on lips that had loosened their smoker's pucker since she quit a year and a half earlier. Marlys's renowned beauty had faded but Dale's sense of style remained strong. She looked the way she had always looked.

That is why Cherie was so shocked when Dale opened the door to her barren apartment with the concrete crumbling around the door frame. For four years in the mid-eighties when Dale was the lead women's buyer for Marshall Field's department store in Chicago and Cherie brought her daughters to visit from Minneapolis during their school break each October, Dale, Cherie, and her daughters had a real relationship, and witnessed Dale living a high-style life. They had developed traditions, like eating the deep-dish pizza that her daughters loved (but Dale and Cherie couldn't stand) each Saturday night after a full day of shopping at Dale's department store. They made memories, like going to the Sharper Image store in Water Tower Place on Michigan Avenue, the girls squishing together in the massage chair as Jessica announced for all to hear that she was "experiencing bliss" as Cherie and Dale doubled over with laughter.

Dale seemed to have it all. When Cherie first walked through the door of that apartment on the seventy-second floor of the John Hancock building, giving her views of both the Navy Pier and Lake Michigan, her jaw dropped. "Is Grandma rich?" Laura had asked. Cherie looked to Dale for her response. "No, dear. Not rich. But someone finally realized I might just know what the hell I'm doing and paid me accordingly."

Dale was being paid enough that if she had lived modestly and saved the rest, she could have had options when she was fired from her job at Marshall Field's after she fell down a flight of stairs after fainting because she forgot to eat during a busy eleven-hour day. Her male superiors said that it was her age. At sixty-two, the stress of daily work had clearly become too much. Wouldn't she be happier if she retired a little early?

But she hadn't lived modestly. She had bought a 1979 Lincoln Continental special edition sedan with Gucci leather interior, even though she rarely left the city and only took cabs when she was in it. She paid nearly half her salary to rent that apartment, because why the hell not? Cherie called Dale a couple of times after she lost her job, asking her what she planned to do next. Dale would joke about putting Grandma Moses in her place, becoming the next famous old-lady painter, and insist, always, that she was fine. Just fine. Until she called Cherie on her birthday. Dale told her how she had moved to Phoenix and was working at a small chain of women's stores. "Oh, that's wonderful," Cherie had said. "I'm so glad someone else realized what a terrific buyer you are." Dale said the next words lightly, but Cherie could hear the pain. The buyer position wasn't currently open, but she was sure it would be soon. In the meantime, she was working as a saleswoman. "Oh," Cherie had said without emotion when Dale told her, "like Dad."

Like Ed. The two people who created Cherie, who had fallen in love with the promise of their artistic talent and their egos as much as each other, both hawking the visions of other people. Cherie remembers going into the bathroom, turning on the shower, and crying. Her dad and Dale, the people who made her when they were still just kids, so far from the places they wanted to go.

After the trip to Chicago that would be their last, just two months before Dale was fired, Cherie had heard her older daughter, Laura, talking to a friend in her bedroom about how amazing her grandmother was, how she had literally sewed her a bubble skirt from, like, the air, in one night (Dale had used a nice black-and-white checkered cotton sateen, not air) and how she had been married eight times (six times, but who could keep track of anything over five?) and how she had actually fought in World War II (she had painted warships at the Charlestown Navy Yard in Boston, where she had met Marlys, who was a welder). In fact, Laura continued, she was going to interview her grandma—Laura had long ago stopped looking to Cherie for reassurance that using that title was acceptable and had embraced it fully—for her next history paper and Mr. Armstrong would be insane not to give her an A.

Cherie stood outside Laura's bedroom door, holding a laundry basket and feeling both proud and immensely sad. Would her daughter learn things about Dale in a single phone call that Cherie hadn't been told her whole life? If she did, whose fault was that? Dale's for not telling, or Cherie's for not asking?

Now, Cherie was with Dale under Marlys's direction, tasked with making everything right and keeping her in the apartment that she liked and that she could afford. There was never any question that Cherie would come to Florida. She had always done what she was expected to do. As a mother, she was a good mother. As a daughter, she was a good daughter, even if less charitable thoughts about lifestyle choices and spending habits sometimes bubbled to the surface.

Evelyn ran her hand through her short hair. "We don't get a lot of children here at Soleil City." She looked at Cherie and saw her confusion. "You. You're a child. In fact, I think the last child that visited was Barbara in unit 4's daughter about six months ago. Barbara's dead now, but she wasn't then, obviously."

"Oh, I'm sorry."

Evelyn shrugged. "She wasn't my favorite. Anyway, the daughter was here for three days, smoked enough marijuana to get a herd of elephants high, broke the ice machine, and had sex with some guy she met in the Denny's parking lot." Evelyn leaned back and looked at the polo horse on Cherie's shirt and tasteful makeup. "She's nothing like you."

Cherie knew what Evelyn saw when she looked at Cherie. A woman of a certain age—fifty-seven to be exact—who lived a comfortable life of which she was firmly in control. It's what Cherie saw when she looked in the mirror. It's what her family saw, too. But there were times when her daughters were younger, so enveloped in this world she had created for them, that she'd want to shake them a little, throw them just a bit off course. Before Cherie even knew what she was saying, the graphic horror stories from her years as a nurse in the emergency room of Minneapolis's busiest hospital would come out. Dolls stuck in lower orifices. Metal pipes stuck in skulls. She'd tell them just enough so that they'd know that she'd had her own life once, that she had existed outside of motherhood. The girls would stare at her as if she were a stranger. "I only like Now Mom," Cherie heard Laura tell Jessica as they walked up the grand staircase of their 6,000-square-foot home. "I think Before Mom scares me a little."

"Yeah," Jessica agreed. "Before Mom kind of sounds like a mess."

Cherie's second surprise since arriving in West Palm Beach was that even though Dale was old, seventy-five years old, she was still so *alive*. Her own messy life had left her broke, sure. But as Dale outran overweight security guards or flirted with the good-looking bartender who was half her age as he fixed her Lambrusco and cream soda, even as she spoke about her regular lunches with Marlys, she was completely animated. It took Cherie a moment to figure out exactly what was happening until it finally hit her: Dale was happy. There were moments when a darkness passed across her face, as if an errant unhappy thought hadn't been pushed down far enough and had managed to bubble up to the surface. But for the most part, Dale was more than content.

Cherie looked at the small woman beside her. She closed her eyes a moment, finally placing Evelyn. "I think we're sharing a wall for a while," Cherie said. Cherie might have been exactly who Evelyn thought she was, but Evelyn wasn't who Cherie had believed she could be at all. Who would have thought that this petite lady could have been capable of *that*? Evelyn, if the previous night was any indication, was also doing a lot of living.

Evelyn didn't flinch. "They all think they have superpowers now with that damn blue pill, that Viagra. Just because they can do it, doesn't mean they can do it well." She raised her face up to the sun, then turned to face Cherie. "This one claimed he had worked for NASA," Evelyn said. "Made a lot of rocket comparisons that didn't hold up, even under basic inspection. Nice cologne though. Expensive."

When Dale heard a man's laugh as they passed Evelyn's door the night before, she had offered Cherie earplugs to silence "the show to come." Cherie had laughed at the offer. These were old people, in the last years of their lives. They were on a first-name basis with their pharmacists, talked primarily in memories and grievances. In that context, what could sex really mean? It was clear, almost immediately, that it meant an act that was energetic and shockingly loud. It meant that even with her arthritic fingers and occasionally sore knees, Cherie, at fifty-seven years old, still had decades of living ahead of her.

Cherie's husband had begun to talk about retirement. Their "next phase," as he said. They should sell their large house and

buy something smaller—maybe one of those new lofts downtown in the old flour mill buildings. They should have a place in
town for the grandchildren and Cherie's charities, but then, a
place for the weekends. They had the condo in Jamaica, but that
wasn't for all the time. Instead, maybe up north, on a lake? He
wanted to sit in a chair and watch the sunset with a glass of wine,
teach the little ones how to fish.

She hadn't said much. What was the point? He could retire
from his life as an attorney, from the sixty-hour work weeks and
months-long legal cases that had consumed him for decades. Her
job, as Cherie's husband once joked during introductions at
some semi-formal event, was as the family's CEO. "She's in
charge of the whole operation," Tom said, his hand on his wife's
back. "No one in the family would be anything without her.
Luckily for my daughters and me, she has been extremely ac-
commodating when presented with regular contract extensions."

Cherie had helped shape her slightly awkward husband into a
respected partner at one of the city's largest law firms with a
closet filled with good suits and appropriate ties, and stores of
prompts for small talk to match whatever new social situation in
which he found himself. There were the years spent helping her
daughters with homework and orchestrating sleepovers and
birthday parties. The hours and hours and hours spent driving
her daughters to dance classes and music lessons. She had organized nearly every moment of their young lives. As a result, they
were both productive members of society. Laura in a more traditional way as wife and soon, a mother. Jessica, the musician, in a
way that none of them could quite understand, except that it
kept her moving, always moving.

If Cherie held the whole operation together, how could she
retire? There wasn't an eager line of applicants begging to take

over the position, and the responsibilities wouldn't just go away. Everyone, eventually, would need something. Sure, Cherie could return to the pottery class she had tried, the golf game she had abandoned. She could shove her day full of leisure activities. But what was the point when, sooner or later, she would just be pulled away?

The night before, while waiting to be seated for dinner, Cherie had looked at the activities board at Hawthorne Haven, a place she had initially mistaken for a new Marriott resort. Surrounded by a full staff and every conceivable amenity—from an on-site hairdresser to an enviable crafts room—Cherie had noticed the activities board. In addition to hand-drawn flyers advertising Body Pump classes and guided meditation was a professionally designed one reminding residents of the 1999 South Florida Senior Synchronized Swim Competition taking place the next month in Fort Lauderdale. "Come support our CHAMPS!" it said at the top of the flyer, just below the case that held the team's trophies, their superiority established in molded metal. South Florida Champions, 1995, 1996, 1998. Champions, champions, champions.

All over Florida were older people, relaxing. Cherie knew that it was possible to walk away—her mothers had left Cherie to deal with her own problems for decades. Her children, marriage, career, and home life? That was all on her to figure out. At the same time, it was just assumed that Cherie would solve her daughters' and her mothers' problems whenever they might arise.

Evelyn turned to her, the story of her gentleman friend from the previous night complete. "Here's the thing. For months, we've had four empty apartments in this place—out of twenty-four, which I'm told is a very bad thing. Also, we might owe a pretty penny in back maintenance payments. I don't think the

Jackass wants to tear this place down any more than we want to leave it. But," Evelyn sighed, impressively, "I'll admit we haven't really given him a choice. We're just . . . stuck, in every sense of the word." She pulled back and examined Cherie more thoroughly. "I like to think of myself as someone who can fix things. But you look like you're someone who could do it even better."

There it was. Cherie, as assumed by Marlys and Dale and probably even by Evelyn, whom she'd known for ten minutes, would solve Soleil City's problems the most obvious way she could. She would buy them out of this mess. She could pay the maintenance debt. She could organize some ads in the paper to fill the empty apartments. She could get her husband, the high-powered attorney, to write some letters that would make the Jackass squirm. That's really what people saw when they looked at her, wasn't it? She was someone who wrote checks to people who needed her money, was thanked at nice-enough banquets to which she wore a dress that cost nearly as much as the original check, and then wrote an even bigger check to feel a little better about the purse she bought expressly for that event. A purse that matched her shoes, which were also new. A purse that was large enough to hold her checkbook to write another check and start the whole sordid cycle anew.

No, not this time. This time, she wasn't just going to pull out the checkbook. She had been asked to help Dale—Dale, her mother who *never* asked anyone for help—and so she would figure out what Dale needed specifically. Dale, who moved on to a new marriage when the last one failed, a new career when the old one tanked. Dale, who had gotten through life on her own, without parents, without a decades-long marriage, without the support of her child. Now Cherie would make it right. In a few days, less than a week, she'd put the pieces all together and make everything whole again. She'd do this because no one else could, then Cherie would return to her home, ready and waiting for the next call for help to come.

"Dale talks about you," Evelyn said.

"It's been too long since I've seen her. Since I've seen either of my mothers." Cherie remembered the last words she said to Marlys in person two years earlier, after receiving her dad's ashes and getting back on a plane without having had even the most basic memorial service. *I'll be back soon.* Cherie hadn't been back at all.

"It's good that you came," Evelyn said as she stood up and brushed her hands against her shorts. She began to walk away before turning back for a moment. "I know both of your mothers. This won't be a quick visit. You're going to be here for a while."

Evelyn had already walked past the ice machine by the time Cherie realized that the words she had heard were exactly the words she knew would come. The lull in her duties had come to an end. She had been called back into action.

CHAPTER 2

23 Days

DALE

Dale watched her daughter's face when Marlys walked through the restaurant door. The weight loss, the heaviness in every step, the coughing. How could Dale have possibly tried to tell herself it was anything else? Marlys was dying. Cherie saw the change in the two years since she had seen her mother instantly. Dale hadn't let herself believe.

But she did know, didn't she? Dale had seen the blood. Dale and Marlys had a weekly lunch in the hospital cafeteria that was eight floors below the room where Ed had died two years earlier, a couple of months before Dale came to town. Any questions about the maudlin location were answered upon eating the cafeteria's tarragon chicken salad sandwiches. Dale knew that Marlys's coughing had become more frequent and her weight loss had become more obvious, but they were old women. There were many less-bad reasons Marlys's health might have changed before jumping all the way to lung cancer. But two weeks earlier, after complaining about the heavy scent of bleach in the air and complementing the staff for keeping spots off the glassware, Marlys began to cough, violently, then pulled one of Ed's old handkerchiefs away from her mouth. Dale saw the spots of blood and felt a wave of ice pass through her body.

If Dale had said the words describing Marlys's illness to herself, even quickly, Marlys had never said the words to her. Dale and her daughter had exchanged a look after Marlys began to cough during the salad course. *I know what this is. You know what this is. If she won't say anything, we won't either.* Dale saw sadness in Cherie's eyes, but there was no fear. Maybe there was time. Hadn't her dad taken years to die?

So, for now, they would ignore the fact that Marlys's shirt was two sizes too large. They ignored the hoarseness in Marlys's voice. They ignored their growing anxiety as they watched Marlys pick at her food. Instead, they talked in cheerful voices that were half an octave too high as they willed themselves to have A Nice Dinner.

They talked about Bill Clinton's just-completed impeachment trial. "I liked him, I really did. I spent every Saturday in October '96 knocking on doors to get the guy reelected. It was the first time I did anything like that since Kennedy. What did that Clinton dedication get me?" Cherie asked. "A lesson in which of my friends whispered when saying the words 'blow job' and which said it loud and proud."

"We always called it 'giving head,'" Marlys said.

"And there you go, Mom. You just proved my point."

They talked about Cherie's hair.

"I like that haircut on you, Cherie. Very flattering," Dale said.

"It's a version of The Rachel."

"Well, she did a great job," Dale told her.

"No, it wasn't cut by Rachel," Cherie said, chuckling. "The cut is called The Rachel. You know, from *Friends*?"

"Oh, a friend."

"Dale! *Friends*! The TV show *Friends*," Marlys said. "It's on NBC on Thursday nights. You have to know it."

"Oh, yes, *Friends*. Sure," Dale said. She had no idea what they were talking about, and still had no idea why this Rachel woman should get any credit.

They talked about Laura's pregnancy.

"My friend Carol told me to establish my dominance as the primary grandmother early. So I invited Justin's parents over for dinner. His dad told us how he's already started a college fund for the baby so that he—or she—can learn the value of compound interest as soon as they can talk, and his mom told us that she'd like to be called Lady instead of Grandma. My plan is to be a—"

"Normal human being who wouldn't terrify a child?"

"Something like that," Cherie said, pleased that her mothers had immediately recognized her leg up.

"You know I don't like him. *Justin*," Dale said as she scrunched her distinctive nose in disgust.

"Dale. Justin is a common boy's name. It's not like a *Dynasty* kind of name or anything."

"He didn't hold the door open for me at the rehearsal dinner before the wedding. He went through the door and didn't even turn to see if anyone was behind him. It nearly hit me in the face. Rude child," Dale said.

"He's a man, about to be a father, and Laura loves him," Cherie said with a shrug.

"A ringing endorsement."

They talked about how the waiter's fly appeared to be down, though it was clear that it wasn't on closer inspection. They talked about how the landscaping crew at Marlys's townhouse development now began mowing at 7 a.m. They talked about how Phyllis, Dale's friend and neighbor at Soleil City, had been one number away from winning the $10 million lottery jackpot.

They talked like it was completely normal for the three of them to be sitting together at a restaurant, as if casually sharing stories and artichoke dip was something they did every couple of weeks, rather than the fact that this was something they had only done a handful of times their entire lives since Dale had left them both for Mexico.

They talked about the new City Place mall going in downtown West Palm Beach and how the area was transforming from an outdoor crack market into a place where people would want to be. "A little late," Marlys said, simply, and looked at her plate.

She was likely thinking of Ed, Dale's first and Marlys's only husband. A man who would have liked to have seen the new mall. Seen, and possibly taken issue with, the new mall. He had written to the city council on five different occasions to ask them to create a beautification board, which he would graciously lead, without ever receiving a response. But none of the three women at the table mentioned his name.

"I'm still surprised that you moved to Florida, Dale. To give up the dry desert air for this godforsaken humidity," Cherie said, with a sigh, her hands going to her head as she tried to pat down the excess volume her hair had gained since stepping off the plane two days earlier.

Dale had seen Cherie's face as they drove to her place from the airport, as they passed the sprawl and the dinge. Her parents, who had met at art school, had three things in common: an appreciation of beauty, frustration at their respective failed art careers, and a daughter who was born when they were barely eighteen. Yet, this was the place, this low-rise town in the western shadow of enviable wealth where her dad, and eventually, Dale, would take their final breaths.

"Who would have ever thought that you and Marlys would end up so near to each other that you shared the same grocery store?"

"And hairdresser. And pharmacist," Dale added.

"And Dunkin' Donuts. Don't forget that too."

Marlys was the only reason why Dale was there, in that place. Dale had walked away and Marlys had always kept a map of where to find her. When Marlys called Dale in Arizona to tell her that Ed had died, Dale went where she knew she would always end up. With Marlys, near her, until the end.

If Cherie hadn't noticed that Marlys had shrunk, in every sense of the word—her body, her voice, the time she had left—Dale could have kept denying what she saw with her own eyes every damn week because the alternative was too much to try to comprehend. Dale had always believed that Marlys would be the last one standing. Ed would go first, because Ed needed to have their full attention, then Dale would go after that. She had lived a full life. Six husbands. A dozen different cities. A single jail cell. She could go. It was Marlys who needed more time. Without Ed. With Cherie. With her granddaughters and great-grandchildren. Marlys would mention the imminent addition of a new generation without blinking. Of course this would happen. Of course they would continue to thrive. Dale would burst out laughing at the absurdity of it—she and Ed had sex on a Tuesday night in the backseat of her dad's car before he could even grow a full beard and *this* is how it all turned out?

"My skin likes the humidity. That dry air was making me more wrinkled than an armadillo's testicles," Dale said.

"Very descriptive," Cherie said.

"Very specific," Marlys said.

If Dale was the last of Cherie's parents hanging around, that meant that Dale would be all that Cherie had left. Dale listened to her daughter and Marlys as they chatted about how Laura's choice to not learn the sex of the baby was causing color drama while planning the nursery as if she were eavesdropping on strangers. When Cherie tried to grab a French fry off of Marlys's plate, she playfully slapped her hand. When Marlys dropped her napkin on the floor, Cherie picked it up and jokingly put it across her mother's face. Together, they were so natural, so easy.

Dale had arrived at the airport almost an hour before Cherie's flight was due to land. She sat in a chair near the window and watched the planes arrive and depart until the gate began to fill up with passengers waiting to go to Indianapolis.

With more than forty minutes to fill, Dale noticed a bar further down the concourse. Having one drink wasn't a terrible idea. Cherie was coming to Florida with two days' notice to see her, to help her—Dale—and frankly, she was stunned. Cherie was getting on a plane specifically for *her*? Dale heard her voice crack as she told Cherie she was looking forward to her arrival.

She and Cherie spoke three or four times a year. Cherie sent checks for a respectable amount of money at Christmas and on Dale's birthday. Unusually, her daughter had called her twice in the three months since Dale had turned seventy-five, as if Dale had crossed the threshold of aging into the truly elderly and Cherie had been warned that parents would need more oversight after that date. Generally speaking, however, theirs was a relationship with guardrails and modest expectations. If Dale wanted more, she also knew not to push. She had walked away. Because of that, there would always be space.

At the bar, Dale noticed a woman around her age with a glass of whisky. She looked at her watch every few minutes, increasing the size of her sips each time until she had reached the bottom of the glass, at which point the waitress put another glass in front of her without exchanging a single word. *Keep 'em coming.*

The woman noticed Dale and smiled, then raised her glass. "You've got to be waiting for your daughter, am I right?" The woman practically shouted across the place, the hum of passing travelers almost drowning her out. "My advice? Keep drinking!" Dale gave her a small nod and turned to face the other direction.

When she told her neighbors that her daughter was coming to visit, Evelyn had let out a low whistle. "Good luck, Dale. You say one wrong word and they fall over as if they've been stabbed." Evelyn and her son only spoke once a year, her son long ago making his preference for his wife's family clear.

As Marlys and Cherie continued their conversation about the nursery and Marlys told Cherie not to be an idiot when Cherie insisted that light gray upholstery would be practical in a baby's room, Dale stiffened. She waited for Cherie to put her napkin on the table, to push back her chair, to stand up and walk away at the insult, leaving her mothers to pay a dinner bill they had no hope of covering. This is what Dale had heard about. Telling your daughter she was an idiot was the misjudged comment that would send the entire night off the rails.

Instead, Cherie laughed and put her hand on her mother's arm and called her an idiot for not knowing about Scotchgard from 3M. The two women smiled and Cherie took another fry from her mom and Dale took a long gulp of wine. This is what a comfortable mother-daughter relationship looked like.

The night before, Dale had planned to take Cherie to an Italian restaurant she had read about in the *Palm Beach Post*. As Dale told her daughter that the recommendation was to order the tiramisu for dessert, Cherie said that the restaurant sounded nice. But there, before the last word, was an almost imperceptible delay. *Nice*. Being with Dale wasn't supposed to be nice. It was supposed to be unpredictable. It was supposed to be a little bit reckless. Being with Dale, Cherie had once said, was like riding in a car with spotty brakes. You wouldn't get into a serious accident, but a little fender bender wasn't out of the question.

So, Dale took Cherie in the other direction for dinner. She brought Cherie to Hawthorne Haven for a little dining and dashing and a quick sprint through the bowels of the upscale senior complex. If the unexpected was expected, Dale could accommodate that belief. But it was clear, once they were back in Dale's car, that Cherie hadn't quite gotten it. Instead, it appeared that she thought that Dale really was that broke. From that point on, Dale vowed to stick to the original plan. No veering off script.

Cherie and Marlys had moved on to talking about Jessica and how she would soon be playing with her band on the *Late Show with David Letterman*. Dale was ready to add what she could, to fall back in line.

"I like to watch that show after I come in from the pool."

"Honey, it's called the *Late Show*. Not early evening. It's on at bedtime," Marlys said.

Dale shook her head. "At eleven o'clock—eleven o'clock *at night*—my friends and I sit by the pool and do our end-of-the-day things. I have a little drink. Donna has her single cigarette of the day. Phyllis has a chocolate bar. Evelyn is allowed to tell us about one of her men. Ilona chews tobacco and spits it into a little cup."

Cherie wrinkled her nose.

"Ilona survived the Holocaust. Look at her arm when you meet her." Marlys spoke in a loud whisper, pointing to the spot on her own arm where Ilona's tattooed numbers lived and bringing the women's attention to her own hanging skin.

Cherie looked startled. "She survived one of the camps?"

Marlys nodded solemnly, then continued the whisper. "She lost a child."

"Okay," Dale said, sitting up in her chair. "First of all, why are you whispering? Ilona isn't here, and even if she was, she knows where she's been. Next, the *rumor* is that she lost a child. Ilona didn't tell you that. She didn't tell me that. She doesn't tell anyone anything. I see the woman every day and I have no idea how old she is. Hell, I don't even know her birthday." Dale sunk down in her chair a little. She was not being playful. She was not keeping anything light. She was not doing this right.

Dale smiled, too widely, then waved her hand dismissively. "Anyway, I watch *Letterman*. The Top 10 Lists are usually pretty good."

Marlys nodded.

Cherie cleared her throat. "It's nice that you and your friends get together at the end of the day. I like the idea of all those people looking out for you."

Dale began to twist her napkin around her fingers. She invited Marlys along for Soleil City's Thirsty Thursday treks to bars and called her for the occasional cocktail by the pool, but it was true that even though Dale had moved to West Palm Beach for her oldest friend, Dale spent most of her time with her new friends. Sure, these women lived only steps away, but they also didn't know everything that Marlys knew. They didn't know what Dale had done wrong. They didn't know everyone she had failed. A few weeks after she had moved to Florida, Dale had invited Marlys over to spend the morning at Soleil City's pool. Marlys had told story after story of Marlys and Dale's first years together in Boston. The problem was that there were only so many shared stories in their lengthy past that would allow Dale to come out on top. So, the poolside invitations to Marlys had lost frequency. Did Dale feel guilty lounging with her new friends as Marlys the widow was left even more alone? She did. Of course she did. But maybe not guilty enough.

"Well, anyway, even if you all have to move, you know you can stay in touch."

Dale felt her stomach drop, and moved her napkin further up her lap as if her daughter could see the movement. So that was it. Cherie wasn't even going to try to help her. She was told that Dale needed help—though not by Dale herself—and she had come to Florida in a matter of hours. She was here. She knew the problem. She had the problem confirmed by a third party—Evelyn—and had said that she would solve the problem (sound carried very well around the grounds of Soleil City). What had Dale said in the hours since then to make Cherie change her—oh, that was it. It hadn't been sadness in Cherie's eyes when she realized Marlys was sick. It was blame. *You knew this. You knew she was like this, and you didn't tell me. All the god-damned secrets between the two of you.*

Dale should have called her daughter when she first saw Marlys's bloody handkerchief. Sure, Dale could say that she was protecting Marlys's privacy or Cherie's feelings. But the truth was that Dale didn't feel like she had a claim to the news. For Dale to tell her daughter something so serious about the woman she saw as her true mother? She didn't get to do that (or maybe, she didn't *have* to do that—remaining, forever, a step removed). So, it had been left unsaid.

Cherie looked away from Dale and smiled at Marlys. "The next few days look like they're going to be really steamy. That sun . . ."

Marlys moaned. "Really? Are we really going to talk about the weather? I thought we had been doing so well."

Cherie smiled. "We are doing well. Great." She wiped her mouth with her napkin. "It was two degrees in Minneapolis when I left. Might get up to thirty by the weekend."

"I can't even remember that. I guess these thirty-five years in

Florida have erased my entire memory of those fifteen years in Minneapolis," Marlys said.

"Since you've never visited me in the winter, it makes sense that memory has gone away," Cherie said, and Dale heard the mumble of words that came next. *Although it's not like you came in the summer, either.*

After connecting with Marlys in Florida in those early months after Ed's death, Dale heard about his illnesses—the diabetes, the congenital heart failure, the lung cancer—and the days and weeks and months in the hospital that ultimately made up almost three years of Marlys's life. It was sometime during the story of the nurse with the tattooed lipstick and eyeliner and the amount of time she saved each morning while still looking her best that Marlys mentioned the fact that Cherie had only come to visit her father three times in as many years. Dale was stunned. She had assumed that Cherie had been in Florida every other month, visiting her dad, relieving Marlys. "No, no. She didn't really come," Marlys said, pressing her lips together before she listed the excuses. "But she's very busy, you know. All those charities. And there was Laura's wedding . . . But she called. Every other day, she would call." Then, finally, Marlys said the rest of the words. "She thought it was just too sad."

Dale cleared her throat. "We'd really like to stay in our apartments. In Soleil City. It's a nice place, a good place. Our other options aren't . . . great. If there's anything you can do to help, we'd appreciate that." Dale saw that Cherie was pushing around a piece of lemon on her plate. She'd ordered grilled fish and steamed vegetables and only eaten half. "If anyone could get through to the Jackass, I have no doubt it would be you."

"Of course," Cherie said, noncommittally. "I have enjoyed sitting by that pool. It's a great pool. Really nice. Better than most hotels."

Dale adjusted the napkin on her lap again. "Yes, well, you are on vacation."

"It's more of a visit—" Cherie began to counter.

Dale didn't let her finish. "So we should make sure you do lots of Florida things while you're here. Going to the beach. Drinking in the afternoon. Buying something with a tropical print and pretending that it's appropriate for every occasion."

That morning, as her daughter joined Dale on the balcony for coffee, Dale was certain it was the moment Cherie would tell her she was moving to a hotel. Cherie had been gracious about the camp bed—"It's really quite comfortable, and great for my back"—but this wasn't how her daughter was used to living. Though Cherie hadn't put a firm length on this visit, it was clear that she didn't intend for it to be a long one. Fly in, poke around Soleil City for a few days, spend time with Marlys, fly out.

"Really, I'm happy with this simply being a visit. We went to Jamaica last month, so I got my tropical time in."

Dale watched as Marlys looked down at the table. Their daughter had flown over them just a month earlier, had possibly even had to change planes in Florida, but had not stopped for a visit. Marlys had proudly told Dale all she had heard about the condo in Jamaica—*she has a full staff, Dale*—but had never been offered an invitation to stay. Now, likely, she never would.

What had made Cherie come now? It couldn't have just been for Dale. Had she intuited that Marlys's health was failing? Had she heard it in her voice? Whatever it was, Cherie was here. Dale would have to make sure that this time, she stuck around.

"I . . ." Marlys began, but she was overtaken by a racking cough before she could continue. Cherie put her hand on her back, but it was soon pushed off from the violence of Marlys's movement. She tried to put her glass of water in Marlys's hand but grabbed it back before the glass fell onto the tiled floor. Dale and Cherie could only watch Marlys helplessly, wincing with each thrust.

When Marlys calmed herself down—Dale didn't look at the napkin she put to her mouth and saw that Cherie also looked away—she told them that it was just a tickle, a reaction to the pollen. It was an excuse so ridiculous that Dale and her daughter immediately accepted it as fact. When Cherie reappeared from leaning down to fetch the napkin that had fallen on the floor, Dale saw her eyes again. This time, there was no mistaking the sadness within them.

"Cherie, honey, as you have quickly learned, the residents of Soleil City lack . . . nuance. If you're able to stay down here for a little while I do think that you might be able to convince the Jackass—uh, the landlord—to drop his ridiculous idea of tearing the place down. It might take a few weeks," Dale said, pointedly looking from Cherie to Marlys, "but if your schedule would allow it . . ."

"Well," Cherie said, twirling the large ruby and diamond ring her husband had given her for their twenty-fifth wedding anniversary. "I can't promise anything, obviously. But there might be a few things that I—we—could try. You're right though," she said, giving Dale a quick, subtle nod, "it will take a little time. This isn't something that can be solved with a few phone calls."

There it was, the unsaid clearly stated. Marlys was dying. Marlys needed Cherie to be with her, now. They could say that Cherie was staying in Florida for Dale, and Dale genuinely needed Cherie's help. But Dale was just a secondary reason to stay.

Marlys smiled. "You're here for a while then? Dale, that spare room you have in your place works out wonderfully."

Dale watched Cherie smile stiffly.

"You two can talk," Marlys said, glancing at her daughter, "to work out a plan, of course." She turned to Dale, who could see the sweat on Marlys's upper lip, the evidence of the effort of her coughing. "Cherie's so good with a project."

Marlys had, in her way, just told Cherie that she was staying in town, at Dale's apartment, for the foreseeable future. Marlys was forcing Cherie and Dale together and if Cherie was going to offer a different scenario, she was doing so at her own peril.

"You can borrow the Lincoln, Cher," Dale offered. "Whenever you need it. Including when you just want to get away from me or Marlys and if you want some time with Fleetwood Mac." It was one of their inside jokes. *Rumours* had been stuck in the car's eight-track player for the last seventeen years.

"'Don't stop thinking about tomorrow,'" Marlys said, and Cherie said nothing until she understood it was just a music reference.

They had to think about tomorrow. To think about Marlys's health deteriorating to a point where they would be able to say, after she died, *At least she isn't suffering any longer.*

"Who wants dessert?" the waitress asked, looking at Marlys as she did.

Cherie muttered something about being full as none of them mentioned the appetites that had deserted them.

"Maybe you could just bring the check," Dale requested, and Cherie gave her a grateful look. This evening was over. Let the rest of the days begin.

CHAPTER 3

22 Days

LAURA

The last six days had confirmed two things for Laura—she loved peanut butter and marshmallow fluff sandwiches and she hated football. She *hated* football.

At some point in the last few weeks, her husband, Justin, had decided to host a Super Bowl party for his friends. It would be a casual event, "guys only," Justin said, waiting for his wife's objection. Laura didn't care. She wasn't going to pretend to start loving a sport she hated just because it was the biggest game of the year.

In response, Justin's friends' wives—Laura's friends—would get together to watch John Hughes movies and eat loaded baked potatoes. "I might even make my own salsa," the hostess, Heather, half-promised.

Before the party Laura had heard Justin on the phone with a friend, talking about the "awesome halftime show," and Laura only shrugged, unaware that her husband was a Big Bad Voodoo Daddy fan. When Laura questioned him about it later, he only said that he loved the band. They were great. That one song of theirs was . . . big and, uh, bad.

On a cold, dark, Sunday night, Laura showed up at her non-football party with hair done, makeup on, and her least-bad maternity sweater pulled over her six-and-a-half-month-pregnant belly and, at the urging of her best friend, Melissa, stayed long enough to watch all of *Pretty in Pink* and half of *Some Kind of Wonderful* and to eat two fully loaded baked potatoes with store-bought salsa. (Laura knew Heather wouldn't come through with anything homemade.) Greeted upon her return home by the stench of beer, the sound of Justin's friends, and five minutes left on the big game's clock, Laura went straight to her bedroom.

The next morning, as her husband remained facedown and borderline catatonic in their bed, Laura went downstairs to begin to clean up. Among the beer can tabs and crumpled paper napkins, she found eight one-dollar bills. The morning sun streaming into the room showed that the carpet was sprinkled with glitter. A lone wineglass rimmed with a smear of red lipstick had been left by the TV, and beside it, placed with intention, was a business card. Crystal Charm, Exotic Dancer.

As the excuses and justifications her husband may try to make about having a stripper in their home ran through her mind, Laura tried to distract herself by rearranging the throw pillows on the couch. It was when she switched the navy blue with the olive green that she found her husband's mobile phone wedged into the couch cushion. On the screen was a notice of six different missed voice messages, all from the same phone number.

Laura assumed the calls had come from her husband's work, trying to figure out if he planned to show up. A wave of anxiety passed through as she imagined Justin getting fired just months before their child was born, weeks after she had quit her job in anticipation of an extended, or possibly indefinite, maternity leave. She picked up the phone and listened to the messages. They were all about Crystal, the stripper. How could Justin do that to her? How could he be so thoughtless? Laura listened to the first two messages, cluelessly believing that the woman on the other end was defending her, Laura, until she realized, finally, that she recognized the voice. It was her best friend, Melissa, using a phone Laura didn't even know she had. She didn't care about Laura. This was about her. Justin had betrayed her.

Melissa felt like Justin had cheated. She felt very strongly that he had cheated. Not on Laura, but on her, which could only mean, as Laura listened to the messages again and again in an attempt to figure it all out, that Melissa was having a relationship with Laura's husband.

Laura ran up to their bedroom, pushed her sleeping husband's shoulder as hard as she could to wake him and as she held his phone above her head, asked the only question she wanted to know. "Are you fucking Melissa?" The quiet moan he gave in response was all she needed to confirm that she had gotten it right.

Laura met Justin in college. He had dated Laura's freshman-year roommate early in the second semester but it hadn't lasted long. Megan had labeled Justin "simple" and moved on to a guy in her art history class. When Laura saw Justin around their small campus over the next few years, she would repeat the word "simple" while noting that Justin was actually pretty hot. Individually, his features were nearly ideal. How they didn't add up to one ridiculously good-looking guy, she wasn't sure. But they did add up to better than average, and in a sea of less than three thousand people, more than half of them female and a quarter of them eighteen, those odds weren't bad.

When Justin started talking to her in a bar one night toward the end of their senior year, Laura moved a little closer to him. When he offered to buy her a beer, she moved closer still. After two more dates with him over the course of a week, Laura felt a weight lift off her shoulders. She felt lighter than she had after arriving on campus nearly four years earlier.

Laura had always had a plan. She would leave college with a boyfriend. She and that boyfriend would move to the same city after graduation. She would get an apartment with girlfriends. He would get an apartment with his guy friends. They would date for another year as they worked their grown-up jobs. Then, they would get engaged. She would spend eighteen months planning the wedding—a spectacular wedding. Soon after their marriage, they would buy a house. They would have a baby. All this, before the age of twenty-seven.

Before that April night when she got close to Justin, Laura thought her plan was as good as dead. The guy Laura had dated her sophomore year (her freshman-year boyfriends—all four of them—were always going to be outside of the framework), wanted to study abroad his junior year. He wanted to go into international business and possibly work for a few years in Japan. Laura let that relationship go. Her junior-year boyfriend wanted to start his own business. "I'm totally fine living in my parents' basement for a few years until I start to make a little money. I don't think that eating ramen packets is punishment. I fucking love that salty shit!" He got pushed aside right before spring break.

Senior year had brought a couple of brief hookups with guys, but nothing serious. Laura didn't panic as she saw the calendar pages turn. She just felt a heaviness. Four years in college and what had she accomplished besides a goddamned marketing degree? She had cycled through a couple of different friend groups, with her freshman-year roommate remaining the only constant, though Laura wasn't entirely convinced that friendship had legs. She hadn't done any useful internships—Laura spent her sum-mers back home at her parents' house, working at the local ice cream parlor. She didn't have a boyfriend. She'd have to go back to Minneapolis—or maybe, possibly, Chicago—and answer an ad for a roommate, find a stupid job, and meet some random guy who she knew nothing about and might be an even bigger waste of her time.

Justin wasn't just kind and a surprisingly good kisser; he was also operating under a plan. He had a job waiting for him in Minneapolis—a friend of his dad's had set him up. He was renting a place with a bunch of friends who all seemed to be named Matt, except for the one who was named Nathan. His friends' girlfriends were renting a place together and could use a fourth woman to fill it out, if Laura was interested. When one of the Matts got engaged right before graduation, Justin told Laura that he was a little jealous, to be honest. He'd love to be at the point of settling down. Laura practically swooned.

It all went the way it was supposed to go. Justin proposed to Laura in a hot-air balloon over the St. Croix River between Wisconsin and Minnesota, presenting the ring they had designed together and continued to pay for to this day. They had an engagement photo shoot that lasted nearly four hours with three different locations. More than one hundred and fifty people were invited to the engagement party at her parents' large house. Laura had four bridal showers. The spring wedding took place in the city's most lavish robber-baron mansion, with events scheduled for three days. Was it all rather extreme or was it extremely well-considered? Laura's color-coded binder holding every last detail for the events would attest to the latter. Her parents joked about the cost but didn't deny her many requests. After all, of the two-hundred and fifty guests, more than a third were invited from her parents' list. They wanted to show off a little. They wanted their place in the pageantry. For months afterward, Laura was told how beautiful her wedding was, how thoughtful, how well organized. How absolutely perfect.

The marriage was good. Fine. Justin wasn't simple as much as he did not like things to be complicated. He liked his job in corporate real estate because the goal was clear—fill empty spaces. When Laura noted some dissatisfaction with her position in the breakfast division at a large packaged-food company, Justin told her that he couldn't understand what the problem could be—her job was to get people to buy cereal. Since people loved cereal, shouldn't her days be pretty easy?

Around the house, they divided the chores down traditional lines, as their own parents had done. Justin paid the bills and did the yard work; Laura made the food and scrubbed the toilets. They watched TV in the evenings, resting their feet on top of one another's as they sat at opposite ends of the couch. On Saturdays, they each did their own thing until reuniting in the evenings to go out with one or all of the Matts. Justin spent most of Sunday on the couch watching whatever sport the season supported while Laura stopped over at her parents' house. They had sex on Sunday nights. Justin seemed happy and Laura was happy enough.

When Laura wanted to be happier, she would walk over to Melissa's house. Melissa had married one of the Matts—Matt Number Three, as Laura thought of him—a couple of months before Laura and Justin's wedding. Melissa had met her Matt through a friend who had lived in the "girls' house," of which Laura had been a resident. It wasn't until Melissa and Laura were neighbors, living only six houses apart, that they became truly close.

It began with a decorative mirror. Melissa walked into Laura's house on a Saturday night—there was a short-lived attempt to establish a game night, which ended when it was clear that the true meaning of the name "Matt" was "sore loser"—and saw that the two women had bought the same mirror earlier that day only hours apart. The next week, they came out of a movie with their husbands and picked apart the same plot points. After they rolled their eyes at Heather's—Matt Number Two's wife's—complaints about her freezer door at the exact same moment, they made lunch plans.

From there, their friendship gained intensity quickly. They talked daily, sometimes more than once. They visited each other's homes three to four times a week. They shopped together. They cooked together, exploring the world of freezer meals with some enthusiasm. They drank the same kind of white wine, immediately alerting the other whenever it went on sale. Once a week, they took a Tae Bo class together at the local YMCA. For the first time since elementary school, Laura had a best friend. Laura loved Justin, but she adored Melissa.

Laura thought that she and Melissa complemented each other well. Where Laura was measured, Melissa could be impulsive. Where Laura liked to spend her time and money on things that were recommended, Melissa would search for the new and unusual. Where Laura accepted nearly any invitation that came to her, Melissa could go weeks without wanting to be a part of any group events. Somehow, they worked. They understood each other. They looked out for each other. There were no BFF necklaces exchanged or friendship bracelets worn, but Laura and Melissa knew what they meant to each other.

Sometime after her second wedding anniversary, Laura introduced the subject of children to Justin one night at dinner. At the time, the subject seemed natural enough. In reality, however, she had thrown a bomb that would start to tick louder by the week until finally, suddenly, it exploded.

Justin agreed that it was time for them to start trying. Matt Number One's wife was pregnant and the only Nathan had just had a kid. "It can take a while, I hear," Justin said, and Laura just nodded, not wanting to consider the possibility.

When Laura showed Justin her positive pregnancy test less than two months later, he asked her what had gone wrong.

"Justin! This is everything going right. This is what we wanted."

"I just thought that we would try. I didn't know that it would work."

"The point was for it to work."

He considered this. "Oh, then I guess it's fine."

She was pregnant; it was fine. During the first trimester, Laura was overwhelmed with exhaustion. She would set her timer and take a twenty-minute nap in her car during her lunch hour at work. Once home, she would put her dish of frozen enchiladas in the oven, go to the couch, and promptly pass out. "Maybe you need to see a doctor about this," Justin had suggested. She reminded him that she had seen a doctor. After penetrating her with an ultrasound wand, he told her the diagnosis: she was pregnant.

At the beginning of her second semester, when her exhaustion finally waned and the reality of the baby was still months away, Laura would spend their dinners trying to engage Justin by focusing on the fun stuff. Did he think it was a boy or a girl? She thought it was a girl. Did Justin want to find out the sex? Laura did not. She wanted the surprise. Did he have any ideas for names? She liked something classic, simple. Maybe something with a family connection?

Justin would reply with a single word most of the time. When he put his hand on his head, she would know it was time to back off.

THE SIRENS OF SOLEIL CITY | 41

"This is the easy part, Justin," Laura would say, and Justin would just look down at his dinner.

Laura didn't even attempt to bring up the bigger issues, like testing for radon in the basement and lead in the water, increasing their life insurance, making a will. Choosing a guardian for their child in case both of them . . .

Preparing for a baby, having a baby, raising a baby was complicated. Justin had wanted a baby. This is what caring for another human being entailed. He was an adult. He could grow up. Except, he seemed to be actively fighting his upcoming responsibility. This couldn't be like their wedding, where she would talk and he would nod along as he pretended to listen.

"It's just all so much, Laura," Justin had said.

She would speak, he would turn away, change the subject, leave the room. He wasn't just ignoring what she was saying. He had stopped paying attention to her. He was shutting down.

He wouldn't touch her belly. He even resisted her larger breasts. (Sunday sex night had been canceled.) Though Laura circled the time and date of her twenty-week ultrasound appointment in his Filofax planner, Justin didn't show up. As she felt ten pairs of eyes watching her in her obstetrician's waiting room trying to figure out her story as she sat alone fidgeting with her wedding ring and fighting the urge to flip all of them the bird, she felt ice go through her blood. This wasn't right. This wasn't how this was supposed to go.

She couldn't do this on her own. She didn't want to do this on her own. Every baby is different, she kept hearing. You'll figure it out as you go. But how was she supposed to do that?

Laura's mom had made it all look so easy. She could mother without trying. Be a wife without any tension. Be a caring daughter to not one but two different mothers. People around town knew her from all her different volunteer positions and they liked her. She scared people with her competence. Laura might bring the best Christmas cookies to her friends' cookie swap and have the cleanest bathrooms, but if she were to be compared to her mom, she would be found to be severely lacking every time.

When Laura was four months pregnant, she and Melissa were having an early dinner at TGI Friday's. At a nearby table, a young mother fed her baby with a small spoon, monitored her toddler as he attempted to feed himself, and talked to a friend who sat across from her. Almost immediately, the toddler began to choke. Laura gasped, but before she could react, the mother reached over, swept his mouth with a single finger, helped him drink water from his sippy cup, gave the infant another bite of food and never once paused her conversation. Laura had to rush to the bathroom before the nausea overwhelmed her.

How the hell was she supposed to pull off something like that? Her mother could have done it. Before she was a mother, she was a nurse. A nurse! That was the right training. Laura was in marketing. What could she do for her child besides make sure that their summer wardrobe and their winter wardrobe were consistent so as not to disrupt their brand?

When Laura returned to the table at TGI Friday's, she found Melissa had ordered three shots of tequila for herself and had already finished off two.

"I can't do that," Melissa said, holding the final shot in her hand and tipping it enough to indicate the young mother near them without spilling a drop.

Laura snorted. "You think I can?"

"I don't want to do that," Melissa said, finally. "Matt wants that. He really, really wants that. I don't. I don't want to have a baby."

Laura felt her stomach turn. She wanted Melissa to get pregnant nearly as much as Melissa's husband did. Laura thought about how good it would be to have babies around the same age. The kids could play together while she and Melissa shared tips and tactics. They could get each other through it, together.

"Ever?" Laura asked.

Melissa looked through the liquor in her shot glass.

"Never?"

"Never," Melissa said, then downed the final shot. "I know that makes me bad."

Not bad, just totally different from all their other friends. Laura and Justin's group of friends had bought homes in one of two different ten-year-old housing developments in the suburbs west of Minneapolis, all the exteriors painted varying shades of beige or gray. Each home had four bedrooms and a mudroom near the back door for little hats and boots. And everyone, except the only Nathan, who had already put the room into use, had designated one of the bedrooms as the nursery, waiting for the day when it would be filled. If there were any discussions on the subject of kids, it was about when and how many. Melissa, Laura had always assumed, was just like her. She was just like all of their friends. A couple of years of marriage, then kids. If Melissa hadn't wanted that, why had she played along?

Laura couldn't do anything about Melissa, but she had to do something about Justin. His baby wasn't hypothetical. It was inside her, growing larger with every hour. After the missed ultrasound appointment, Laura sat next to her husband on the couch, turned off the TV, and took his hand. They would have a real discussion, just like the magazines said to do. *Communication is key.*

"I know this all seems like a lot. But look what we've done in the last few years. We started careers. We planned a wedding. We bought a house. We figured all that out. We'll figure this out too," Laura said.

"I need more time," Justin said, pulling his hand away from his wife's. "I'm not ready."

"We still have time. I'm not going to have this baby tomorrow."

Justin leaned away from her on the couch.

"Justin. I can't do this without you."

Silence.

"Together, we'll get there. You and me."

He looked at her in a way she hadn't seen him look at her before. He was meeting her eyes but looking right past her.

In the last couple of weeks before Super Bowl Sunday, Justin had seemed to move toward acceptance. He hadn't taken more interest in her pregnancy or health in general, but he had stopped trying to actively deny the inevitable. He wouldn't shut the door to the nursery as he walked past. He had spent approximately forty-five seconds looking at the instruction sheet for putting together the crib. He had started storing his video game controllers on a higher shelf in anticipation of tiny hands. When he told Laura that he wanted to host a party for his guy friends and compared it to the baby shower that her friends had thrown her the previous month, she thought that it was a big step forward. He wanted to celebrate. What, she still wasn't entirely sure. But she decided to see it as something positive.

Sometime while they were watching *Some Kind of Wonderful* at their Sunday night party, Laura told Melissa about how Justin had been the one to suggest that they trade cars after the baby was born so that Laura could reach the car seat easier in the backseat of his SUV. "It's slow, but it's progress. Little by little. We'll get there," Laura had said. Melissa had smiled and nodded her head.

How the fuck could Melissa have done this to her? She had never seemed particularly taken with Laura's husband at any point in the past, but now Melissa was stuck with him. By throwing the complete contents of Melissa's closet out of their bedroom window and onto the fresh snow of their front lawn, her husband's feelings about the whole thing were clear. Matt Number Three was out. But even if Melissa was fine with the end of that relationship, what about her best friend? Melissa had to know that the loss of Laura would be far greater than the addition of Justin. Justin might not have been able to demolish his marriage to Laura without Melissa's help. But Melissa didn't need Justin to start over, to choose a life where the expectation of children wouldn't have to hang over her. She could have ended her marriage without ending her friendship with Laura. The fact that she chose to take both relationships out at the same time was a definite choice.

Hours after Justin left with a single suitcase, Laura learned that he and Melissa had actually taken everything with them. As she walked through the grocery store pushing a cart full of marshmallow fluff and white sandwich bread, Laura ran into Heather, the baked potato party hostess. When Laura burst into tears, Heather simply tilted her head and put her hand on Laura's arm. She knew. She knew that Melissa was sleeping with the husband of her pregnant friend, and she hadn't said one goddamned thing.

"Melissa loves you," Heather said. "They're both a little freaked out by this whole baby thing and kind of found each other. But it'll pass. Once the baby is born, they'll both come around. Justin will be back. Melissa will be there for you. It'll all be fine. You can forgive her."

Laura was stunned by what she was hearing. Melissa hadn't slept with Laura's husband once. Laura had spoken to Justin just long enough before he walked out the door to learn that he had been sleeping with Melissa regularly over a period of months.

Her husband had betrayed her. Her best friend had betrayed her. Her friends—all the wives of all the Matts and the Nathan too—had betrayed her. How could they have talked about anything but this affair? Laura knew them! They would have run with this news faster than Olympic sprinters. How could Laura have scooped sour cream onto a baked potato the previous night while these women who knew a devastating fact about her made small talk about pregnancy cravings and maternity jeans?

As Laura finished her second peanut butter and marshmallow fluff sandwich on her first Matt-free Saturday night in months—no, *years*—using the Boppy she had received at her baby shower to support her plate, her phone rang. She carefully reached for it on the side table that she and Justin had picked out at the Dayton's furniture sale two springs ago. It wasn't Melissa, who still hadn't called Laura, six days in. It wasn't even Justin. It was her mother.

"Laura, hi! How did Justin's party go? Listen, I'm working on a plan right now and I could really use your help. How would you like to come to Florida for a few weeks?"

Ten minutes later, her bags were packed.

CHAPTER 4

21 Days

DALE

"How do you pronounce it properly, Donna?" Evelyn asked while picking at the box of croissants Cherie had brought to the pool area. Cherie had asked to borrow Dale's car over an hour earlier, telling her only that she had to run a few errands. She returned to Soleil City humming "Gold Dust Woman," a Target shopping bag holding a small appliance for squeezing orange juice slung over one arm and a bag of roadside oranges slung over the other. She held the box of pastries in between.

"*Kraw—*" Donna said, raising her hand while holding the pastry as if she were conducting an orchestra, "*—san.*"

"Donna taught French," Ilona told Cherie. Cherie nodded, impressed.

"Where did you get these, dear?" Phyllis asked. "They're absolutely divine."

"Oh, they are," Evelyn added. "This is what the croissants from Darla's on Main Street wish they could be."

Donna frowned. "Darla's? Darla's croissants haven't been any closer to France than you have. Though"—Donna patted her tote bag—"that soap she keeps in the bathroom is very nice."

Evelyn and Ilona patted their own bags.

"Um," Cherie said, looking down to make sure her own purse was buckled closed. "I got them from Palm Patisserie. I had them the last time I was down here and stayed at The Breakers. Did you try the ones with chocolate?"

"With my diverticulitis?" Donna asked. "No thank you."

"The Breakers?" Evelyn asked, arching her brow. "Well, that's a nice little place to lay your head."

"Is it true that the fruit plate is $35?" Phyllis asked.

"It was right after my dad died. I wanted to give my mother some space. My husband's secretary made the reservation. It was May. The rates are lower in shoulder season," Cherie said, defensively, adding, "I didn't order fruit."

Dale looked at her daughter among her friends. In the three days that Cherie had been in Florida, she knew they had been observing her. What had they seen? Cherie, deadheading flowers, straightening chairs, wiping down tabletops. They had seen Cherie, in her thousands of dollars of jewelry and designer sportswear, keeping busy, smiling when someone passed, spending as little time in Dale's apartment as she could.

The last impression Dale had of Cherie was at Laura's wedding three years ago. Cherie greeted most of the people in the large ballroom of the robber baron's mansion that Laura had rented for her extravagant affair—Dale couldn't remember if the guy had gotten rich off timber or railroads, or maybe it was both?—with a fixed smile. Cherie nodded politely and said the right things, but even as she spoke, Cherie's eyes drifted away, on to find the next person who needed her attention. Cherie clearly cared something about these people—she had put them on a list and paid for all of their dinners. The people cared something about her—they had decided that the wedding was an event they should attend and bought a gift to put on the heaving table.

Were Cherie and Tom trying to impress them, or did they want to impress Cherie and Tom? The longer Dale watched, the clearer it became. People wanted to impress Cherie. They might have admired Tom, but they wanted Cherie's approval.

Now, was Cherie trying to impress Dale's friends? Is that what the croissants were about? Or was she trying to establish that she wasn't like them? They were doughnut kind of people and she was an authentic French pastry.

Dale watched as Phyllis tried to wipe the crumbs from the side of her mouth. Phyllis's husband had died the same year that Dale's last husband, Frank, had. Phyllis had technically been married three times, though since they were all the same man, no one was exactly sure how to count. Though Dale still talked about Frank, Phyllis never spoke of her husband. She did, however, speak often of the son who was institutionalized after returning from fighting in Vietnam when he refused to come out of the basement for more than twenty months. He hung himself within months of moving to the institution. Dale reminded herself of this every time Phyllis's constant indecision made her want to scream.

Evelyn had moved closer to Cherie after the mention of Palm Beach's most expensive hotel. Evelyn was a hustler—anything for money. As a seven-year-old dropped at an orphanage during the Depression by her destitute parents, this lifelong quest for more made sense. She had been a medium after the war, channeling the spirits of dead soldiers for their grieving wives and mothers. "They all wanted to hear the same things. The soldier hadn't died alone. He hadn't died in pain. Their names were the last thing to pass his lips before he quietly died. All lies, most likely. But it made them feel better and made me a little cash." In the seventies, she was Maryland's premier Tupperware saleswoman.

Donna had never been married because, in her words, she never met a man who she thought she'd like more than a Seagram's Seven and Seven, a hot bath, and a good book at the end of her day. She thought of the high school students, who she seemed to loathe and miss in equal measure, as her children. One of them invited her to his family's house every Thanksgiving for dinner. Having spent thirty-four years teaching teenagers, she had very little patience for bullshit. Or for Phyllis.

Ilona intrigued them all. Beyond the physical clues to the past she would never speak of—the numbers tattooed on her arm, the mastectomy scar, the Caesarean wound, all visible because of the tiny bikini she wore every single day—were the occasional dropped hints. When Dale mentioned her Murray Hill address in New York during a conversation, Ilona had let her know that she had a salon in the same Manhattan neighborhood in the 1950s. Dale remembered some of her uptown clients combining a visit to her dress shop with a facial from Ilona of Buda—their secret weapon, they whispered reverentially—and when Dale asked Ilona if that had been her, Ilona had simply walked away. When Dale had a mild sun rash two weeks later, Ilona disappeared to her apartment and returned with a small baby food jar filled with an oatmeal-based concoction. The rash was healed by dinner.

"You stayed at The Breakers after your dad died?" Donna asked Cherie, then looked at Dale. "Not your husband, right?"

Dale shook her head. "Not since 1948."

"If there's one thing you shouldn't do while you're here in Florida," Evelyn said, "it's to ask this group for marriage advice. How many husbands have we had between us?"

"A hell of a lot," Ilona said.

"Really?" Cherie asked, shifting uncomfortably. "Well, I just celebrated my thirtieth anniversary. With my first husband. My only husband. So I'm not sure what advice I would need."

The women exchanged looks. "You're definitely not like Dead Barbara's daughter, I can tell you that. And not just because you didn't have sex with a man you met in a McDonald's parking lot," Phyllis said, wiping the croissant flakes from her sun cover-up.

"Denny's," Donna corrected. "They have table service."

Phyllis shrugged. "Anyway, you drove past three Dunkin' Donuts to give us this taste of France. Dead Barbara's daughter sure as hell wouldn't have done that."

"Dead Barbara's daughter had her buried in a pauper's grave," Donna said.

Ilona shook her head. "It's back of cemetery, no headstone. Not good, could be worse."

"What would be worse? Actually being buried on the grounds of the sewage treatment facility rather than just ten feet from its gate?" Donna asked.

"The point is, Cherie, you're not cheap. In men or baked goods. That's a good kid."

Evelyn had a son who lived in California. He was married to a woman with a strong and supportive family who had adopted him, more or less. He spent every holiday with his wife's family. Apparently, they even took vacations together. Evelyn hadn't seen him in more than five years. Ilona had a daughter that she never spoke about. Though, even if they were the best of friends, Dale wasn't sure if any of them would know. The only thing they did know was that the daughter had never come to visit.

With Dead Barbara's mess of a daughter, the women could temporarily feel like they hadn't gotten everything wrong. Their kids might not visit, but at least they hadn't turned out like that.

Dale put down her croissant for a moment. Cherie had turned out great, and here she was, visiting. But even with that, her friends still had an excuse. Dale hadn't raised Cherie. Marlys had.

Marlys, who they knew and liked. Marlys, who taught the women the right way to apply mascara to their lower lashes.

Was there any of Dale in Cherie? They didn't look like each other. They didn't share any mannerisms. The only thing that Dale saw of herself in her daughter was her mother, Elizabeth.

Physically, the resemblance was startling. The other day, when Cherie told Dale that Laura was considering the name Elizabeth if her baby was a girl—the name that all three women shared as their middle name—Dale went to her bedroom and returned with a photo of the grandmother Cherie hadn't seen since just after Dale left when Cherie was four years old. Cherie took the photo in her hands and went silent. "Why haven't I ever seen this picture before?" Cherie asked about the lovely portrait of the woman who had been dead since the early 1950s. Dale didn't have a good answer.

But the similarities weren't only physical. As Cherie and Dale were leaving for dinner with Marlys, Dale had chided Cherie for not bringing a sweater.

"A sweater? Dale, it's still seventy degrees!"

"You're in South Florida, Cherie. That's practically arctic here."

Cherie had laughed. "Aren't we supposed to be from hearty New England stock?"

"Oh, no, my dear, you must have misheard me. Haughty New England stock. Our people were tremendous snobs. Rarely lowered their noses long enough to see the ground in front of them."

Dale's mother, Elizabeth, might have been the worst snob of them all. They were Irish, but a different kind of Irish than Dale's husband's family. Ed's family were laborers. His dad was practically straight off the boat. Elizabeth's family had arrived in Boston decades earlier, after the potato famine. "Our people didn't come because they were starving," Elizabeth had said. "They had food. They just wanted . . . more."

Was Cherie a snob? Dale wouldn't say that exactly. But her daughter had become accustomed to a certain standard. She had certainly seemed startled by Dale's apartment. Dale didn't have clutter. Hell, she barely had furniture, beyond what had been left behind by the previous tenant. When she left Arizona, a place she had stayed far too long, everything she owned fit in the trunk of the Lincoln. What more did she need? Everything she had— even, it could be said, every man she had—had served a purpose at the point that she had acquired it. Once she didn't need it—or him—any longer, she let it go.

Cherie's large house in Minneapolis was filled with things. Useful things. Decorative things. Old things, with a provenance. New things, with a label. She seemed to love her things, told Dale some of the stories behind them, saying names and places that she assumed Dale must know. Dale could only wonder how long it would take to pack it all up if Cherie ever wanted to leave.

Beyond the similarity of their eyes and mouth and their awareness of a standard that Elizabeth tried to reach and Cherie had surpassed, was the final thing that would have served as the strongest connection between grandmother and granddaughter: disappointment. Dale's mother and her daughter had been, and continued to be, disappointed in Dale for not being the person they wanted her to be. If Dale traveled light, that was the baggage she carried with her wherever she went.

Cherie leaned forward in her chair. "This is a wonderful community you have here," Cherie said, continuing the conversation. "You have each other. You can check in on someone who might need it, share things someone else might not have."

"How's that camp bed working out for you?" Evelyn asked.

"It's surprisingly comfortable, thank you," Cherie replied.

"The sex bed? She's staying on the sex bed?" Donna asked, and Cherie jumped a little.

Evelyn raised her hands to calm the women. "We don't *do* anything there, of course. Just some of my, uh, friends, shouldn't drive after dark anymore. So I have the cot for them. I haven't actually *slept* in my bed with anyone since Paul, my last long-term lover, died two years ago. And I won't." Evelyn looked at the women around her. "It's not like I have this allegiance to Paul. It's just that . . . the men snore. And the ones who don't snore fart in their sleep. Not to mention the fact that most of them can't reach down to cut their toenails all that well. I'm not dealing with that shit. Once the evening's business is done, they're off to the camp bed until dawn, when they need to get themselves the hell home."

Ilona shrugged her shoulders, then returned to picking at the layers of her pastry.

"Yes, well, anyway," Cherie said, then wiped her hand on the napkin she held. "Dale took me to that other place up the street for dinner. What was it called, Dale?"

"Hawthorne Haven," Dale said. Here it was. Cherie had made a plan.

Dale's daughter always had a plan. Cherie kept a small note-book in her large purse and Dale was certain that it was filled with so many plans for so many people that executing them would take her the better part of a decade. Now, Cherie could add the women of Soleil City to her book, turning their parts into a whole.

"Hawthorne Haven. That's right. I thought it was a Marriott! It was very nice, of course, but it lacked a real sense of *commu-nity.*"

Phyllis waved her away. "She must have shown you the flaws

in their security. To be able to eat in the restaurant and then go down two different out-of-the-way hallways without anyone noticing? That isn't a well-run operation."

"Ah, yes, the flaws. Anyway, I know your landlord thinks that this place"—Cherie said, motioning to the pool instead of the rust on the cement from the balconies surrounding it—"should be that place. But we need to make him see what it is that you have here."

Dale looked around her, at the complex that Cherie was referencing. It was light-years away from the corner apartment on the seventy-second floor of the John Hancock building in Chicago. But Chicago had been the exception, not the norm. The point when Dale and Cherie were the closest was during the most financially stable time of her life. Her daughter had never seen the apartment at the top of a hilly street without indoor plumbing and with an abusive husband in San Miguel de Allende. Or the bungalow with the peony bushes and dull husband in West Hollywood. Or the tenement apartment that was hers alone in Greenwich Village, or the penthouse on Park Avenue where she was a wife to her fourth husband for less than a month. Cherie had seen her adequate one-bedroom where she lived with her fifth husband on a lonely block in Murray Hill, and one of the apartments that she and Frank, her sixth husband, had lived in outside of Atlanta. But they had never felt like homes.

"So what do you think?" Evelyn asked. "What's the plan to save this place?"

"Well," Cherie began, "I think we could add a little programming here. Maybe ask the library if there are some volunteer speakers they could recommend. Maybe someone could come and explain the whole Y2K thing. That might be appealing for prospective tenants."

No one reacted to the suggestion.

"You could also put some flyers up at Albertsons advertising your Thirsty Thursday events to see if anyone else would like to join you. That could be a way to get one of the apartments rented."

"Nope, no way," Phyllis said. "That's our time."

"Sure, but let's be honest, ladies. You have nothing *but* time. And you don't have many other options."

"Listen," Ilona said. "We will never be them. They have Body Pump. We have an ice machine. We lose. They win. They always win."

"Screw 'em," Donna concluded. "No offense, Cherie. I know you've got a little money." Donna looked at a frowning Dale and began to talk faster. "But they think they're so special with their tennis whites and their golden anniversaries." Donna hit her leg. "Dammit, Cherie, I offended you again. Congratulations on that big, long marriage of yours."

"You haven't offended me. But we need to think about—"

"I have a plan," Evelyn said, her voice confident. Dale looked at Cherie, who seemed to be looking at Evelyn with some annoyance. Was Evelyn stepping on Cherie's toes? "It's a way to get people interested in Soleil City and to make a little money to help pay the maintenance debt."

Cherie motioned for her to share it.

"We're all good at something," Evelyn began.

"Oh Lord, this could go many different ways," Donna mumbled.

"And we could share those things with others."

"I think this will go the way I thought it might," Donna said.

"This new pill, this Viagra, has changed things around here. The men want one thing and the women often want another and no one wants to talk about it, and I could talk about it all day. So if I could just get them speaking . . ."

"You want to be a sex therapist," Dale said.

"Sure. I guess you could call it that."

"People would probably pay for that," Ilona offered.

"Yes! And Ilona, you could teach people Hungarian . . ."

"Who the hell wants to learn Hungarian?"

"And Dale, you could help people dress better. Get them away from those godawful white capri pants. And Phyllis, you could . . . uh . . . um. Donna!"—Evelyn said, turning herself away from Phyllis—"you could host book clubs, lead the discussions since you read so damn much."

"Like a teacher."

"Sure, kind of like that."

"I was a teacher."

"I know, Donna. That was the whole point of mentioning it," Evelyn said, irritated.

"But I'm retired. Which means I'm done teaching. Which means I'm not going back to work. This sounds like work." She stood up from her chair and stood over Evelyn. "Listen. We aren't Hawthorne. We can't be Hawthorne. That's just a fact. If we're going to put our energy into anything, it should probably be trying to find a new place to live."

Cherie moved next to Donna. "Sure. You could all just give up. If you want to do that."

"I don't think we want to do that," Dale said, trying to let Cherie introduce the plan she had no doubt concocted.

"Okay, so maybe you can't be Hawthorne," Cherie said, swatting away a fly. "Maybe you can be better than Hawthorne."

"How the hell would we do that? We have no Body Pump," Ilona said.

"What about the synchronized swimming squad? The champion Hydras of Hawthorne Haven? That team put Hawthorne on the map with their TV appearances and newspaper articles.

They had an entire article in *Southern Living* magazine. Not to mention all the money they've made."

"Money?" Evelyn asked, her ears perking up.

"Money," Cherie confirmed. "Real money, too. The South Florida Senior Synchronized Swimming Competition on March 12th has a $10,000 first prize."

Phyllis stood up from her chair and flakes of croissant fell off her. "Hold up. They twirl around a little, smile in a swim cap, and get $10,000? Well, I'll be goddamned." She shook her head and looked at the pool.

So this, Dale mused, was how Cherie would stay in West Palm Beach with Marlys for the next three weeks. It was rather brilliant, actually. Convincing Dale's friends to go along with the idea, then working feverishly for the next few weeks to help Soleil City avoid public humiliation, might have seemed completely out of left field in any place but South Florida. Here, it was a cover that Marlys might just believe. To the women of Soleil City, Cherie could be a hero. (Or she could fail miserably, but her dying mom was a hell of an excuse.) Dale looked at the pool. If anyone could try to get this group of women in line, it would probably be her daughter.

"What would we need to do," Evelyn asked, "to get the money? To try to save ourselves," she said with a wink that almost seemed casual.

Cherie smiled. "Well, you'd need to compete. You'd need to put a team together, learn the basics, choose some music, and then master a routine. All this in"—Cherie looked at her gold watch, but Dale knew that Cherie knew the exact timing by heart—"twenty-one days."

Ilona laughed. Evelyn leaned back in her lounge chair and raised her face to the sun. Phyllis squirted a pump of lotion into her hand from the bottle she kept on the side table and began rubbing it into her knee. Donna continued to chew her second croissant.

"Come on!" Cherie said, the subtlety gone. "Why can Hawthorne Haven do it and not Soleil City?"

"Because they've been practicing for years?"

"Because they have a professional coach on staff?"

"Because they've already won before?"

Cherie tried to wave away these valid points.

"You would be our coach?" Ilona asked, skeptically.

"No. I would be your manager."

Dale frowned.

"My daughter would be your coach."

"The one who's in the military band?"

Cherie began to laugh. "Military?"

"She plays American music, right?" Phyllis asked. "Like for the government?"

"Oh! No. Their type of music is called *Americana,* whatever that means. Not American," Cherie said.

Phyllis shrugged. "With the government, she'd get a pension."

"But isn't your other daughter very pregnant?"

"That's the one. Laura."

The women exchanged looks and Cherie began to speak quickly. "She took dance for fifteen years, twice a week. In high school, she captained the danceline and led them to a state championship."

"What the hell is a danceline?"

"They're dancers. Performers."

"Like the Laker Girls?"

"Kind of. Just not as . . . sexy." Cherie considered this. "Maybe as sexy. Anyway, the danceline usually performs during the halftime show. It's very competitive to get on the line," Cherie said. "Winning State was a very big deal. She'll do a fantastic job."

Laura? Cherie hadn't said a word to Dale about the nearly six-and-a-half-month pregnant Laura coming to Florida. Who had Cherie asked Laura to come to Florida for? Was it for Marlys, or was it for Cherie? It couldn't have been for Dale.

"And we'd do this in less than three weeks?" Phyllis asked, walking over to the edge of the pool.

"It's not Olympic-level competition. It's geared toward . . . uh, well . . ." Cherie stalled.

"Old broads," Evelyn said. "Yes, we know that. It's nothing too complicated. Put your leg up, move your hand around, swim in a circle, create a star formation. But we'd have to do it together. We'd have to do it at the same time."

"Well, yes, that's the synchronized part of synchronized swimming," Dale said.

"What do you think, Dale?" Evelyn asked.

"I think it'll be a challenge," Dale said as she looked at her daughter's face. In the last few days since Cherie arrived, they'd already begun to have a routine. Breakfast together, mornings apart, Cherie would have lunch with Marlys and then return to Soleil City, where she and Dale would watch *Jeopardy!* together while they yelled the answers at the screen and called the contestants idiots when they didn't get it right. Then, a drink by the pool, dinner, and as Dale went to sit on the balcony to inhale the night air, Cherie would go into her room and cry herself to sleep as she no doubt thought about losing yet another parent. It hadn't become comfortable yet, but it was also not strange. Now, that seemed like enough.

Dale continued. "But I also think we can do it. I think we should do it. And not just for the money. We've figured out how to do harder goddamn things than this our whole lives—without activity kiosks or professional coaches or any of it. We can figure out how to float on our backs and raise our legs."

"Oh honey, I've got that move covered," Evelyn said.

"That's the whole truth," Phyllis murmured.

"Okay," Ilona said, now adjusting the straps of her bikini top. "Let's do it."

"Really?" Phyllis asked, stunned. Dale saw Cherie try to suppress her smile.

"Why the hell not? What other option we have? This makes people know Soleil City, so they maybe rent one of the empty apartments. And there's money."

"Okay," Phyllis said, "I'll do it. It'll make my doctor happy that I'm exercising my knee. It's nice to have a happy doctor."

"You know that I'm in," Dale said.

Donna threw her hands up in the air. "You do all know what you're agreeing to here, right? We can barely even manage a successful duet at karaoke. That's two people! You think we can do a whole goddamned routine? In the water? Together?" When no one said anything, Donna took a different approach. "You'll get your hair wet, Evelyn."

"I'll wear a cap."

"You'll have to go in the deep end, Phyllis."

"I can swim just fine, Donna."

Donna sat back down heavily and pulled at the towel behind her. "Fine. I'm not going to just sit here and watch."

The women looked at Donna, waiting for her to continue.

"I'll do it. What the hell, right?"

Cherie clapped her hands together. She had her project. She had three weeks with her mom. And three weeks with Dale, whatever that might mean.

"Well," Dale said, getting up from her lounge chair. There

was a hierarchy to the chairs, and Dale was currently in the number two spot. Ilona had the best chair because of the fact that she had lived at Soleil City the longest and most of the residents were scared of her. Dead Barbara had had the number two spot. Dale wasn't entirely sure why it was given to her after Barbara died, but she willingly took the upgrade. She no longer questioned goodness.

"There's only one thing to do now." The women looked at Dale, watching to see what came next. She slipped off her kimono robe, turned toward the pool, and dove in.

CHAPTER 5

20 Days

CHERIE

Cherie hadn't slept more than four hours a night since she first saw Marlys. After spending the afternoon at the Palm Beach County library looking at a videotape of the women's synchronized swimming finals at the 1996 Atlanta Olympics while flipping through instructional books on the sport, she returned to Dale's Lincoln, drove to the beach, rolled down the windows to listen to the waves, and promptly fell asleep. A half hour later, she was awoken by a cop knocking on the windshield to ask if she was okay. Cherie wondered what the thirtysomething man standing above her saw when he looked at the sight in front of him. This middle-aged woman with her modified Rachel haircut and good gold jewelry, sound asleep in a car often associated with pimps. When she saw him drive away, Cherie knew the best next move was to find a bar.

She was a wine drinker but this time, she needed something stronger. She thought she should have a cocktail, but Cherie only knew drink names, not contents. Sex on the Beach. Cuba Libra. Old Fashioned. Vodka, rum, bourbon? Or was it whisky? Didn't she drink whisky sours a couple of times in college? She shuddered at the thought.

In the end, she ordered a Painkiller and drank the whole thing. It tasted delicious and went straight to her head. There had to be a catch, right? It was probably packed with calories. If she had another, she would see it on her hips in the morning. She was nearly sixty. She couldn't just drink delicious, alcoholic things and not think there would be some kind of consequence. Wasn't there always some kind of consequence?

Besides, now Cherie would be spending time in a swimsuit. She put her head in her hands. What the hell had she been thinking? She had told a group of seventysomething women in various stages of physical fitness that they could be a powerhouse synchronized swim team capable of winning a large cash prize in less than three weeks. She couldn't make that happen. Laura couldn't make that happen. Her stomach sank with each additional page she flipped through in the second edition of *Coaching Synchronized Swimming Effectively* that a kind librarian helped her find deep in the stacks. The Alligator Scull? The Shark Circle? Cherie pulled at her shirt's neckline, trying to loosen its grip. The sharks would be circling soon enough. She sucked the straw in her empty drink.

She had thought the synchronized swimming competition was a stroke of brilliance. Three weeks in Florida would give her enough time to research the best local doctors and the most aggressive treatments for Marlys. Her dad had tried nearly everything and had died anyway. Being in Florida without her father wasn't as strange as Cherie thought it might be, which made her feel almost worse. She thought that if she missed the last, bad days of her dad's life she could be left with only the good memories of the man she had loved. Instead, she had good memories, and she had guilt, and the guilt sometimes threatened to overwhelm everything else.

Even if her mom was determined to let nature take its course,

Cherie wasn't going to let her go without even attempting to fight. She felt the knot return to her stomach. No, she couldn't think of losing her mom. Not yet. At night, when she was alone in her tiny room she could cry. But the days were for business. The days were for trying to help her mom stay with her longer.

The days would also allow her to help the women of Soleil City. They were growing on her, every prickly and obstinate one of them. The synchronized swimming competition might do something to hold off destruction, but Cherie also planned to meet directly with the Jackass—Curt, she had to start calling him Curt—to see if she could convince him to delay any plans he might have to change the complex. Maybe South Florida would have an active hurricane season. Maybe the downtown West Palm Beach mall development would be a flop. Maybe Y2K would screw them all. Wouldn't it make more sense to wait three years, four years, even five years to make any radical changes? Wouldn't that be enough time for Dale and her friends to vacate their apartments naturally and definitively?

And then, there was Laura. Cherie had learned from Tom two days before she left for Florida that Laura had asked him for the name of a divorce attorney. Laura wasn't exactly a pleasant pregnant woman and Justin wasn't exactly a patient man. The combination couldn't have equaled a wonderful home life. This time away from each other that Cherie had arranged would be good for them, bringing them happily back together in enough time before the baby's arrival.

The bartender caught Cherie's eye and made a motion that seemed to ask her if she wanted another drink. Screw the calories. She nodded vigorously.

Cherie hadn't returned the message Tom left that morning saying that he was "just checking in." Her general annoyance with her smart and capable husband had lately turned to resentment. What did she resent? That his mother, of which he only had one, had died peacefully and suddenly of a brain aneurysm less than a year after her husband had died of a heart attack, leaving Tom with a few days of shock, a few days of planning and travel for the funeral, and an easy sense of grief—they had worked until their deaths on their eastern South Dakota farm when their bodies had finally called time. They hadn't smoked themselves to an agonizing death.

But was that all it was? What else could it be? She couldn't resent the fact that she had spent the last three decades with this man who still seemed to genuinely like her company. Who still told her she looked great each morning? Who made a point to kiss her before he drifted off to sleep with a pile of papers next to him each night?

Did she resent the fact that Tom had seemed to completely accept that Jessica had essentially removed the two of them from her life? Did she resent that he didn't lay in bed each morning staring at the ceiling, wondering where Jessica had spent the night after playing at yet another club in yet another town being praised by yet another group of strangers?

Cherie looked at the eleven-foot marlin mounted above the bar. Taxidermy was such an utterly bizarre human occupation. What was the message? *Members of the natural world, take heed. We can possess you entirely.* This poor fish, ready to spend its nine to ten years on this earth happily swimming around in the warming waters of the Atlantic Ocean, was now stuck, glassy-eyed, watching people sit uselessly while drinking enough to forget who and where they were. Poor thing.

"Nice, huh?" the bartender asked, following Cherie's eyes to the fish as he put her new Painkiller in front of her. She smiled tightly.

The messages from Tom were on Dale's answering machine. Cherie had a mobile phone, but he must have wanted greater accountability. He shouldn't have bothered. Dale wasn't Marlys. Dale hadn't told her daughter to make sure she called her husband. She hadn't told her daughter much of anything.

Cherie had tried to have a deeper conversation with Dale only once in her four days in Florida. She had asked her mother about the painting of the ocean that hung to the side of Dale's dresser in her bedroom. It was a beautifully powerful painting of a beach as a storm came in. At the bottom of the painting was a young child's sun hat, abandoned as she was likely swept into someone's arms as they ran to escape the storm.

Dale admitted that she painted it. Cherie complimented her. This was Dale's work, and she was talented. Wasn't this, at least, something they could discuss? "It's Cape Cod," Dale said, then said nothing more.

Dale had always held back though, hadn't she? Cherie didn't know anything about the years Dale spent in Mexico after she left her daughter. What had been so wonderful to keep her away from her child for five full years? Dale didn't tell her daughter when her dressmaking business in New York failed. Cherie found out when she went to visit Dale in New York after she graduated from high school and realized that Dale's days were free. Dale had barely told Cherie anything about Arizona, the place she had spent the last ten years. Cherie found out from Marlys that Dale had moved to West Palm Beach—her mothers with their strange, complicated relationship that Cherie would never understand—now living less than three miles away from each other. Dale hadn't told Cherie that Marlys was sick.

No, Marlys wasn't just sick. Marlys was going to die. Wasn't that the real reason that Cherie had come to Florida so quickly?

She had heard the change in her mother's voice, those times her mother got off the line at the beginning of a coughing fit. Cherie had known that something was different. If she wanted to blame Dale for not telling her that her mom was sick, Cherie also had to blame herself. She'd known that something wasn't right.

Sitting in that restaurant her second night in Florida, watching helplessly as Marlys nearly hacked out a lung, Cherie thought of her first snow day after they moved to Minnesota. She was five years old. Her dad was on the road with his sales job and after sitting at the kitchen table chain-smoking for over an hour while watching the snow fall, Marlys told Cherie to close her book, pull on her new snow pants, and meet her downstairs. There, Marlys stood in front of their apartment building holding two garbage pail tops. "Sleds," she said, and pointed to the hill across from their place.

For the next hour, Cherie and Marlys—Mom now, no longer "Mar-lips"—went up and down that hill, giggling and screaming as they went, taking the occasional break to lie on their backs and make snow angels before they went on.

It was Cherie who exhausted first. Marlys smiled, then half-pulled her daughter back inside their home. While Cherie soaked in a hot bath to warm up, Marlys made her hot chocolate, complete with whipped cream. The whole memory couldn't have been more than two hours of her life. In all the years since, even with all the spas and the retreats and the in-home massages that Tom arranged for Cherie each year on her birthday, no one else had been able to match the perfect comfort of that day. Then, as a young child in a completely new and sometimes confusing life, Marlys had given Cherie the thing she needed most.

Cherie closed her eyes, then ran her hand through her hair. She had missed the appointment with her colorist in Minneapolis that afternoon. Her roots would soon be obvious, gray streaks waiting at the top of her head until they could slowly take over the rest of her brunette hair, telling the world exactly what she paid thousands of dollars a year to conceal. She was getting old.

She took a sip of the new drink that had been placed before her. Oh yes, this was going down nicely. Why wasn't coconut cream a bigger part of her life?

Cherie hadn't yet told Tom that she would be in Florida for the next three weeks. This was the longest time they had ever been apart from each other. There were periods, during major cases, when they barely glimpsed each other for weeks at a time—Tom came home when she was already half-asleep and left in the morning before she was again conscious—but he was still there. They were technically together. Now, when he eventually learned how long she'd be away, what would he say? Would he offer to join her? Not likely. It wasn't that he didn't like her mothers; he was just very, very confused by the whole situation. He wasn't sure if he should be grateful to Dale and Marlys for the daughter they had produced or be amazed that Cherie had come out the way she had in spite of it all.

With Tom, Cherie had married well. She had been sitting in a bar near the University of Minnesota with a friend and her boyfriend after a shift at the hospital. The friend was a teacher and her boyfriend was in law school. He nodded toward Tom. "Cherie, if you're looking"—she was twenty-seven years old, of course she was looking—"set your sights on that guy. He's brilliant. Going to be a great lawyer. Going to be a rich lawyer," he said.

Cherie had expected she would marry a doctor. Wasn't that how it went? The pretty nurse grabbing herself a nice doctor. After she quit her job to raise their children, he could still talk to her about work and she would understand the words he said. But that hadn't happened. The doctors at her hospital were older. If they weren't already married, they were simply uninterested.

She had almost married for love before. His name was Randy and he and Cherie had talked about marriage. They were young—she wasn't even twenty-one, he was a year older—and still in college, but that wasn't terribly unusual in the mid-sixties.

Randy, her dad thought, wasn't the right husband. Sure, he was kind and thoughtful and seemed to worship Cherie. But Randy wasn't a "man's man," as her dad pointed out. He wouldn't fight in his war like her dad had fought his war, valiantly, in the Pacific. Instead, Randy wanted to be an elementary school teacher with a little house and a couple of kids and summer camping trips. "Is this what you really want?" her dad had asked her. It was. She was tired of her consistently broke parents always talking about money. Couldn't she just be in love?

Then, Randy asked Cherie to lunch on a Thursday and wore a tie, and stammered that he had been accepted into the Peace Corps in western Africa as a single man and was determined to follow it through. She cried, he left before they even ordered, and the waitress gave her a free cup of coffee, and then, when she continued to cry and didn't leave, a piece of cherry pie. She cried every day as she checked her mail for the next four months and never got a letter.

During the fifth month, she got a letter from Ella, a friend from high school who went to the University of Iowa. Ella claimed she saw Randy walking around Iowa City wearing a nice tweed blazer and holding the hand of a redheaded woman. It was a throwaway line at the end—though knowing Ella, it was also the entire point of the letter—but Cherie never believed her. He was attractive, but not distinctive. Ella had gotten it wrong. Randy wouldn't have done that to her.

Then, the moment from her wedding that she remembered as if it had happened the day before.

"I didn't do such a bad thing, did I?" her dad had whispered into her ear as they watched Tom joke around with his best man. At the time, the hair on her arms had stood on end, as if her body had figured out what her brain wasn't computing. The fact that her dad was looking for praise wasn't unusual. But this was more, this was different.

On her last trip to visit her sick dad, Cherie resolved to confront her dad with the question that had stuck in her mind for decades: Was he the real reason that Randy went away?

But then, sitting next to him, seeing how frail and weak and helpless he was, she lost her nerve. What if he said yes, that he had driven Randy away? How would she respond? Her last months or weeks or days with this man that she had loved so much, spent rehashing something that had happened half her lifetime ago.

I didn't do such a bad thing, did I? Her dad knew there was a Tom out there for her, and she was wrong to settle for anything less. After nearly five years and a series of short and insignificant relationships, the brilliant lawyer in the university bar interested her very much. As Cherie approached thirty, she had soured on love. It was time for strategy.

When Tom suggested marriage after they'd dated for a year, she readily agreed. This was exactly what she wanted, wasn't it? Cherie could imagine building a life with him. She enjoyed his company, looked forward to seeing him at the end of the day. This wasn't like Dale and her fifth husband, a marriage that Cherie was only made aware of moments after getting off her plane to New York a few weeks after she graduated from high school. Lenny was old. He was loud. But Dale had just lost her dressmaking business and Lenny had a decent apartment in Murray Hill.

Tom wasn't about convenience. He was the right man to become her husband. Besides, Cherie wanted children. She wanted her own home. She wanted to know that she wasn't broken.

Theirs was an adult relationship. She and Randy had been kids. Tom called her his partner. That was nice. That was mature. Randy had once called her his goddess. It was after she told him that her full name was Ceres, after the Roman goddess of fertility, so there was some context to the pronouncement. When she told Tom her legal name, he chuckled and said that her mom clearly had some delusions of grandeur, after which Cherie wasn't sure if he had insulted Dale or her.

Now, half of Cherie's friends were divorced. Two-thirds of the partners at Tom's firm were paying alimony to at least one former wife. Her friend Susan joked about her well-known affair with her tennis coach. "How was I supposed to resist? He was good-looking and available and knew how to serve." Susan was gorgeous and careless and extraordinarily unhappy. She could do impulsive, dangerous things because she felt she had nothing to lose. In the end, she didn't lose. She got an incredible divorce settlement—her single infidelity was no match for the half dozen a detective dug up on her husband—and she spent another six blissful months with the tennis coach until she finally decided that she wanted more than sex. "Just imagine how much sex we had to actually reach that conclusion. Time to stand on my own two feet. Ha! Get it? Because I've been horizontal for so many hours?"

Even if there were times when Cherie had been unhappy or even just unsatisfied, it was never bad enough to risk everything. She tried to do what was right, and she tried to tell people what she thought the right thing was. Maybe that made her seem judgmental. Maybe that made people hold a little back.

If Laura knew that Cherie could just keep her mouth shut and listen, would Laura have come to her with her marriage problems? If Cherie had just sat with her daughter and asked what she needed, would her daughter have listened to her advice? Cherie hadn't ever truly believed that Justin could give Laura everything she needed—both emotionally and materially. But was that something that she would ever let her daughter know?

Tom had only told Cherie that Laura wanted to talk to a lawyer. But what else had he been told? "She came to me because of my connections, Cher. Not because she likes me better," he said, though they both knew that she did. But what had Tom done to help? He had said words like "settlement" and "full custody" and "child support." Cherie was the one who had picked up the phone and told her to come to Florida. She was the one who had given her something to do.

Because that's what she did. She didn't only say the words she thought that others should hear, she did what she could to make things right. She was a daughter who would play along with her mom's absurd plan to pretend that nothing was wrong, that the coughing they could all hear was just a tickle in her throat. That the pain she felt in her chest was mere heartburn, a reason to drink a little less coffee. There were words that Marlys should hear, but this time, Cherie didn't want to be the one to say them. *You're dying, Mom. Just tell me you're dying.*

The bartender put a new drink in front of Cherie. "No, I'm fine. Thank you," Cherie said, but he shook his head. "It's from the one with the mustache, end of the bar."

Cherie looked down the bar and saw him, a handsome man around her age with a Tom Selleck mustache and blue eyes. He smiled at her and made a motion with his head that invited her down to his end of the bar. She felt her heart leap a little. She made the same vague head movement in response. *No, you come to me.* She nearly gasped when she saw him lower himself off his stool and begin to come toward her.

She was alone, in a bar. This is what happened in that situation. If this had happened to a married friend of hers, Cherie would have chastened her for not knowing that this might come next. What should she do now? While Cherie was playing with her straw and stewing about the needy people in her life, mustache man had been hatching a plan. He probably took her to be a new divorcée. Maybe a widow? In any case, he likely didn't think she was married and sitting at this nautically themed bar drinking alone.

What would he want? Sex, right? He didn't just want to chat, that's not how this kind of thing worked. Well, she'd give him a few minutes and then use Dale as her excuse. She caught a glimpse of her watch. Honestly, she should be getting back.

Actually, should she? Couldn't she just admit to herself that she was sick of her own shit? Loosen up, Cherie! Live a little. Pretend to be a single woman in a bar for one night. Talk to an attractive man and bask in the fact that someone found her appealing. Someone wanted her.

Besides, if everyone around her wanted to play their little games of make-believe, why the hell couldn't she? Marlys wanted to pretend she wasn't sick. Dale wanted to pretend she had been some kind of great mom, taking credit for the daughter she didn't raise to her friends. Laura said she wanted nothing more than a little break before the baby came, a nice little stint in the sun. Maybe Cherie was at this bar as a woman who wanted to talk to a new man. Maybe she was someone who wasn't just a wife and mother, a daughter.

"You looked thirsty," the man said as he took the stool next to Cherie's.

Cherie stifled a laugh. Whatever she had expected his opening salvo to be in the battle to bring her home, she hadn't expected it to be that clunky. Did that mean that his blue eyes usually got him what he wanted without trying, or maybe he was new to this game?

"I haven't ever bought a strange woman a drink before," he said, then quickly corrected himself. "You're not strange! Not strange at all. I just meant 'strange' in the sense of stranger. We haven't ever met."

Cherie stuck out her hand. His voice was slightly higher than she expected. *Not a manly man.* "Cherie. Nice to meet you."

"John. John Blunt."

"Well, that's very to the point."

"Yes," he smiled. "It's how I was raised."

"So you come from a Blunt family?" Cherie asked.

He laughed. "I do, in fact."

"When my younger daughter was in elementary school, her art teacher was named Art, and her gym teacher was named Jim. When she found out, her little mind was blown. She was heartbroken to learn that her reading teacher was named Sandy and her math teacher was named Steve."

He laughed again. "I had a school friend, Chuck Butcher. He became a surgeon. I think it was only because of his name. Too good of an opportunity to pass up."

"I knew a surgeon named Dr. Hope. I assume their offices would have been on opposite sides of the hall."

He laughed again, then pointed at the drink he bought her but that she hadn't touched. "If I guessed wrong, I could certainly get you something else."

"Oh," Cherie said, looking at the drink. "This will work. I just wasn't sure if . . ."

"You wanted to bother with me."

"Something like that."

"So, you have a younger daughter. Which means you have an older daughter as well," he said, settling in.

Cherie looked at him. He was probably a few years younger than her. His clear blue eyes were definitely the trait that had gotten him the most attention over the years. Which made the decision to keep such a prominent mustache puzzling. What was it covering up?

Maybe John Blunt just had thin lips. Or maybe, back in the height of Tom Selleck's fame, he grew the mustache, someone he cared about told him they liked it, and he'd kept it ever since. Cherie imagined what it would be like to be kissed with so much facial hair brushing against her mouth. Wouldn't it itch?

"Yes. I have two daughters," Cherie said.

Should she be giving this John any personal information? What would he do? Find out when Jessica's next show was with her band and try to show up? Go to Target to find Laura's baby registry and send her a gift?

"What would they say if I offered to buy their mother dinner tomorrow night? I know a place with a nice sea view."

This was actually happening, this attractive man at a bar, trying to pick her up. Cherie looked at his fingernails. They were trimmed and clean. Then, down at his shoes. He wore a pair of leather loafers. They were broken in but cared for. Were they handmade? The stitching made her think they were. Possibly Italian.

She could feel divorced Susan with the tennis coach lover slap her on the back like a frat boy. *Get it, girl. Who will know?* But that was it. Cherie wouldn't get away with this. She would never get away with having a brief fling with a handsome man in South Florida. She wouldn't get away with it because she wouldn't even know how to try. She had no idea how to operate inside of a relationship where she was wanted. All she knew, now, was what it was like to be needed.

If she was the one who was needed the most, she was the one who couldn't be left behind. Tom needed her. He wanted her, but those moments were situational—after a racy movie, a few too many glasses of wine. He needed her to help him find a clean shirt. He needed her to talk to the mechanic about the clank in his engine. He needed her so much that she almost forgot it was she who had first needed him.

Marlys needed her, and not just her money or her care. She needed her to be her daughter so she could continue to be a mother. But still, Marlys would leave. They would all leave. Dale had left her. Randy had left her. Her dad had left her. Jessica hadn't been home for more than three nights for the last five years. It would be nice to be wanted, but this handsome man in a bar in South Florida couldn't change that Cherie had been good, that she had done what she was expected to do—she had done more than was expected—and she was, once again, about to be left behind.

She sighed. "My daughters would remind me that I'm married." Cherie took five dollars out of her purse and put it into John Blunt's hand as she hopped off her barstool. "I'm sorry I wasted your time."

CHAPTER 6

19 Days

MARLYS

Marlys's weekly class at the hospital provided her with a pencil and a piece of paper. She had been told, in a rather firm voice, that it was time to write.

Marlys Claire Kelly was born in Youngstown, Ohio, on June 16, 1927, the sixth and final child of a mother who had lost interest in her offspring sometime after she pushed out the second one and a father who was a good delivery driver but a bad thief, constantly getting caught selling the goods he was transporting, avoiding jail but ensuring long stretches of unemployment. Frankly, with that beginning, it was a goddamn miracle she ever got out.

"So, Marlys," Pam, the Living with Dying class's leader said as she read over Marlys's shoulder, her voice slow and quiet. "We'd like this to be an obituary that would be suitable for publication."

"Yes, Pam. I am aware. This is hardly the beginning of a bedtime story, is it?"

Pam cleared her throat. "To have this published in a newspaper . . ."

Marlys looked down at her page. "Would 'damn' be more acceptable than 'goddamn'?"

"Sure. Let's start there," Pam said, dropping a second pencil onto Marlys's workspace. Marlys picked it up, trying to figure out Pam's coded message. She was not Pearl, the woman sitting about ten feet from her, staring at the letters on the side of her pencil and moving her mouth slowly as she did. Marlys's cancer had started in her lungs. Her mind still worked perfectly fine. Check the damn chart, Pam. Check the goddamned chart.

Marlys picked up the lips, the cheekbones, the hair, the waist, and the breasts that were missing from her siblings, and on her, they had landed perfectly. She was beautiful, so at the age of seventeen, she boarded a bus to New York.

Pam dropped the sheaf of papers that she was carrying across the room. Marlys heard her swear under her breath. How old was Pam, thirty? Thirty-five? Not much older than her grand-daughters. She still thought of them as kids. But they weren't. They were adults. Married, having children, managing their own careers. Old enough to have come to visit their grandfather when he was dying, something they had not done. Old enough to know that soon she, too, would be gone.

Marlys went to St. Mary's Hospital at least three days a week. Tuesdays she had lunch with Dale in the cafeteria. Both women enjoyed the chicken salad made with a generous amount of tarragon—a bold decision for a hospital cafeteria that she had discovered early in the first year of her husband's illness. Wednes-days she had her Living with Grief support group in room 107, which she had joined a week after Ed died. And for the last three weeks she had been attending the Living with Dying class in room 109 on a strong recommendation from her oncologist after she had refused treatment for her advanced lung cancer.

Marlys remembered looking down at her feet while she sat in the exam room waiting for the doctor to come in to go over her treatment plan. She began laughing, almost hysterically, when she saw that she was wearing two different shoes. A brown sandal and a black flat. She was wearing two entirely different shoes.

The doctor didn't even notice. He barely looked at her, yet another woman in her seventies with cancer in her lungs due to her decades (and decades and decades) of smoking, and knew how this would go. One more that he couldn't save.

Marlys waited for him to sit down in the chair across from her—wasn't this usually done in wood-paneled offices with diploma-covered walls?—before announcing that this meeting would be quick. She wasn't seeking treatment.

"But without treatment," the doctor paused for effect, running his hand through his red hair, "you will die."

"It's lung cancer. I'm dying either way," Marlys had countered.

Dr. Ginger cleared his throat. "Well, yes, but we might be able to give you more time."

"Yeah, well, my husband got that time. He got those miserable, pathetic months. It was a terrible end to a difficult life."

Her strongest emotion after the death of Ed, her husband of fifty-one years, was anger. She shared this fury in the only place she felt she could, the grief support group in room 107, though it didn't necessarily make her popular. "It seems like you're having a really hard time moving on from anger," the young widow of a heart attack victim said.

"Well, woman-who-went-on-a-date-less-than-three-months-after-your-husband-dropped-dead, have you considered, perhaps, that you're moving on a little too fast?" Marlys had asked in a room divided neatly in half by guffaws and gasps. She was asked to take a little break after that, give the next week's session a miss.

Ed had taken nearly three years to die. When he got sick, Marlys was still beautiful. Older, but no less lovely. She had been regularly asked on lunch dates by unfamiliar older men as she bagged lettuce in the produce section of Albertsons grocery store, men who were genuinely disappointed when she let them down. By the time Ed died, she had gotten old. Haggard. She didn't turn a single head, didn't disappoint a single grocery shopper.

By taking so long to die, Marlys lived in a state of half-mourning for those years. While he was dying, she stopped living too. She dropped out of book club. She didn't sleep more than three consecutive hours a night. She missed Laura's wedding. Two hundred and fifty goddamned people eating free beef, and not one of them was Marlys.

She had wanted to die first. She didn't want to be the one who was left behind. But she also wanted Ed to live alone. She wanted Ed to know everything she had done for him, how big a space she had held in his life. She wanted him to know that emptiness.

But she didn't die first. As a result, her daughter, who is still grieving the loss of her father, will now have to say goodbye to the mother that raised her, too. A double dose of grief was more than Cherie should have. So, Marlys had decided. She wouldn't tell her daughter anything. Not about Dr. Ginger, not about this class in room 109. She'll know soon enough. For now, they could pretend all was good. They could have a nice visit.

Pam put a plate of packaged cookies from the elf company down on the table nearest to Marlys. Marlys looked at Pam, who was attempting to artfully arrange the cookies. What would it be like to spend your days with dying people? To look around the room and know that everyone in the place probably won't see another Christmas, another presidential election? Would it make you appreciate your life more, or just feel resigned to the unfairness of it all?

Pam noticed Marlys's gaze and smiled at her. She then walked to her and looked over Marlys's shoulder. "Oh," she said, taken aback at the next paragraph she had written.

"I was beautiful. It's just a fact. I modeled in New York for a while at the beginning of the war, but these things," Marlys looked down at her substantial breasts, "got in the way. Too much for high fashion, but just right for smut. So, I became a welder for the Navy."

"Are you going to mention that?"

"The smut? I only posed once. But hey, why the hell not? Not many people can say they've been featured in a girlie magazine."

Pam shifted her weight to the other leg. "Your work during the war."

"I suppose that's the thing to do, isn't it?" Marlys asked, and Pam told her it was something she should mention. "People seem to care about that war again," Marlys said, and Pam followed her eyes over to a small man around her age wearing a baseball cap with the name of his platoon.

At the doctor's appointment when she sat alone across from the man with the red hair in the white coat and was told she had cancer, Marlys wasn't told how much time she might have left. "We're not fortune-tellers, Mrs. Kelly. There are too many factors to consider, so anything I would tell you would be a guess."

"But I should get my affairs in order."

"Yes."

Before she finally went to the doctor, before her primary doctor ordered the X-ray that had told them what they both already knew, she could pretend. Her cough had been getting worse. Climbing the stairs to her bedroom had become difficult enough at the end of the day that she had begun to sleep in Ed's old Barcalounger. But maybe it was a cold. Maybe allergies. Perhaps it was a bronchial infection.

Until, after a morning coughing fit, she pulled her hand away to see blood. The blood meant that she couldn't pretend anymore. She had lived the same life as Ed, smoking almost continuously, drinking prodigiously. Why shouldn't she also die like him?

But she wouldn't die like him. She wouldn't die with bedsores because she'd been in the same hospital bed for too long while knowing the first names of all the nurses' children. She would spend her last months—weeks?—in the world, a world that would have no idea that her own time within it was limited. Other than Pam, of course. Pam knew. She would leave the world on her own terms, the way she wanted it to be.

Even if her coughing shook her, even if her clothes had started to hang from her frame, she wouldn't say that she was sick. Dale would go along with it. At the end of their lives together, Dale would take her cue. Cherie would too. Cherie had always done what she was told. They would all play their parts in Marlys's stupid play.

Besides, if Cherie was told that her mom was sick, she would have to act. There would be appointments with specialists. There would be reams of photocopied articles from medical journals. Their conversations would become nothing but wellness checks. She would be a patient first, a mother second.

There were moments when Marlys was filled with bitterness knowing that the mother who had left her child, Dale, was also the mother who would be the last one left. But even if they got more time together, even if Dale got to be a great-grandmother to Laura's child—Marlys ached at that reality—she would still be Dale. She would always be Dale. Not Mom.

In New York, Marlys worked as a model. Knowing she could do more to help her country in its time of need during the war, she did a short course in welding and got a job at the Brooklyn Navy Yard. Marlys chuckled. She went to the Brooklyn Navy Yard because they paid well and she needed money. She wouldn't have flashed her ass if she wasn't broke, would she have? God bless America.

She left Brooklyn for Boston . . . Marlys stopped. She was done. She left Brooklyn because she had been raped. Should she mention that? Should she finally say in writing what she hadn't even told Ed in person?

Should she talk about how she fled Brooklyn and ended up in Boston, where she met Dale and her adorable daughter, Cherie? Should she mention how after the war she accepted each one of Ed's advances while Dale confided in her all the ways their marriage was falling apart? Or maybe why Dale ended up going to Mexico alone?

Nope. She was done here. There was nothing more she wanted to say.

For the first time, Marlys noticed that she and Pearl were the only two people in the room not silently weeping. Were they crying for the lives they'd be leaving behind or the ones they'd never lived?

Marlys stared out the window. She'd lived in Florida longer than anywhere else in her life, yet it still didn't fully feel like her place. Did she have a true hometown? Marlys, Ed, and Cherie left Boston for Minneapolis as soon as Marlys and Ed married, "a new start," according to Ed. The cold, the snow, wasn't unfamiliar to Marlys, but the winter days seemed darker, shorter. Especially since Ed was rarely there.

Ed was a traveling salesman. He was an artist. Marlys should say that. She should always say that first. He was an artist who also happened to work as a salesman who traveled throughout the upper Midwest selling Dalton cashmere, and only Dalton cashmere, which was a very particular choice since there was only so much Dalton cashmere that a woman in Iowa might need. Marlys would make Ed a sandwich or two and a thermos of coffee and send him off in his huge Chrysler, along highways from one reasonably sized town to another, for days and nights on end.

"I'm gone for two weeks, but then I'm home for a week. I can paint. Think how much I can get done. Then, when those paintings start to sell, I can quit this salesman gig altogether."

But he didn't paint, not really, so there was nothing to sell.

"He's a snob," Dale said to Marlys once after she had called to speak to Cherie on her birthday. "If he just switched to something with a lower price point, he could actually make a little money. The man looks like a movie star." When Dale showed Marlys Ed's picture for the first time, she actually gasped. His dark curls dipped down onto his forehead and made his eyes look even bluer, even in black and white. His nose was strong and straight, his lips pink and full, his jawline was almost chiseled. He was gorgeous. He knew he was gorgeous. A gorgeous man didn't sell girdles. He sold luxury goods, even if those luxury goods barely sold.

At the end of Cherie's second year at the University of Wisconsin–Madison, Ed said he was done with winter. He wanted to move to Florida. Marlys was ready to try something new, but Florida? The humidity, the sprawl, the sedentary nature of the days. When Marlys thought of Florida, she thought of sitting somewhere and sweating. Sitting and sweating and having other middle-aged women judge her because her necklace was too big or her hair wasn't permed.

But Ed wouldn't let it go. So, they moved. "You're going to God's waiting room, Marlys," her neighbor told her as Marlys carried the last of the boxes to the car. Her life with Ed, snuggly packed into the smallest trailer U-Haul had to offer. "You're too young!" She was barely forty.

Now, almost half her life later, the waiting would soon be over. For the last three decades, she had been surrounded by visions of what would come next: Her skin would wrinkle. Her hair would go white. Her body would get bigger and her knees would go, or it would get smaller and her back would curve. Then, finally, it would be done. Until then, she would call the shots.

Pam approached her. "Is something wrong, Marlys?"

"I don't want to do this."

Pam looked at Marlys's paper. "You know, you aren't dead yet."

Marlys laughed. "Thanks, Pam. That's really helpful."

Pam shrugged, then squatted down next to Marlys. "Listen, I've heard some crazy shit over the years. Deathbed confessions, that kind of thing."

"Oh, yeah? Good stuff? Probably a lot of affairs, maybe some petty theft?"

"You'd be surprised. Your generation went to war. That does things to people."

"Don't I know it. But I don't have any manslaughter in my past."

"But if there is something—someone—that you want to revisit, this is the time to do it. You can still rewrite part of your story."

Marlys put down her pencil. Dale. They had been best friends. During those first few months in Boston—after Brooklyn, where Marlys's landlady's son crawled in through her window because she had put a chair against the door—Dale had helped bring her back to life. Dale helped the nightmares come only at night, the sensation of the man's bulk on top of her as she uselessly tried to fight back fading each time she picked up Dale's child. How had Marlys repaid her? She took her husband. She took her daughter. It was Dale who didn't come back for Cherie, but it was Marlys who pushed her away. She closed her eyes.

After Ed died, Dale called to tell Marlys that she was moving to Florida. She had heard about an apartment in West Palm Beach and had nothing to keep her in Arizona. She was ready for something new, she said.

Then, she heard nothing more until one afternoon when Marlys was at Albertsons, shopping the recently remodeled aisles, and noticed a woman pull a couple of bananas from a bunch. *Ha!* she thought. *That's something. That woman looks exactly like Dale might when she's old.* It had been thirty years since the women had seen each other, back when they still felt young. When the woman looked up from the bananas and met Marlys's eyes, then began to walk toward her and said Marlys's name, she still wasn't exactly sure who was speaking to her. When the woman stood before her, looked at Marlys's widow's shopping basket—a single baking potato, a single lamb chop—Dale's eyes filled with tears. "Marlys," Dale said, again, then, "I'm so sorry about Ed." Marlys pulled the woman to her, put her head on her shoulder, and sobbed.

They were kids when they met. Kids who had adult problems. When they made sure to be at the same place at the same time to smoke a single cigarette during the course of their workdays at the Navy Yard in Boston, they could say everything they wanted to say, everything they thought no one else would want to hear.

Now, when Dale and Marlys met for chicken sandwiches each week, they spoke about Ed. They spoke about Cherie, Laura, and Jessica. They spoke about the people they shared, the people who filled out their lives. But they didn't speak about everything that had happened between then and now. Marlys couldn't leave Dale without telling her what she had done to her that day in Boston and what she owed her for giving her everything she took.

"There's someone," Marlys told Pam, who had stood up again. "Someone that should hear the things I don't want to say."

Pam nodded, pleased with herself. "Good." She turned around as she walked away. "Keep the pencil. You might want to pick it up again soon."

CHAPTER 7

18 Days

LAURA

Three hours after arriving in Florida, Laura was already standing at the side of the pool at Soleil City, full of regret for not trying on her maternity swimsuit before buying it. She wasn't sure who had devised the design for this particular garment but was absolutely convinced it was done without an actual pregnant person being within ten miles. It was enormous in the chest, tight around her belly, and nearly obscene around her ass.

Now, there were five elderly women ("Oh, honey, do not say 'elderly' out loud around that crew," her mother had said) standing in the pool and looking up at her for direction. Laura was glad that the heat provided an adequate explanation for the sweat pouring from her armpits. She had agreed to come to West Palm Beach because it wasn't Minneapolis. Other than that, she had little confidence in her abilities.

On the plane ride, as Laura sat with a pad of paper and pen on her tray table, ready to work out a comprehensive coaching plan, she had gotten no further than the first item of business: a pep talk.

"Who can do this?" Laura shouted.

"Possibly us. I'd put the chances at around thirty-seventy at this point, and the odds are not in our favor," Phyllis declared.

"No! That's not what I want to hear!" Laura said, attempting to channel the kind of male sports coach who wore a full warm-up outfit on the sidelines instead of a suit as if he might be called onto the field to play at any moment. "Who can *do* this?"

"Us," the women grumbled, knowing that any other answer would prolong this exercise.

"I can't hear you!"

"Us," they said with enough power that the response was deemed sufficient.

"We'll get there, ladies," Laura said. "Every day, we'll build up the power of possibility and see that this journey is taking us to places we only thought we could go."

"What the hell does that mean?" Ilona asked Dale. Dale shrugged in a way that imitated Ilona's own usual response.

The women looked away from Laura and immediately continued their own conversation about the flowerpot that had fallen from a second-story balcony onto the cement below just before this practice, barely missing Donna in the process. "It was Dead Barbara!" Evelyn had said. "That bitch is haunting us because we don't miss her." Laura thought that the missing balustrade in front of where the flowerpot had been and the rocking chair behind the pot probably had a lot more to do with its movement, but she sensed immediately that her opinion on the matter wasn't needed.

When Laura was the captain of her danceline, her teammates were a group of girls who had been taking dance classes nearly as long as she had. They had auditioned for their spots, with the coach leaving out anyone who had less than superior dance skills. When dance-specific language was used during practice, there was no need to pause to define a single word. Everyone was on the inside. Everyone was ready to go the moment they stepped foot in the gym on the first day.

Everyone was sixteen. At sixteen, you could be coached, then molded. At sixteen, you would listen to the thing that the person in front of you had learned to say through their own years of hard-won experience. At seventy-five, you didn't want to listen to shit.

Knowing only that she had to get the women moving, Laura sent them on a series of "sprints"—swimming back and forth across the width of the pool. After they had completed six of these, she asked the women to form a line in the pool so they could all catch their breath.

"Listen," Donna said. "You're going to try to make us do some backflips, aren't you? I'm telling you now, if you make us do backflips, we will drown. We will go into the water and we won't resurface. So, you can decide if you want to deal with that."

"There are actually a lot of moves in synchronized swimming that use a backflip," Laura said. "The Vertical and the Jumpover, for example." Though she hadn't written much in her notepad on the plane, Laura had managed to read a few chapters of the synchronized swimming workbook she had checked out ten minutes before her local library closed the previous evening.

"Laura, honey," Evelyn tried, gently. "This isn't about not wanting to ruin our hair. There's a hell of a lot we can do, but that's not one of the things. No backflips."

"Also," Ilona began, "sometimes people are thrown into the air."

"I think that's more in cheerleading," Laura responded.

"Oh no, I've seen it at the Olympics," Phyllis clarified. "We can't do that either."

"Got it," Laura conceded, easily. She smiled.

"And anything where our heads are very close to each other. That might be hard. A few of us—like Donna, for instance—have terrible eyesight and it will end with a cracked head."

"Phyllis, that's a goddamned lie and you know it. My eyesight is fine."

"You can't drive anymore! You lost your license," Phyllis said.

Donna flinched. "Because that damn cop had it in for me. He made me retake the driving test after one little mistake."

"You hit a child who was crossing the street in front of a school!"

Donna swatted away the accusation. "I tapped him. He got right back up. He barely felt it," Donna offered.

"He broke his arm. He was supposed to pitch at the Little League World Championship. The highlight of his young life."

"Well. Everyone has disappointments. A good lesson to learn at eleven."

"If we're being honest here," Phyllis said, "my left knee is just about shot, but I can still climb those stairs each day. Which reminds me—Laura, when you talk to the Jackass—"

"I won't. That's my mom's deal."

"Sure. Ask him why he bought an apartment complex specifically built for seniors that has the majority of the units on the second floor."

"I'm sure it has something to do with hurricanes," Laura offered.

"Well, whatever the hell the reason, it means that we're climbing stairs, all day long."

"We aren't invalids," Evelyn said. "One set of stairs is hardly an insurmountable challenge."

"Wait until your knees start acting up, Evelyn," Phyllis said. "Because they will, let me tell you. You think you aren't slowly falling apart too?"

"I keep active," Evelyn said defiantly.

"You know who else kept active? Dead Barbara. Who is dead. And clearly not very happy about it, throwing flowerpots all over the damn place."

Laura tried to get the women back on track while barely containing her exasperation. "Let's try this circle move I was reading about."

The circle move wasn't a "move" as much as it was the women simply swimming in a circle. Donna swam too slowly, leading to Phyllis bumping into her, which led to Donna stopping to curse Phyllis out. When the order was reversed, Ilona got kicked in the back by Donna, which led to Dale jumping in between them to prevent a physical altercation. A bird flying above would have seen chaos. Wet, angry women who couldn't swim together in a simple shape.

"I'm an independent spirit! I can't be expected to follow in the paths of *these* women," Evelyn declared, causing almost-simultaneous snorts from Dale and Donna. Ilona just rolled her eyes and shrugged. Phyllis swam away from the group, then swam a full circle on her own.

Laura put her hands on her head for a moment, then took a deep breath. "Let's just pause on this for a moment. Maybe we should talk about music possibilities for the routine."

"Sure, I have ideas," Evelyn said.

"Good," Laura said. "I was thinking 'Under the Sea' by Bobby Darin."

"Oh, hell no," Evelyn said. "I think my granddaughter danced to that when she was a toddler. They slapped makeup on her face, gave her something frilly to wear, and pushed her onto the stage with the instructions to spin. For this, $100 a month in lessons."

"That isn't actually that bad. I think my friend's daughter was paying closer to $200 for her kid," Donna said.

"The makeup they put on those children. Like streetwalking clowns."

Laura looked at the women in the pool wearing lipstick and waiting to be pushed onstage with instructions to spin. For this, Cherie had admitted to Laura that she had paid a $60 entrance fee per participant.

"I like that song 'Come Sail Away.' I think it's by Creedence Clearwater Revival," Dale said.

"Styx," Ilona corrected, and every head in the pool turned in her direction.

"How about 'Sitting on the Dock of the Bay?'" Evelyn asked.

"But we aren't sitting. We're supposed to be twirling and sticking out our limbs," Dale said.

"Then compared to the lyrics, we'll look energetic."

"Do we have to have a water-based song? Isn't that a little on the nose?" Donna asked.

"What are you thinking?" Laura asked, losing patience.

"'Money (That's What I Want),'" Phyllis said, and everyone laughed.

"Now, that's on the nose," Donna said. "But also, motivating."

Laura knew that the prize money was the major reason these women were in the pool. Evelyn told Cherie, who had come to say hello before taking off and leaving Laura all alone, that she had called and confirmed that the amount was accurate. There really was $10,000 waiting for the winning team, put up by a large West Palm Beach–based orthopedic practice who wanted to "encourage the benefits of water-based exercise," which seemed kind, but not wise. "Shouldn't they be sponsoring a senior hurdles competition instead?" Dale had asked. "Seems like that would have made a little more business sense."

The women had spent their time before practice talking about how they would use the influx of cash if it were theirs to keep. Evelyn wanted to buy a new mattress, a potential purchase that went without comment. Donna wanted to take a vacation to Vermont to see the maple leaves in the fall. "It's nice not being cold, but goddamn, I get sick of this every-day-the-same weather."

Ilona said she would invest in the stock market. "Buy the dip," she said, to blank looks.

Dale would buy a selection of flat shoes that would be comfortable with her bunions.

Phyllis hadn't decided what she wanted. "Maybe I'll pre-pay for my funeral," she said. "Or maybe I'll go on a cruise. But I don't know. I'm just not sure."

The money, if they won it, would go not in their pockets, but to a landlord they barely knew. A man who they hoped would allow them to stay in Soleil City, doing what they already did with people they already knew. "My whole life with these goddamned landlords calling all the shots," Donna mumbled. "But hey, you can't take it with you, can you?"

Evelyn threw her hands in the air. "All the other teams will do their routines to some kind of golden oldie. Why do we need to age ourselves like that? Why not something sexy? 'I'll Make Love to You' by Boyz II Men." She shuddered. "That song *gets* me."

"Okay . . ." Laura tried, her smile tight. "We want to excite people, but we don't want to *excite* people."

"What about that God is watching us song by Bette Midler?" Phyllis asked.

"What the hell, Phyllis? No."

"How about 'Girls Just Want to Have Fun' by Cyndi Lauper?" Laura asked.

The women considered this option.

"Then we must convince the people that we are having fun," Ilona said.

"And we'll do that!" Laura said.

"I will not smile," Ilona said.

Laura's face fell and she walked away. It was too hot for this.

"Ilona," Dale said quietly, "be good. She doesn't have to do this."

"Then why? Why is she doing this?"

Laura was doing this because she had no idea what else she should do. She had quit her job weeks earlier in anticipation of the baby. Even if she had wanted anything to do with her friends, they were all at work. Even Nathan's wife went back to her job eight weeks after giving birth. If her friends—former friends—had aspirations of wealth, no one had come close to achieving it.

Even watching TV all day hadn't been terribly satisfying—Laura had stopped watching soap operas in college and had no idea what was happening when she had turned them on, though she was also fairly certain it would take her less than two days to catch up. The game shows were equally unsatisfying, as the hosts seemed to be phoning it in and the guests seemed to be too aware that they would be endlessly replaying this moment in their lives.

If her mother had told her to come to Florida because she had a great plan that involved digging ditches, Laura would have mentioned her physical limitations, then gotten on the plane just the same. Also, Laura wasn't entirely sure that during that phone call with her mom asking her to join her in West Palm Beach, she would have been able to say no. Laura's mom had a plan. Even if her mom knew exactly why she was so willing to leave, Laura believed she would have been offered exactly what she was given—an assignment.

Her mom thought action was the best form of comfort. It came in the form of a request for a favor, but Laura knew this game. She would con Laura into believing that she really did have the powers that her mom claimed she had. *Laura can definitely coach this group of uncoordinated amateurs into a regional win*. It was said with conviction and enthusiasm and Laura was the idiot for falling for the whole thing.

Laura was standing next to a pool filled with winded and disgruntled women because her Grandma Marlys was sick. It wasn't about Laura. It wasn't even really about Dale. It was about Grandma Marlys and her mother's belief that there was something she could do to change the inevitable.

Dale had been the one to call Laura the night before she got on the plane to say that Grandma Marlys was sick. She was noticeably sick.

"Like, are we using the word 'sick' to really mean that she's dying?" Laura asked.

"We are."

"And are we using the word 'sick' because no one is talking about the fact that she's dying?"

"*We're* using the word 'sick.' She's not even saying that."

Laura rolled her eyes. "God, this family."

She thought of her grandmother's lung cancer—she assumed it was lung cancer, but of course she wasn't allowed to say the words within earshot of anyone she was related to—as a sad thing for her mom. She would lose two parents in just over two years. Laura could understand the devastation in that.

Laura was in Dale's Lincoln after being picked up at the gate and was on her way to her Grandma Marlys's townhouse before she thought about what it meant for her.

She hadn't come to visit her Grandpa Ed when he was sick. When Laura expressed regret about that after he died, her mom excused her. "You were so busy. You had the wedding. And the new house with the first-floor powder room that had to be re-painted. He understood that you had a lot going on." Laura and her sister should have visited their dying grandfather. He wasn't their favorite grandpa—that was Grandpa Niels, who let them hold baby chicks—but whether or not they actually liked him didn't seem to be the point. Laura and her sister should have made an effort.

Her mom should have also made more of an effort. It was the one thing about Laura's mom in her recent memory that didn't really make any sense. Laura's grandpa was hospitalized, on and off, for *years,* and her mom had only come to Florida a few times? The single instance when Laura had specifically asked her about it, her mom had shaken her head sadly and said, "I just didn't want to get in the way."

To her grandpa, Laura knew she was just another girl with little to distinguish her from all the other girls in the world. Jessica was the one who stood out because she had musical talent. Still, even that preference hadn't meant much more attention from Grandpa Ed.

One of the few memories that Laura had of her grandpa was a visit he had made to Minneapolis when Laura was in first grade and Jessica was in preschool and they were still in the house with one TV. He watched some weekly Wall Street roundup show, yelling at the TV that they were goddamned capitalist thieves, instead of letting the girls watch their Saturday morning cartoons. "The Christmas toy commercials are on now, Grandpa," Laura had said mournfully, and without turning to face her, he told her that she had enough damn toys already and to give it a rest. Laura promptly went to her room, ripped out the page featuring the World's Greatest Grandpa mug from the JCPenney catalog that she had considered giving him for that year's gift—

her mother had just explained the concept of a white lie: something that wasn't completely true said to make someone feel better—and threw it away. The lie would no longer be white.

She liked Grandma Marlys the way you'd like a teacher who you've never met but would always smile at you in the hall anyway. Was the feeling more like fondness? Laura knew something about her life, especially the drama of living in a high-crime area of Miami in the 1980s before they moved to West Palm Beach. But still, she didn't feel close to her.

Why hadn't her mom prioritized her children's relationship with their grandparents? Why hadn't they come to Florida more? Laura's grandparent memories—baking with Grandma, Grandpa sitting awkwardly on a child's classroom chair for Grandparents' Day—were there, but with her dad's parents. When those grandparents died, separately but suddenly, Laura cried. Jessica came home from college for her grandma's funeral. Even fucking Justin took a couple of days off from work to drive to South Dakota with the family. Back when he still loved her, Laura thought. Or back when he still cared to pretend?

If it were Dale who was dying, Laura would have felt differently. Dale, she knew. It had been years, but when she thought of her Grandma Dale, she thought about walking through the fancy women's department at Marshall Field's that smelled like beautiful perfume as all the salespeople greeted Dale. She remembered sitting on a bench with Dale at the entrance to Water Tower Place as her mom took Jessica to the bathroom, ranking the fur coats that passed in 1980s Chicago. Being with Dale felt like being with an adult who had guided you into a special world. Being with Marlys felt tense as she swatted at her grouchy husband while telling the girls that she would tell them a special story about her brother who had died in the war if they lowered their voices for the next two hours. Laura and Jessica would whisper to each other while walking around on their tiptoes, waiting for a story that never came.

When Grandma Dale's Lincoln pulled up to Marlys's townhouse—this place with the same copper planter that her mother had given Laura for a housewarming present, though this planter contained a single plant trying to hang on—Laura suddenly felt nervous. What was she supposed to say to this grandmother? She felt bad for her mom that Marlys was dying. She felt bad that her mom was going to lose her mom. She didn't feel terrible for herself. Laura couldn't miss what she hadn't truly known.

Dale threw Ilona a pointed look, then loudly cleared her throat. "Because, Ilona, she thinks this can work. That's why she's coaching this team, or whatever we are." Laura turned, smiled at Dale, then walked to the edge of the pool.

"'Girls Just Want to Have Fun,'" Laura said, clapping her hands. "We'll have the music tomorrow. In the meantime, I want you all on your backs, next to each other. We're going to work on raising your right legs at the same time."

CHAPTER 8

17 Days

MARLYS

Marlys had watched as Dale sat down at their usual table at their usual time in the hospital cafeteria of St. Mary's for their usual Tuesday lunch of chicken-tarragon salad sandwiches.

Dale was good. She had looked Marlys in the eye and didn't let her expression or body language give anything away. They would have lunch, just as they always had lunch. Just as if there were weeks and months and maybe even years of lunches ahead, instead of a handful or two. Marlys knew what she saw when she looked in the mirror every morning. She was a sick woman who looked sick. Even at that, Dale wasn't giving anything away.

As a reminder of what was to come, Pam, the leader of Marlys's Living with Dying class, was paying for a bag of chips at the cafeteria register. Would Pam try to say hello? Would she try to say more? *No,* Marlys thought, *not Pam.* She knew to keep her mouth shut.

"This whole synchronized swimming competition is such a Cherie type of thing to do." Marlys put down her napkin and watched as Pam left the cafeteria without a single look in Marlys's direction. "It's nice that she's staying in Florida to spend more time with you."

Dale nodded vaguely as she looked at her sandwich.

"But there has to be more to it than that. She's probably feeling old. Becoming a grandmother, Tom talking about retirement options, that arthritis in her left hand."

"That looks painful."

"She's reminding herself that she can still do things. Getting that Soleil City crew to win a prize would certainly be an accomplishment."

"But wouldn't it be Laura's accomplishment? She's actually the one leading the charge."

"But Cherie orchestrated it, so it's still Cherie's win." Marlys put her hand to her chest as she felt a cough start to brew. She took three small sips of water, as she had taught herself to do, then exhaled slowly. "In 1960, she was in love with Kennedy. Adored him. This was her senior year of high school, our fourth year of living in Edina, that wealthy suburb outside of Minneapolis where we rented the worst house in the best place because Ed wanted Cherie to be surrounded by 'kids whose parents would make damn sure they were going places.'" Marlys rolled her eyes. "Women wore white gloves to drop off a letter at the post office. Anyway, Cherie and the boy she was dating noticed that the place was covered with Nixon signs as far as the eye could see. Cherie bet this boy—Wally, maybe, I don't remember—she bet him $50 that she could convince ten houses to change from Nixon to Kennedy, lawn signs and all."

"Do I want to know how this story ends?" Dale clearly hadn't heard it before. When Dale called her daughter every couple of months, she generally heard a list of Cherie's greatest accomplishments. "It's like she writes them out," Dale had once lamented to Marlys. That's exactly what Cherie did. Academics, extracurriculars, social life—it was all there, with three to five examples of success in each area.

"You were raised Catholic. Who's the patron saint of lost causes?" Marlys asked.

"St. Jude. That one I know. Don't ask me about the rest."

"Jude. That's the one. Cherie's favorite saint. Ed got her a necklace she wore for years. Probably wore it as the doors of Edina were slammed in her face."

"They stuck with Nixon and she lost the $50," Dale guessed.

Marlys laughed. "She got the $50. It included a trip to the police station in the back seat of a squad car, but she got her prize."

"What?"

Marlys played with her earring and looked at Dale. "Cherie got a couple of wives to agree to the sign change, but their husbands changed the signs back to Nixon as soon as they got home. When Cherie saw the Kennedy signs she was holding, she realized that she had been making this much harder than it had to be. She didn't have to convince people, she just had to win the bet.

"Those fancy neighborhoods had very few streetlights and Cherie had lots of Kennedy signs. So, she decided she'd just swap out Nixon for Kennedy and take the Nixon signs with her. So, she calls up old Wally and tells him to take a look the next morning—Kennedy signs all down the street. She got her ten converts. He gave her the money and she decided that it was too easy. Why stop at ten? She went out the next night with twenty signs and was in the process of pulling up a Nixon sign from some neoclassical heap when the cops grabbed her. Ed gets a call to go down to the station and since he knew one of the cops—I don't know how and I didn't dare ask—they let Cherie go with a stern talking-to. She gave the Kennedy campaign $20 and kept the rest. She bought a new coat and Kennedy won Minnesota. Barely, but he won."

"What's the message here, Marlys? That Cherie will do anything to win?" Dale asked.

Marlys shrugged. "You want to win, don't you?"

"We'd all like a win sometimes, wouldn't we?" Dale said. She looked up at Marlys, then cleared her throat. Marlys tapped her foot impatiently. Was this worse? Was pretending that all was well worse than admitting it was not? "It's great to see Laura. I haven't seen her since her wedding."

"It's been longer than that for me," Marlys said, pursing her lips.

"Well, it's nice that you're getting time together now," Dale said, then caught herself. "Before she gets busy with the baby, of course. Those early months are all a blur."

Dale had known the early months, but Marlys never had. She had known that she wouldn't be able to have children since she was sixteen years old. Her mother finally dragged her to the doctor when her older daughter told her that it wasn't normal that Marlys hadn't ever had her "monthly," as she called it. After an aggressive pelvic exam that she endured through tears—her mother sat on the other side of the room, repeating, throughout, that she had been through childbirth six times and a simple poke and prod was nothing to cry about—Marlys was sent to a teaching hospital. A room full of men just a couple of years older than her watched her endure a second pelvic exam and discussed her future as if she wasn't also in the room. She had a severely misshapen uterus. She would never have children. She was, however, pretty enough that it might not matter to a certain kind of man.

A certain kind of man like Ed, who already had a child of his own.

When they first met, the attraction between Marlys and Ed was mutual and immediate. The picture of Ed that Dale had showed her during the war that had made Marlys gasp showed a teenager with the last vestiges of baby fat still settled in his face. The man she met was older, leaner, sculpted. Marlys felt a physical need to rest her hand on his cheek, to push his dark curls from his forehead.

For his part, Ed could only stare at Marlys, then smile slyly when caught. Once he understood that she was real, that she could smile back, he began his flirtation in earnest.

They were careful around Dale, taking Cherie with them when they were together under the guise of "giving Dale a break." It began aboveboard, playing with a chatty Cherie, laughing as she said the kinds of things that only an adorable toddler would say. It stayed that way for nearly four months. But then the pull was too strong. Ed and Marlys went from flirts to lovers to spouses in less than a year.

Ed knew he thought Marlys was gorgeous. But he also knew that she wasn't Dale. Marlys didn't ask to see his work and have a comment or "suggestion" once she did. She didn't ask him where the $10 she had given him earlier in the week had gone. She didn't have her own special language with Cherie, a language that communicated to Ed how much of his daughter's life he had missed. Marlys was easier. Marlys didn't want much. She wanted him. She wanted Cherie. She didn't seem to want too much more.

Now, in a hospital cafeteria, the women ate in silence for a moment. Ever since Marlys hadn't put that handkerchief away fast enough and Dale had seen the blood, it had been like this. Quiet. Stilted. Pained. The two of them, only touching the surface.

"Has Cherie asked you about Ed's paintings?" Marlys asked.

"Me?" Dale asked, startled. "Why would she ask me?"

"About a year ago, she asked me about them. I told her that you knew an appraiser and he was evaluating them for insurance value but he had a long list of clients and it was taking some time."

Dale wrinkled her forehead. "Why did you say that?"

"Well," Marlys said, pushing her own plate away from her. "I sold them all. Kind of. For the price I got, it was more like I gave them away. Anyway, they're gone."

Three weeks after her husband died, Marlys brought all of her husband's paintings to a cut-rate "pre-used home décor" store in Fort Lauderdale and sold the lot for $400. The woman she dealt with frowned as she looked at the work but told Marlys, "At least he used good frames. People will like the frames." Marlys had no idea if the paintings still hung on the store's walls or if they were on someone else's walls or if they were in a dumpster behind the store's strip mall.

Dale looked horrified. "You did what? Marlys . . . speaking purely as his former art school classmate, I have to say, that is not something that you should have done."

Marlys knew it was the worst thing she could have done. Which is exactly why she had done it.

On the drive back to West Palm Beach from Fort Lauderdale, Marlys turned up the radio, slammed her hands on the steering wheel and screamed. It was gone, his whole artistic life. Every painting he had kept, given away as scrap.

As the weeks passed, her anger was paired with guilt. He was scared of dying—he had said so more than once—and he wanted her, his life's partner, by his side. His selfishness reflected his own physical pain. He was angry that all the choices he had made in his life had caught up to him, so he was taking out this anger on her. All these things were true. And she still couldn't let her anger go. She had been by his side for more than fifty years. She had given him his way for more than fifty years. She hadn't wanted more for half a goddamned century. But those years of dying had nearly broken her. She had gone from terror at the thought of losing him when she first learned of his diagnosis, to disappointment when she went to his bed in the morning and saw that he was still breathing, ready to live another painful, helpless day.

Missing Laura's wedding was an example she could cling to of all that had been lost as the days and weeks and months and years—years!—of Ed's illness crept by. All she had wanted, since the day she saw Laura smile when her sister joked with her about a boy she liked when she was twelve, was to go to her older granddaughter's wedding in a new dress, to bask in the pride of having made this family, to be acknowledged for her life's work as a mother, to even be fêted for it. Instead, Marlys stayed by her husband's hospital bed and the honor went to Dale. Dale, who hadn't put in the work.

Marlys couldn't hurt Ed in life. That would have been cruel, and cruel she was not. So, when he was gone, she took away his legacy. Marlys had considered returning to Fort Lauderdale for the paintings. For Cherie, at the very least. Once, Marlys had even gone twenty miles down I-95 before exiting and turning around. She hadn't tried again.

"I did it because . . . I needed the money." She couldn't tell Dale the real reason. She couldn't tell her about being angry at her husband for not dying soon enough, for asking for every treatment to try to cure an incurable mess because he couldn't accept that his body wasn't listening to his mind. Marlys couldn't tell Dale that she was angry that by the time Ed was finally gone, her beauty, her energy, her desire to do anything that would only be for her, had gone too.

"But like that?"

"You sold Frank's paintings after he died," Marlys countered, and she saw Dale flinch at the mention of her favorite husband.

"Under his direction." Dale fingered her necklace. "I didn't want to do it, but I needed money. Besides, painting was Frank's job. The paintings I sold were paintings that he always intended to sell. It's how he made a living. Ed's paintings weren't done for money."

Marlys laughed. "Only because no one would buy them! The man had every intention of making a living from his art. Edward Kelly, American artist. But he didn't. He couldn't."

"Yeah, well, he wasn't the only one to think that his art career would go differently than it had," Dale said.

"Maybe you weren't painting, but your dresses were beautiful. All those years as a couturier—"

After Dale left her job teaching art in Mexico, she had worked on the Paramount lot in Hollywood as an assistant in the costume department, leaving after nearly three years to move to New York where she started her own small dressmaking business. She could do it all—day dresses, suits, eveningwear. Sometimes she'd design the dress herself, sometimes she would copy a Paris original. Dale would say she could draw and she could sew and she could make a little money doing both things together. But the truth was that she was excellent at what she did. Her business failed, ultimately, as fashion changed with the era, but for a time, Dale made many women very happy.

"I was a dressmaker, Marlys."

She put up her hands to object. "You designed a completely different dress for each woman who walked into your salon."

"My Midtown shopfront."

"You created, Dale. You created gorgeous things. You had a career."

"I had a few careers. That was one of them. And in the end, I'm right back where I began. Broke."

"But goddamn if it wasn't a good ride," Marlys said.

"At times a little bumpier than I would have liked."

Marlys smiled at Dale. She could catch her friend by a certain angle and still see her at twenty. She could hear her laugh and go right back to Burt's bar near the Charlestown Navy Yard in Boston where they had first met, and hear Burt tell them, "You ladies deserve a drink more than the bums that are hanging around here. If one bothers you, let me know and I'll throw him out on his ear." She could see Dale at twenty, forty, seventy-five.

"The other day I was thinking about you and me and Ed back in Boston. The way things went at the end—" Marlys started and Dale shook her head and waved her off.

Dale was quiet. She picked at the sandwich on her plate, opening her mouth and then closing it again. Finally, she looked at Marlys. "That was a long time ago, Mar. But I did think about Ed yesterday."

Marlys was taken aback. Ed and Dale hadn't been in each other's lives in decades. Marlys handled all correspondence with Dale. When Marlys tried to talk to him about her—another marriage, another move—he would wave her off. *Doesn't matter, don't care.*

Until about a month before Ed died, when he asked Marlys to call Dale. He wanted to talk to her.

His bad health was getting worse. The chemo had nearly incapacitated him. "I think this stuff might actually be what's killing me," Ed said as he threw up his chicken soup lunch, and Marlys had to leave the room because it was so clear to everyone but him that the poison that wasn't doing much to fight his cancer was doing a fine job of taking him down.

On this bad day, when he asked to speak to Dale, Marlys left the room. When she returned from getting a cup of coffee and stood outside the door, she heard his laughter. "The old bastard never knew what hit him!" he exclaimed, and then began to cough.

Finally, after listening for another ten minutes, Marlys entered the room and motioned for him to put the phone down. She rubbed her thumb and fingers together to indicate money being spent, and Ed's face immediately changed. He quickly told Dale that it was nice talking to her and that they'd see each other again someday. And then, a final, resigned, goodbye.

"I forgot about the cost," Ed said, apologetic. "We were having a nice talk about Boston, our parents, the kids in our art school classes. The old days."

It wasn't the cost. It was jealousy. Irrational jealousy. Marlys was supposed to be Ed's whole world, knowing him better than he knew himself. She was the one who had given almost everything to this man. But there was one person left in his life who knew things that Marlys didn't know, that she couldn't know.

Dale.

Dale got everything first. She was Ed's first love. She was the first woman he slept with. She was there for his first joyful days of art school, watching as he understood he was free to be both proud of his talent and excited by what he could do, no longer the nancy boy who got slapped upside the head for always sketching. She got to introduce him to his daughter. She got to know the first Ed, the man he was before he went away to war.

Dale knew the Boston that Marlys hadn't gotten to know during her time in the city. The streets and corners and seasons and years. She knew his brothers—the older one who was killed on D-Day and the younger one who moved to Alaska and never came back. She knew his parents. She knew his dad's thick Irish accent and his mother's muted one. If a shotgun wedding could be accepted, divorce could not. Ed was out of their lives the minute Dale walked away, knowing all the things that Marlys didn't.

"Ed?"

Dale nodded. "This whole thing with Laura wanting to name her baby Elizabeth if it's a girl. My mother's name. I wanted to hear how Ed would have arranged the expletives in his sentences as he gave his opinion on the matter. He really hated that woman."

"Wasn't the feeling mutual?"

"Completely. I was supposed to marry William McMullin, a man I had met a handful of times whose mother would lead my mother into a world of upper-tier church committees and Christmas cocktail parties. A better Boston. But I married Ed, the bricklayer's son after he knocked me up like an overheated sow."

"You do remember that my mother was a complete bitch?" Marlys asked.

"Sure. But you had a couple of decent sisters and a brother who adored you. I had Elizabeth, a woman who held her granddaughter one time. Once. To show the postman. When Cherie was crying for hours every day the first five months of her life, do you know what Elizabeth did?"

"Nothing?"

"Oh no, she did something. She locked the door to my bedroom during dinner so I couldn't bring the baby out and disturb her meal."

"Jesus, Dale."

"What kind of mother did she set me up to be? I knew that I had disappointed her. I was her only child, and I wasn't at all who she wanted me to be. But when I became a mother, a mother who desperately needed help that she refused to give, it was clear that she despised me. She told me I was a terrible mother and I believed her."

Marlys put her hand to her chest, willing her lungs to not try anything.

"Do you remember when I took the train to Minneapolis after I left Mexico? I was going to talk to you and Ed about taking Cherie for the summer. Maybe longer. Maybe forever. But then, the way Ceres looked at me . . . she wasn't that girl anymore. She was Cherie and she was never going to think of me as her mother again. You were. So, I left."

"You didn't come back."

"What would have been the point? She was yours."

Before that, the fear had lived between them, but Marlys and Ed never talked about it. Marlys had seen Ed look at his daughter quietly reading a book on the couch after dinner with love, then look at the door and frown. There could always be a knock, and Dale could always be behind it. Dale was Cherie's mother, with all the power that fact had.

But there were also moments when Marlys was alone with Cherie when Ed was on the road. When Cherie was saying so many words so early in the morning while her head was feeling so heavy and Marlys would look at the front door, close her eyes, and wish Dale was on the other side of it.

When Dale came to visit just before Cherie's ninth birthday, when Cherie looked at Dale with a mixture of confusion and intrigue—emotions that held to this day—Marlys understood that she should stop watching the door. It was locked, and she and Ed held all the keys.

"I wasn't perfect, Dale. You can't believe I was."

"But you were enough. More than enough. I wouldn't have been."

"You would have been. You had done just fine before me. I made mistakes." Marlys sighed. "I made some big mistakes."

Dale shrugged. "Whatever they were, they don't matter.

Cherie loves you. She—" Dale stopped herself, and Marlys heard the catch in her voice. "She cares about you."

When Marlys died, her daughter would mourn her. That's what Dale was telling her.

"I don't live with regret. I did the right thing. You were better. I knew that. You knew that. I didn't know if Cherie knew that. But when you told her that I needed help with the apartment, she came. She came to me. She'll never forgive me, and I don't expect that. But she's here so I guess that means something."

Marlys had heard how Laura rushed to give Dale a hug when she first arrived in West Palm Beach, doubling over in laughter as her pregnant belly bounced off Dale's soft post-menopausal stomach. She heard how Dale had calmly explained that Laura had the Rowen women's pregnant ankles and there wasn't a damn thing any of them could do about it.

Later, she had seen Laura bend slightly to allow Marlys to kiss her cheek. It had been done out of duty, not affection. The looseness she had with Dale grew tight as soon as she saw Marlys. There was no ease between them.

Dale had been a part of her granddaughters' lives. Not regularly, not consistently, but distinctively enough that they remembered her. They loved her. They were pleased to see her again. Maybe it had just been proximity that had brought them together during that time—the drive between Minneapolis and Chicago taking just over six hours. But Dale was in their lives enough that her older granddaughter wanted to name her daughter after a part of Dale. The wrong part, but a part nonetheless. Marlys was their mother's mother. Someone else.

Dale got to see what would come next. She got to look ahead, learn things that Marlys would never know. If Dale got to be a part of her daughter's and granddaughter's future, would it matter if Marlys told her the truth about the past? What would change if Marlys told Dale that she didn't just walk away, Dale had been pushed? Hadn't they both gotten what they wanted? Dale got to leave before failing. Marlys got Cherie.

"Well. Anyway. This chicken salad needs more salt." Marlys began to rise from her chair when the dizziness overwhelmed her. She sat down again.

Dale's face revealed nothing. Marlys had saved her. Instead of losing, she had pulled out of the fight. She had disqualified herself from competition.

Dale pushed her chair back, stood up, grabbed a handful of salt packets by the register and put them in front of her friend.

"I'm here, Mar. I've got you."

CHAPTER 9

15 Days

CHERIE

Even after Tom made partner at his firm, even as they began to look at homes that were quadruple the size of the house to which they had brought their children home from the hospital and could pay their household bills without waiting for a paycheck to clear or dividing the balance between two months, Cherie didn't really understand what having money truly meant.

It meant that she slept better at night, sure. It meant that she could quit her job at the hospital as the nurse scheduler threatened her with a Christmas morning shift. But those were pleasant byproducts of having a checking account that made the bank teller raise her eyebrows a little higher. What having money really meant, Cherie came to learn, was that you had power.

You could change outcomes so that you could get your way. Laura could practice her dance routine for two hours a night, but Cherie could even better ensure that her daughter would be chosen for the most selective show unit at her dance school by donating a sizable sum to the travel fund. It meant that Jessica's musical talent could be fully recognized by offering the most sought-after tutor double their normal hourly rate to take her on as a student. It meant that Cherie's driveway would be the first to be plowed out after a snowfall by topping up the driver's account at the local gas station.

"I have an appointment at 11 a.m.," Cherie told the man in white in the gatehouse at Hawthorne Haven. "I'm expected," she said and the man she spoke to, a man in his thirties, didn't look at her as she drove past the gate.

Cherie parked her car and smiled at the unenthusiastic woman in white who pointed her toward the lobby. She knew where she was going.

Cherie had come to Hawthorne Haven to find a ringer. Laura was doing as well as she could coaching the women she was given to coach. But the clock was ticking. They didn't have the time to wait for the team to figure out how to work together. Cherie needed to get someone on the inside, swimming with the women to make them better. A teammate, but an example. She needed to find someone who had won this competition before, who knew exactly what it would take to get them that prize.

Cherie had watched the beginning of the previous day's practice at Soleil City. The women were acting on every third command that Laura issued. Though they had figured out how to swim in a circle and had even managed to do it fairly well a couple of times, the next ten minutes were a mess. There were crepe-like arms shooting to the sky at mismatched intervals, veiny legs attempting to rise above the water but rarely breaking the surface, heads—

"Ow!" Donna cried just as she cracked her head on Phyllis's.

"I told you you're blind!" Phyllis shouted at Donna as both women held their heads and cried real tears. Laura called a ten-minute break and told the women, not kindly, to pull it together. The women swam to the ladder one by one until they had all exited the pool. Only Dale looked at her granddaughter, and even that glance was without a smile.

Cherie knew what she had to do. She drove over to Hawthorne Haven, in her imperious rich-lady voice told everyone she came across that she was expected, and went straight to the bar to hang out with the bartender, Shane, a man who reminded the women of Hawthorne both of their grandsons and the fact that sexually, they weren't yet dead.

For $40, she asked for a club soda with lemon and a little information. He knew the women of Hawthorne Haven. The bar, of which Shane was in charge, was possibly one of the busiest drinking establishments in town. "There aren't day drinkers and after-fivers here. There's just drinkers, all the goddamn day long," which pleased him just fine. One hundred bad tips add up when you get them every day.

Who, Cherie wondered, could be persuaded to flip on her synchronized swim teammates? Who had been on the team since the beginning and could remember how they started? Who had a grudge and could be easily convinced to side against the other women? Who was a croissant instead of a doughnut, a woman who was refined and sophisticated enough to both infuriate and inspire the women of Soleil City into action, so they could prove to the Hawthorne women that they weren't second-class? Shane thought he had just the person in mind.

Cherie veered into a glass-domed conservatory ringed with tropical plants. She inhaled deeply but didn't smell anything. Had the rich and elderly managed to crossbreed the scent out of their flowers? Was it clashing with the women's Chanel No. 5 and Shalimar perfumes?

She saw two men sitting in the corner, deep in conversation. The man with hair was holding up the newspaper in his hand, moving it up and down as he tried to make his point. The bald man had a slight, smug smile on his face. *I'll let this fool rant, until I will calmly and completely shut him down.*

Cherie couldn't hear the short, pointed answer that the bald man finally gave, but she did see the immediate flash of anger from his companion with hair. The man with hair threw the paper down, furiously glared at the bald man, and stormed off.

The memory hit her as she watched this unfold. It was about three weeks before her sixteenth birthday. Cherie's bedroom door in their small rental house was open, and she listened closely as her dad said that he wanted to give Cherie a gift of $50. Her mom said, calmly, "I think you should paint a portrait of Cherie."

Her dad claimed he was too busy, that he didn't have the time. Her dad said that his favorite art supply store had closed and he hadn't found a new one. Her dad said that the winter light wasn't strong enough to give him the look that he was after. Her mom listened without comment until she said the one line that would stop his excuses. She told him that he was scared.

He yelled, he stomped, he slammed the door. He opened the door and came back inside, only to continue to yell.

Cherie remembers her dad going through a list of her mom's shortcomings with her mom silent in response, which infuriated her dad even more.

"I didn't ever think this would be my life. But I was left with the kid, wasn't I? So I have to do things I don't want to do. Because I'm trapped." The door slammed almost immediately after.

Cherie didn't move from her bed for the next two hours. She barely tried to breathe. She looked out of her third-story window, trying to judge if anything would break her fall if she decided to jump. And run.

She was the reason her dad was always gone. She was the reason they lived in an apartment and had to ride the bus when her dad was off with the car. She was the reason he didn't paint, that he wasn't a painter. An artist. Cherie got the $50 for her sixteenth birthday. The portrait she had of her younger self that hung on her bedroom wall was painted by Frank, Dale's last husband. Her father had never managed to paint her a picture.

"Is everything all right?" Shane the bartender asked as he approached Cherie. Shane put his hand on her shoulder, a look of genuine concern across his face. Cherie could see why Shane could tell his supervisor that he was taking a half-hour unscheduled break at the beginning of his shift. They would do anything not to lose him.

Cherie smiled her frozen smile and assured him that all was well. She realized that Shane was alone. "Did she flake?" Cherie asked, as she did quick mental calculations as to what she could offer to up the ante.

Shane shook his head. "She decided this was too public of a meeting place. She invited us up to her apartment."

They went to the fourth and farthest bank of elevators. When they got in, Cherie and Shane were alone.

What would life have been like if Cherie's dad had gotten to be an artist? Forget wealth and fame. What if he had been able to simply be a working artist? Would that have brought him more happiness? She thought of her dad, her handsome, brooding dad, and knew that wouldn't have been enough. When his friend Walt, a successful wildlife artist, had one of his paintings chosen for a postage stamp, her dad was dismissive. "It's only being issued for a month," he said. "If the painting were hanging in a museum, it would be there for decades." If her dad couldn't have had it all, he wouldn't have any of it. Which meant she and her mom couldn't have it either.

They had moved nearly every year when she was growing up, except for the four years they spent in the tiny house in Edina so she could go to high school with the "good" kids. The kids that were supposed to show her what she should have while confirming exactly what she didn't have. The one constant in their many apartments was a decent-sized window in the bedroom so her mom could lie on her bed and look at the world and Ed's paintings hanging on the wall. Even when she was young and her dad would put on his paint-stained clothes, even if he didn't go anywhere, the paintings on the wall never changed.

When Cherie asked where the new work was, her mom told her, "He has his favorites," and she knew by her expression not to ever ask again.

The elevator bell dinged as they reached the fifth floor. "It's worse than high school here, in a lot of ways. You know why Patty is turning on her teammates to come swim with you, right?"

"Something about Patty's boyfriend? One of the other women tried to move in on him?"

Shane laughed. "That might make sense. No. It's because of a towel."

Cherie furrowed her brows. "Like, a towel, towel?"

"A towel, towel. A $12 towel. Patty would bring her own white towel down to the practice because she didn't think the Hawthorne-issued towels were soft enough. Gladys, one of the other women on the team, took Patty's towel one day after they got out of the pool, insisting that she had brought it from her apartment and refused to return it to Patty. After that, Gladys brought Patty's towel to practice every day in a small footlocker that she would actually lock up during practice so Patty couldn't take the towel back. When Patty took the entire footlocker, Gladys knocked her down, grabbed the locker, took the towel out, and ran over to the restaurant, where she took a glass of red wine and poured it all over the towel as Patty watched."

"This can't really be about the towel, though, right? This has to be about something else between the women."

"Apparently they barely knew each other before Gladys took the towel."

"So, she's motivated by revenge. Revenge for the integrity of a $12 towel," Cherie said.

They walked down an open hallway that faced the parking lot, just like at Soleil City. There, the concrete was crumbling in places and the wooden frames around the aluminum windows needed paint. Here, there was no disrepair.

When Patty opened the door, Cherie could see that the inside of her apartment was laid out virtually the same as Dale's. But instead of carpet, Patty had ceramic tile on the floor. Instead of white-painted walls, Patty had grass cloth wallpaper. Instead of a single couch and a few pieces of furniture, Patty had two couches and knickknacks everywhere. Cherie could see through the kitchen window—in the same exact place as Dale's kitchen window—that the balcony faced the pool area. Cherie had entered an alternative universe of better finishes, but the same guts.

"This isn't just about that bitch, Gladys," Patty said by way of introduction.

Cherie looked her over. She wore the same uniform as the other women of Hawthorne Haven, with white cotton capri pants and a pastel polo shirt. But there were signs she wasn't quite like the other women Cherie had seen walking around. She wore earrings in the shape of skulls. Her nails were painted a deep maroon, almost the color of dried blood. She had a prominent scar that ran the length of her right arm.

"You're looking at the scar?" Patty asked, as she saw Cherie's eyes on her arm. Cherie could feel her cheeks flush red. "A hard day. That's all I'll say."

Cherie nodded and accepted Patty's offer of a glass of iced tea.

Shane sat silently on his chair, looking at the framed photos Patty kept on her end table. Had he been inside one of the units at Hawthorne before? Cherie looked at his full lips. The more accurate question was probably how many other units at Hawthorne had he been in before?

The photos showed Patty and three teenagers. Patty and two middle-aged men. Patty and Nancy Reagan.

"That was at my dead husband's cousin's funeral. She and Nancy were classmates at Smith. Was it gauche to ask for a photo at a funeral? Probably was. But we do both look very good."

Cherie agreed that they did. There was a moment of silence as the two women looked over at the silent Shane to begin the conversation. Instead, Cherie cleared her throat.

"I think you know the basics here. My team, Soleil City, plans to compete at the South Florida Senior Synchronized Swimming Competition in two weeks and, well, we could use someone with a little more experience on the team."

"How much experience do the rest of the women have?"

"In synchronized swimming?" Cherie asked. "Absolutely none."

"In men and mischief, however," Shane added with a twinkle in his eye, "a hell of a lot."

Patty howled and clapped her hands together. "I love it!"

Cherie turned to Shane and looked past him. Patty lived here alone, Cherie was sure. She saw a single orange juice glass on the dish rack next to the sink. It looked almost elegant, this lone glass with a sole purpose. A glass only for juice, as indicated by the printed oranges on it, and nothing more.

Since she'd been staying with Dale, Cherie had been trying to slowly, quietly, buy Dale things she might need. There were new towels, costing significantly more than $12. New sheets. A small throw blanket Dale could pull over herself if the air-conditioning felt too cold while she was watching TV. There was a new toaster that was in no danger of catching on fire, unlike the ancient model Dale had kept on the counter. New coffee filters, so Dale didn't have to keep reusing the same one five times. Cherie wanted to buy a new microwave but realized that she hadn't seen Dale use the one she had, even once.

Every morning, Cherie put her suitcase on her camp bed, ready to pack it and finally, finally move to a nice hotel. And every morning, she had heard Dale squeezing oranges for their juice in the kitchen and put the suitcase away after she imagined Dale quickly composing her face to look disinterested, to tell her daughter that she completely understood. She should stay somewhere else. She could do better.

What was better? A bathroom to herself? A more comfortable bed? Halls of rooms filled with people she didn't know, who she'd never know, who didn't care, who didn't need her, or want her to know them in any way? Was that better? Better than being greeted and cared for and appreciated by the women of Soleil City every damn day?

Cherie had sent Laura to stay with Marlys, not because she'd be more comfortable with a bedroom all to herself—as cluttered with boxes and newspaper stacks as it might be—but because Cherie could admit to herself that she had screwed up. She hadn't given her daughters enough time with Marlys and now time was running out.

When Cherie was raising her daughters, time with Grandma Marlys and Grandpa Ed meant time spent hearing many, many opinions about Cherie's home, Cherie's car, Cherie's neighbor's car, Cherie's lack of pets, Cherie's neighbor's abundance of pets, Cherie's daughters who spoke a little too loudly at the dinner table. Spending time with Grandma Marlys and Grandpa Ed wasn't the easiest way to spend time. So, what wasn't done then would have to be done now. Cherie would force the matter. Laura would be comfortable enough while she spent these weeks with Marlys and they would grow close and when Marlys died, there would be one more person to mourn her.

Cherie noticed the candy dish on Patty's side table on the far side of Shane. Such a grandmotherly thing to have. How well did her grandchildren know her? How big a role had she played in their lives?

She inhaled deeply. Was Cherie ready to be somebody's grandmother? Did she know what to do? She didn't have a candy dish. She didn't keep a container of Tic Tacs in her purse that she could offer the child as both bribe and reward. When she saw Laura for the first time down by the pool after she arrived in Florida, Cherie had felt her stomach lurch. She was carrying a baby. Not the idea of one, but an actual child who would be in their lives in a matter of weeks.

Cherie looked back at the orange juice glass. Laura had been in town for three days, and neither woman had even begun to approach the subject of what would come next. Laura didn't know that her mom knew that her marriage was ending. One more secret that had to be told.

"So you want me to be the coach?" Patty asked.

"Oh no, my daughter is the coach."

"What does she know?"

"Well, she's a state champion dancer, and has come to Florida to choreograph and organize the team."

"Dancing isn't the same as synchronized swimming."

"It's close enough. Listen," Cherie said, trying to move these negotiations along, "I need you to be . . . a good teammate. No one listens. I need you to listen and to lead. To be the best so that the other women want to be better."

"The teacher's pet, then."

"Yes. In a way that annoys the others just enough to want to prove that they can be better than you."

"I am one of the best," Patty said, without modesty. "So it's good you came to me." She cleared her throat. "You probably want to know why I'd do this, switch teams."

"There isn't a . . . a residency requirement for the team, is there? Before we go any further?"

Patty chortled. "This isn't the Olympics, despite what Coach Diane down there," she gestured to the pool, "may think. This is a local competition. There's an age requirement, so you couldn't go get some twenty-four-year-old to join up—strictly fifty-five and older—but beyond that, who the hell cares?"

Cherie and Shane continued to look at Patty. She leaned her body closer toward them. "I'm switching teams because . . . could it be as stupid as that you asked? That you'll appreciate me? That the Hawthorne ladies might actually realize that I was worth something to them once I'm gone?"

"I don't think any of those reasons are stupid. Don't we all just want a little recognition? A little respect? I know that I—"

Patty interrupted Cherie. "I want them to lose. When Gladys stole my towel, my good towel that I bought for full price at Macy's, and then ruined it, I asked Coach Diane to do something. To show Gladys that there were some consequences for what she had done. But nothing happened. The rest of the women didn't turn against her. The coach kept her on the team *and* moved her up a woman in the Pyramid formation. Everyone just pretended like it didn't happen. That I was the crazy person because I cared so much about a goddamned towel. That's not how it should work. If you do something *insane,* like lie about stealing a towel, there should be consequences for your actions. This is the consequence. I will join a different team, and I will make sure that team wins."

Cherie smiled. Consequences. Finally, someone, somewhere, would get some. No one ever had to pay.

Shane clapped his hands. "So, that's settled. Everyone wants to be a winner." After they left Patty's apartment, Cherie would give Shane his agreed upon "finder's fee."

"Absolutely! We definitely want to be winners." *Or even competent,* Cherie thought.

Patty began to rise from her seat and Cherie followed her lead. "It's nearly lunch," Patty explained. "I need to get a chair closest to the soda machine. Those are the ones everyone wants."

So this is how it went, this generation that made it through a Depression and a world war, who raised children who fought in or against a different war, who watched as phones and radios, then TVs, and finally computers became common in homes, a generation who had struggled and succeeded. A generation that was about to see a new century. A new millennium. Now, in the last decades of their lives, they cared about chairs. Chairs at lunch. Chairs next to the pool. Chairs in the deli area of remodeled supermarkets. This is what her future would be. Chairs. Just the thought of it made her want to run away and leave Tom to the rest of it all by himself.

"So we'll see you this afternoon? For practice?" Cherie asked.

"Sure, yeah," Patty said distractedly, and Shane looked at his watch. He had to get back for the lunchtime crowd.

Patty had her lunch chair; Shane had his tips. Cherie was meeting a recommended oncologist in his office for twenty minutes to talk about what other options Marlys might have. Cherie was the manager. She managed things.

"This will be great," Cherie said. "It will all be great."

Patty shrugged. "Revenge is a decent way to pass the day."

CHAPTER 10

13 Days

DALE

Ilona, as usual, hadn't said why she needed to go to Fort Lauderdale that morning. She had only casually mentioned that she was going and only nodded silently when Dale asked if she could come along. Now, thirty minutes until they returned to Soleil City, Ilona reached to turn the classics station that was playing on the radio up louder. "Patsy Cline," she said and mouthed the words to the chorus of "Crazy." "Patsy Cline, John Kennedy, Dinah Washington, all dead in 1963. Bad year."

"That was the year I met my sixth husband, Frank. The one I loved the most," Dale said.

It was stupid, spending an entire morning driving to Fort Lauderdale and back, but ever since Marlys had told Dale that Ed's paintings were gathering dust while hanging on a pegboard wall in a secondhand furniture store in the city, she had fought the urge to jump into the Lincoln and drive down to see them for herself.

Dale had no plan to rescue the artwork. She wasn't going to buy what she could and surprise Cherie—a misguided peace offering that neither of them would really understand. Dale just needed to see them. She needed to remember who Ed had been.

Who they had both been, all those years ago when they still thought they could be whoever they wanted to be.

"You know, it was only a few weeks ago that I realized that Frank has been dead almost four times longer than we were together. But I still miss the hell out of him," Dale said, expecting no response.

How could Frank have been dead almost thirty years already? How could Cherie be nearly sixty years old? How could Dale have spent nine years and eleven months as a saleswoman in a small store in a suburb of Phoenix, Arizona? What had she done with those years?

"My daughter misses my last husband. I do not," Ilona said.

"How long have you been widowed?"

Ilona shrugged. "Long enough."

Dale decided it was better to not ask any clarifying questions. Ilona had mentioned her daughter in the present tense and her husband in the past. That was more information than Ilona had released in the last six months.

Both women watched the man in the car next to them eat a sandwich as he steered the car down the freeway with his elbow. Ilona grunted in disgust, then pressed on the gas to get ahead of him. She turned up the music even more as if she were trying to keep the outside world away.

"Cherie has very good taste," Ilona said, pointing to the radio. "She said she loves Sarah Vaughn."

"That's her father's influence. She was one of Ed's favorites."

Dale was going to Fort Lauderdale because she wanted to be reminded of the talent she once thought she had. When Dale was twelve years old, she took her first art class. Her mother had signed her up. Not because she was convinced Dale had any talent—despite three different nuns at her Catholic girls' school telling her mother that she did—but because Bridget O'Malley's daughter Eloise was in the class, and if Bridget O'Malley deemed the class worthwhile for her dear Eloise, Dale should be there too.

During those two hours on Saturday afternoon, time stood still. Dale moved from pencil sketches to watercolors after the first week, supplies she would later beg her parents to buy her for her thirteenth birthday before she received a pair of white suede gloves instead. The teacher told Dale that she had unusual talent. She told Dale's mother the same thing. "I see. And how is Eloise O'Malley's talent?" her mother asked. "Extremely usual," her teacher replied, and Dale's mother frowned.

Dale continued to stand out as she started art college, and not just because she was one of only six women in a class of twenty-five. In class, her canvas had her full attention. After class, she couldn't stop staring at Ed Kelly, then found him staring right back.

Ed would watch while she painted, often neglecting his own canvas in the process. He praised her paintings almost continuously, though he also had a list of reasons why he was at a disadvantage. These fine arts classes were his first formal training. He didn't have great nutrition when he was growing up. His hands were large, so holding the paintbrush was more of a challenge.

Dale's appearance was "distinctive," as Bridget O'Malley once told her, to her mother's eternal shame. She had a big nose, big eyes, and prominent ears. But she knew how to dress. She knew how to talk. She knew how to talk to Ed—to compliment him, to challenge him, to charm him.

From the first time Ed and Dale kissed on the corner of Museum Road and The Fenway, everything about them existed with urgency. Within three months, after making her friend Agnes pull her dad's car over so she could throw up on their way to a night out at Blinstrub's, Dale realized she was pregnant. Two days later, after telling the news to Ed, who promptly proposed even though he had enlisted only a week earlier, she told her parents, who cried and stomped and ultimately called the priest to set up a Tuesday midday ceremony. Four months later, she was a noticeably pregnant new bride saying goodbye to her husband as he boarded the train for boot camp, unsure if she would ever see him again. Three months later, as she was in labor with their daughter, Ed was on a ship to the Pacific, headed into war.

As she stayed in the childhood bedroom she had so desperately wanted to escape at her parents' house, Dale spent hours and hours and hours holding her colicky baby to keep her from screaming. During the brief moments when Dale put the baby down so she could bathe or change her clothes or eat a meal or just rest her arms, Cherie cried like the world was ending. Despite the baby she held in her arms, Dale felt utterly alone. Agnes visited once during a crying fit and left after twenty minutes complaining of a splitting headache. Dale's parents were only feet away, yet her dad stayed at work as long as he could and her mom entered the room only to drop off the day's newspaper, opened to the latest published casualty lists, Dale's daily reminder that this, single motherhood, could be the reality for the rest of her life.

"You got what you wanted, didn't you?" her mother sneered as Dale begged her to hold her granddaughter for just a few minutes. With the baby, she had gotten Ed. Ed was the one she wanted. Ed was the one she dreamed about, imagining his fingers running through her hair, his full lips pressed on her own, the electricity that passed through them both each time they touched. Ed was the one who could make her sob with fear that she would never see him again. Ed was the one she cursed for leaving her all alone.

By the time Ed returned from the war, nothing was the same. Dale's father was dead from brain cancer. Her mother had been taken to a sanitarium in Western Massachusetts. The casualty lists that Dale had only scanned had become too real for her mother, leading her to imagine that the son she never had, that she had always wanted, had been killed in Monte Cassino. Ceres, Dale's daughter, was a chatty, active three-year-old who memorized library books and claimed she could read. Dale had her own set of rooms at a boardinghouse in the North End, rooms that were paid for with the money she earned at her job at the Charlestown Navy Yard, all made possible by the landlady who cared for Ceres all day for just a few dollars more. Her friendship with Agnes had ended when she moved to California, replaced by her friendship with a woman from work named Marlys.

Ed wasn't the same, either. He was confused by the changes that had happened in his absence, haunted by what he had left behind. His three closest friends in his platoon had been killed in the last months of the war. He and Dale had been apart more than three times longer than they had been together. The reunion they had both mentioned in every single letter and thought about every single day was interrupted by the little girl who wouldn't leave her daddy's side.

The only thing they both knew, that was certain, was that Ed and Dale wanted to paint again. The money that Dale had managed to save from working six days a week painting warships was enough to save Ed from finding a job for a while. His plan was to make paintings, to get a gallery to show his work, to sell it all, and to get commissions to sell more. He was going to be a famous painter. Dale could be a wife and mother who could paint.

It didn't take long for their little home to become heavy with tension. It wasn't that so many of their conversations ended in arguments with each of them unwilling to concede their point. It wasn't that the money, Dale's money, was running out. It wasn't even the attention that Ed had begun to pay to Marlys, really. It was that Ed would never create what he, or the world, thought he should. And they both knew that Dale could.

Before she knew she was pregnant, but after she thought she was in love, Dale invited Agnes to her first exhibition at the School of the Museum of Fine Arts. Dale proudly showed Agnes her own paintings—two of them, hung on the back wall with the other women's work—and then showed her Ed's contributions. Agnes looked at Ed's painting, looked at Dale, and frowned. "But Dale, this isn't going to work," she said. "You're so much better than he is."

It was never going to work. And then, of course, it didn't work at all.

When Ilona had dropped Dale off at Second Season Home Décor, Dale stopped for a moment at the entrance to take stock. The scene was chaotic. It didn't appear to be a store as much as a dumping ground. If Marlys wanted to park Ed's work in the most disagreeable location in a one-hundred-mile radius, Dale was fairly certain she had found it. Unlike a Salvation Army or a charity shop, there were barely any shoppers. Dale looked around the store to count. There were three people inside, total. Dale, a cashier, and one man who was standing behind a velvet high-backed chair, bobbing up and down in her field of vision while making barely disguised moaning noises. Dale turned and walked in the other direction.

She walked past the shelves of glasses and silverware, of wedding china and pewter frames. The things people needed and the things they wanted. Cherie had been filling Dale's cabinets with new and better things, hiding the Target and Dillard's shopping bags at the bottom of the trash. Dale noticed all the new items and the replacements, but the hidden bags told her she shouldn't say a thing. For both of their sakes.

On the back wall of the store, Dale found the framed artwork. There were framed paint-by-number paintings that looked to be done with a fairly precise hand. There were five different paintings of palm trees, six different paintings of the beach. Two dogs and one teen girl whose artist seemed to struggle with scale, painting her nose smaller than her eyes, which were smaller than her lips, which were all smaller than her ears.

There, at the end of the row, were six of Ed's paintings. They stood out for their skill and were priced between $75 and $200 and were gathering dust.

Dale stepped back, knocking over a stack of encyclopedias, to see them better. Four were landscapes, all of them very dark. While the cigarette smoke that had settled over the top of each painting in a deep fog had contributed additional shading, Ed had painted a bleak world. Grays, darker grays, some black.

Dale moved forward to see the date next to EDWARD KEL-LY's outsized signature. They were all painted right after the war, in those first months Ed was home. Dale recognized two of them, maybe, but they weren't at all what she remembered. Had she not seen the darkness then, or had she been so desperate to find some light that she hadn't let herself notice? It was a bleak world that Ed was letting out of his mind. A world where death and destruction and loss overshadowed everything. The seemingly simple cityscapes hid something darker, something deeper. Dale slept next to Ed as he thrashed through his nightmares. She saw him pour himself a third or a fourth drink on a Tuesday night. She watched as he fell to the ground when a car backfired outside their window. The Ed she had said goodbye to at South

Station in 1943 was a completely different Ed than the one who slept next to her in late 1946, than she left her daughter with in early 1948.

She shook her head as she looked at these paintings, these canvases that Ed thought would support the family he barely knew. They weren't going to match the drapes or pick up the red from anyone's rug. Ed had painted pieces that people would not want. Dale leaned closer to see the clearance sticker on the bottom of the frame. He had painted pictures that people still didn't want.

Dale's sixth husband, Frank, had painted pictures that people wanted, because he painted their portraits. He showed up in a wealthy community, talked to the bartender at the local country club about who he should approach, and then, once he had a client, he'd get a dozen more. He painted quickly and well. He made women handsome and men stately. He painted them the way they wanted to be seen. Then, once his sittings began to drop off, he'd pack up and move to the next enclave. He had done this for over a decade when he and Dale met. With Dale, he'd do that for nearly a decade more. They'd move from apartment to bungalow to townhouse. In Charleston, they lived in a charming old carriage house. They'd take what they could get from the community, and then they would move on to the next. After he was done with his portraits for the day, he would walk around and sketch whatever caught his eye. He would re-create some of these charcoal sketches in oil and sell them just as he sold the rest of his paintings. He would keep a few.

Frank, like Ed, like Dale's second husband Bob, like her third husband Harry, had fought in the war. Frank, like Ed and Bob and Harry, could slip into a world she had never known. What had Frank painted before Dale met him? She wouldn't know.

Frank had sold almost everything he had done. "I paint so I can eat," Frank said.

Ed's works were angry. They were dark. And they were what he thought would allow him to feed his family and make him a star. Had Dale ever truly believed that too? He carried Cherie on his shoulders and held Dale's hand as they walked through the high-rent Back Bay area of Boston, Ed pointing to his favorite homes and telling Dale that he would buy a place for them someday. Dale felt her throat grow thick. What else during that first and last full year that they spent together had she not seen? What else had she allowed herself to believe?

She had seen him fall in love with Cherie. She had only seen him fall in love with Marlys after it was too late, after he had already decided that he didn't still love Dale, after Dale had wondered if she had ever loved him at all. She had seen some of his pain, but not all of it. Some of his anger, but not all of it. Some of his desperation, but not every single part. Ed, she was sure, hadn't seen Dale at all—her pain, her anger, her desperation. For Ed, the end of the war meant he could regain his freedom. For Dale, the end of the war meant that her freedom would all be taken away. The woman she was then—independent, self-assured, liberated—was not the woman she was expected to be once the men who would return came back.

On Dale's first trip to Minneapolis to see Cherie after she left Mexico, after she had to start all over again, Dale helped her former husband do the dishes in the kitchen while their daughter played with her new mother in the next room. "When you gave me Cherie, you gave me my purpose. I can thank you for that," Ed said.

Dale had told Ed that he was a good father or that Cherie seemed happy or that Minneapolis seemed nice. She couldn't remember what she had said, but she knew what she had wanted to say. In giving him Cherie, Dale hadn't given him a purpose; she had given him an excuse. He said he couldn't paint because he had a child to raise. He said he couldn't paint because he needed to make a living. Dale thought he couldn't paint because he had lost his nerve.

She remembered a conversation she had with Marlys sometime when Cherie was a teenager. Marlys was angry with Ed for something, an emotion she rarely let Dale see. Dale tried to lighten the moment, the long-distance phone charges ticking up.

"I guess that's what you get for marrying an artist," Dale joked.

"No," Marlys said, her voice flinty. "You married an artist. I married a salesman who can draw."

When Dale turned to leave the store in Fort Lauderdale, to stand outside and hope that Ilona returned for her, Ed's large signature caught her eye on a sixth painting that was hung away from the others. The painting, dated 1955, was a picture of a lovely lake, most likely in Minnesota, with a pair of loons on the water and a child's sun hat on the grass in the foreground. The picture was surrounded by a perfect blue sky. It was peaceful. Bright.

Ed could see the light. Whether it was just for that day or week or month, he had found it. Dale believed she did too. When she met Frank, she woke up one morning next to him and felt almost weightless. She had shed her own darkness.

At the secondhand store, Dale pulled Ed's painting off its hook on the pegboard and held it. In 1955, the year that Ed found this blue sky, Dale was in Los Angeles, married to her third husband, Harry, a contract screenwriter at Paramount, and working in the costume department of the same studio. She would divorce Harry the next year and leave Los Angeles for

New York, where she would live alone for the first time in her adult life.

Dale saw a sticker on the bottom of the frame and realized it wasn't a clearance tag like the other paintings had. It was a SOLD sticker. Ed had sold a painting. Someone had looked at this sliver of contentment in this chaotic place and found a moment of peace. Dale put the painting back on the wall, whispering her congratulations to a man she once loved, the father of her daughter.

Now, returning to West Palm Beach with Ilona, her friend turned down the radio.

"Has Cherie always called you Dale?"

"No. I was Mama once. She was called Ceres. But that was a long time ago."

"Before Marlys came into the picture."

Dale looked out the window, saw a car abandoned because of a flat tire. "We were at the beach one day. I was painting. The sky was changing quickly because a storm was coming in and it was . . . gorgeous. It was dark—" Dale stopped herself. Dark. Did the darkness inside Dale keep her from finding Ed's paintings disturbing? Was it her own fury, her pain for being dismissed by her mother? Dale exhaled. "I painted the storm. I didn't hear Marlys shouting for Cherie or Cherie crying in the water. I didn't notice any of it and Cherie almost drowned. Marlys saved her. When Ed told me that he was in love with her, it was almost a relief. Marlys would be a good mom. I was not."

Dale couldn't paint without guilt after that day. The guilt took her talent. The war had taken Ed's. Had Marlys gotten rid of Ed's paintings because she no longer wanted to be confronted with the disappointment of Ed's limp ambition? Or was it the reminder the paintings provided that within Ed still lived a war from which he would never really return home, a darkness that he would never truly shake? When he kept his paintings on the walls of their many different homes, he was bringing with him his ghosts—from the war, but also from his ideas of who he once thought he could be.

Ilona kept her eyes fixed on the road as she spoke. "My daughter was riding bike when she was little girl. We were visiting a friend I knew from Hungary in New Jersey and Vanessa was riding bike and got hit by a car. She was in hospital, they tell me she might die. I was talking about Hungary, about dead people I wouldn't see again. I didn't protect my daughter." Dale watched as Ilona took a breath. Had there been a first child that she hadn't been able to protect either during the war? "I never talk about Hungary again. Not about country, not about war. Then I watch daughter too close. She moved away as soon as she could."

"I gave up. But I gave up because there was someone better," Dale said.

"You would have been fine," Ilona said.

"Is fine enough?"

"Fine is very good in world that isn't perfect." Ilona looked quickly over at Dale. "But Cherie wants perfect, doesn't she?"

"In me, or in life?"

Ilona shrugged.

"She does very much like when everything works out," Dale heard herself say and knew that with every day that went by, each conversation with Cherie got shorter. Each cocktail hour by the pool had Cherie's attention focused on the other women. Dale knew that while Cherie would try to solve Dale's problems, she was less concerned with solving her problems with Dale. Their relationship was what it was, and it wasn't going to become something else.

"She's doing good things for us. I like her," Ilona said. "Patty was good idea."

Dale smiled. Cherie had put up her hand as the women began to howl their complaints when they learned that Hawthorne Patty would be joining their squad.

"We want to win. We have to win. This isn't just for a trophy. This is for Soleil City. For you, all of you. Patty knows how to do this. Let her in. Let her get us where we want to go."

Ilona had moved to Cherie's side. "She is right," Ilona said, and the grumbling grew quieter. "This is how we stay here."

Now, Dale looked at the woman next to her, a woman whose early life she couldn't even begin to imagine. Ilona didn't hide her scars. But she also didn't share them. But what did Dale's friends in Soleil City know about her either?

Her friends did know about her bunions. Just as she knew about their high blood pressure and bad knees. It's what they cared about in these last years of their lives. They would sit by the pool and rate local doctors, discuss vitamin combinations. Before each doctor's appointment, there was a collective intake of breath, exhaled as soon as a test came back requiring nothing but a new medication. For now, they had all been lucky, their declines slow and manageable.

They had all lived. They had all loved. They had all lost. They had all landed here, in the end, together.

"I tell you something," Ilona said, the synchronized swim competition forgotten. "Ilona of Buda was me. You said first, so I can say now. I was aesthetician. One of the best." Dale bit her tongue to stop from speaking because she thought Ilona might give her more. "I'm actually Ilona of Pest," she said, laughing. "But they don't know. No one knows. No one cares." She looked at Dale. "So now you know something about me."

"I never told my fourth husband that I was a mother. I never told my fifth husband that I had been married four other times. Now you know something about me, too."

"We say what needs to be said," Ilona concluded.

"We do what needs to be done," Dale agreed.

"We don't always get it right," Ilona said.

"Enough. We got it right enough," Dale said, and Ilona shrugged her signature shrug. "We got through it, anyway," Dale concluded, and at that, Ilona finally smiled.

CHAPTER II

11 Days

LAURA

Laura looked at the drink the waitress at the West Palm Beach Veterans of Foreign Wars post put in front of her. "This is Diet Coke, right?"

"We serve Pepsi products," the woman said, walking away.

Laura pushed the drink to the middle of the bar table. She would drink it, eventually, but for now, she would pout. A gaggle of elderly women had gleefully taken advantage of her alcohol-free status and had gotten her to drive a large Lincoln Continental to this VFW outpost for karaoke night while they sang along to Fleetwood Mac songs and screamed out the window that it was Thirsty Thursday and they were ready to get sloppy. This was the second-to-last place she wanted to be. The absolute last place she wanted to be, however, was back at home.

Justin had called her two hours earlier. If she wasn't staying at their house, could he stay at their house? He was tired of his room at the Radisson and besides, it wasn't her house, it was their house and if she wasn't there, why couldn't he be?

"Is Melissa with you?"

Silence.

"Shouldn't the two of you be at an adults-only Sandals resort in the Caribbean or a casino in Las Vegas or some other place that prohibits children?"

"Laura," Justin said, and Laura could faintly hear him cracking his knuckles, a sound she could never stand. "I do feel bad."

"I'm sure you do, Justin. But I don't think you feel bad about the thing you actually need to feel bad about."

Laura got off the call knowing that however long it lasted, Justin would likely not acknowledge the upcoming birth of their child. She thanked the difference in time zones for giving her another hour to find a locksmith still on his regular clock (though for this, she would have paid time and a half), and got the locks changed—front, back, and garage entrance. The Asshole and the Traitor would be kept out.

Marlys beckoned toward her. "You're my duet partner, Laur. 'Summer Nights' from *Grease*."

Marlys appeared to be drunk. On Laura's twenty-first birthday, Cherie told her the story of her first drink when she was three weeks old. Marlys had come to stay with them to help with baby Laura and between stepping out to smoke cigarettes and keeping the TV volume up way too loud, she had spilled her whisky on Laura's head. Cherie hadn't thought any had gotten near Laura's mouth, but then Laura slept twice as long as she normally did between feedings. "It had to have been the booze," her mother concluded. "Your grandmother thought she had cracked the code for sleeping babies and suggested that adding a few drops of whisky to your bottle before bed every night could only be good for all of us. She was puzzled when I refused."

Laura knew that giving her baby brown liquor might bring unwanted attention from the authorities, but she didn't know much else. She didn't know how to get a baby to sleep. She didn't know how often a baby needed to eat. She didn't even know how to change a damn diaper. Her friends had mentioned something about the hell that was clipping a baby's soft fingernails. Until that moment, she hadn't even considered the task. She didn't know any of it.

During practice at the pool that afternoon, the baby had kicked Laura so hard that she had bent over in pain. Who the hell was this inside of her? The older women laughed, "You've got a live one, watch out," but Laura didn't laugh. If the baby could kick her that hard, the baby was becoming the size of a baby. Not a grapefruit or whatever the hell kind of fruit her pregnancy book used as visual aids. If the baby was almost as big as a baby—and Laura's belly was evidence that it certainly was—that baby wasn't far away from being outside of her, crying, sleeping, pooping, needing care. Needing her to know what the fuck she was doing.

Laura reached for the diet Pepsi and took a sip. Man, she hated this stuff. Why was it even considered an alternative to Coke? The two products were absolutely nothing alike. They were probably actually virtually the same, brown-colored fizzy sugar-substitute water, but a person's allegiance lies with one or the other and if you favored Pepsi, you usually kept that to yourself.

"Laura!" Marlys shouted. "Do you want to be John Travolta or Olivia Newton-John? I'll let you choose, but you've probably guessed which one I want to be."

"Olivia?"

"Olivia? Not that prissypants! I want to be John."

Her Grandma Dale sat next to her. "I'm sorry that can't be a glass of something stronger."

"Did you drink when you were pregnant with my mom?"

"Of course. Drank, smoked, worried that her dad was going to be killed by enemy fire, and look how she turned out."

They looked over at her mom wiping the edge of her wine-glass with a paper napkin, turned to each other, and began to laugh. "I'll stick with the Pepsi." Laura picked up the glass to have a sip, then put it back down. "Do you guys hang out here often?"

Dale shrugged. "When I need even more old people in my life."

Laura yawned.

"You aren't just tired," Dale told Laura.

"I am very tired," Laura said. "Grandma Marlys has that high-powered air filter going all the time to help clear out the smoke. It's loud."

"She's still smoking?" Dale asked.

"Why not, right?" Laura said, then saw her grandma's expression. "Not in the house. But there's enough residual smoke in that place to keep the filters going for the next decade."

"I wish I had more room at my place."

Laura waved her off. "My mother has now told me three times how nice it is that I get this time with Grandma Marlys, so none of this is on accident. I don't really know her, Marlys."

Dale only nodded.

They watched as Marlys took another sip of her drink across the room as she listened to one of Evelyn's stories. "I'm not just tired," Laura said and Dale sat quietly, waiting for Laura to continue. "Was there ever a point, maybe a few months after one of your divorces, when you were sitting at the kitchen table, worried about what the hell you were going to do next, and you thought it might just have been easier if you had just rode out the whole thing?"

"No."

"No?"

Dale wrapped her hand around her glass. "The fastest way to divorce my third husband was to live in Reno, Nevada, for six weeks."

"That was fast?"

"As the speed of light, compared to the alternatives. Anyway, I sat in a hotel in town—there were these lovely ranches where you could stay that had horses and swimming pools and handsome ranch hands, but I didn't have the money for that—and I played cards with the other would-be divorcées until the day I could go to the courthouse and make the whole thing legal." Dale smiled. "I remember walking down the hall of my hotel, past the other doors, listening to the music playing in each room. There were these two radio stations—one that played sad ballads about lost love, and one that played happy swing songs that made you want to dance. Some of the rooms never moved from the ballads. But most of the rooms, by about week three, had moved to the swing. The more you talked to the other women, the more they told you about the husbands they were leaving behind, the more you realized that the man you were crying over wasn't worth it. Men had the power. Men had the law on their side—I couldn't even open a bank account without a man's signature until the 1960s. You, as a woman, didn't get a hell of a lot of your own. But you could get a divorce. You could get rid of your useless husband. Or boring husband. Or mean husband. Or just plain stupid husband. As long as you were able to do that, why would you settle for a dud?"

"You never settled."

Dale shrugged.

At her wedding, Laura overheard one of her mom's hair-sprayed friends nod toward Dale, whose back was turned but whose ears were opened, and ask, "Is that the oft-married mother?" How had Cherie described Dale to her friends? Did she talk about her during cocktail parties in an attempt to scandalize her friends the way she told Laura and Jessica stories from her days in the emergency room? (Laura would sometimes look at her mom setting the table for dinner, adjusting the silverware just so, and wonder why the hell she had told her grade school–aged daughters about the man who had shoved a Barbie doll up his ass.)

What reaction did Cherie want when she told her friends that Dale had been married six times? Did she want them to be impressed by her unconventional upbringing or did she want them to pity her?

About six months into her wedding planning, when the number of checks that had to be written began to increase by the week, her mom had softly asked her if she really wanted such a grandiose wedding. Laura had been confused. Her mom had seemed quietly supportive of everything until that point. "Why would I not?" Laura had asked, and her mom, in halting language that only partly made sense, said something about memories being longer when you make something unforgettable.

It was a year and a half later, after Laura had received a dozen carnations with baby's breath that Justin had picked up from the grocery store for Valentine's Day, that she finally understood what her mom had been trying to say. *This might not work out. If it doesn't, everyone will mention your wedding and what a waste the whole thing had been.*

Her parents never actually told her that they thought she could have done better than Justin, but their body language communicated their beliefs loudly. Was it right, that they had let her make her own decision and deal with whatever consequences, or had they failed in not telling her what they had obviously felt in their gut? What would her mom say now that she had been right? Justin was wrong. Laura had chosen the wrong man to marry.

"I'm going to divorce Justin," Laura said, leaning back on her stool. "My mom doesn't know. Yet."

Dale's face remained neutral. "When are you going to tell her?"

"Have you ever had to admit to my mother that she was right?"

Dale pushed Laura's drink toward her.

"He slept with a friend of mine," Laura clarified, taking a sip. "My best friend, actually."

"I see."

"For three months, at least—actually, it was probably longer—a couple of times a week. Quite a commitment for a man whose attention wanders during a half-hour sitcom."

"Then you're right to leave him."

"The thing is, I don't miss him one bit. I truly don't. But her—Melissa—I miss her. I miss her more than I ever thought I would."

Every morning, Laura grabbed her phone from the floor near her guest-room bed, closed her eyes, counted to five, and opened them. And every day, no matter how elaborate she made the ritual—she had also begun to twirl the phone over her head three times—there weren't any messages or missed calls from Melissa. It was as if she had simply disappeared.

Dale put her hand on top of Laura's. "Don't I know it, sweetheart."

Phyllis, who wobbled slightly as she walked, approached their table. She had a single bandage above her eye where she had been nicked by a piece of concrete that had fallen off her building at Soleil City.

"I've been meaning to tell you this and I can't wait any longer," Phyllis said, her black hair styled into soft waves.

"Ah . . ." Laura tried, looking behind her to see where Phyllis had come from and how much she had heard.

"Do not overpluck your brows. Ever. I had lovely eyebrows like yours once. But the fashion was to pluck them into a line. So I did, again and again and again, and look," she said, shoving her face close to Laura's. "I have just a couple of wisps left. I have to draw them in each day or I'll scare dogs and small children." Phyllis pointed her finger at Laura, then pushed it into her shoulder. "Listen to me on this. Really."

"Message very definitely received," Laura said, as Dale shook her head and Phyllis walked away to dispense drunken wisdom to the next poor sap.

"I don't have a plan," Laura said, returning to the subject. To her surprise, she felt a lump form in her throat. Why shouldn't she cry? Hell, she should be sobbing, right here, into her diet Pepsi. When your best friend is the other woman in the whole equation, it removes a major shoulder to cry on. "I don't have a plan, or a job, or any money, and I'll soon have a baby. What a fucking mess," Laura concluded.

Now, a swaying Donna approached them.

"Laura," Donna said, pulling a stool from a nearby table and nearly tipping over as she tried to mount it. "I have a few questions I've wanted to ask you. You know, as a young person." She pulled a piece of folded paper from her bra.

"You've written them down?"

"Oh honey, I've got a memory like a sieve." Donna unfolded the paper. "It's not right to ask you anything at the pool. You're at work then."

Donna, the former teacher, hadn't ever been as much as thirty seconds late to a practice and hadn't ever crept toward the stairs in the three minutes before Laura dismissed the women like the others did. "That's just disrespectful," she had murmured as she watched the women quit before the time was up.

"Okay, then, what do you got?" Laura asked.

Donna cleared her throat. "Mobile phones—are they the future or just a fad?"

"The future, definitely. You'll have one within the year, mark my words."

Donna rolled her eyes.

"Y2K—on a scale of one to ten, what should my concern level be?"

"I don't know, I guess a three?"

"Really? Less than five? Tell that to my refrigerator repair guy. He's turning his garage into a bunker. I told him I've lived through the Great Depression and a goddamned world war. I'm not putting all my money into canned peas because of a computer glitch."

"Obviously, I don't actually know."

"None of us do." Donna squinted to see the next item on her list. "Will China accept the Dalai Lama's invitation to talk about the future of a free Tibet?"

"Um . . ."

Dale chimed in. "That report on *60 Minutes* a few weeks ago didn't paint a rosy picture. I thought, well, hell, add it to the list."

"Isn't that the truth? Sometimes I think that maybe it's not a bad thing I don't have another twenty years in me." Dale and Donna laughed.

"Hello?" Laura asked.

"What is it, dear?" Donna said.

"I do have another twenty years in me. This baby has twenty years times four. At least."

"God willing," Donna said, slamming her palm on the table.

"And good luck. It appears as if you'll both need it in this world. The ice caps are melting too, just so you know. Ah, it's time for my song." Donna jumped off her stool without falling on her face and rushed to the stage.

Once there, Donna picked up the mic that had been left on the ground, burped as she stood up, then steeled herself as the opening notes to "Total Eclipse of the Heart" began to play. Donna, who had also sung the loudest to Fleetwood Mac in the car, launched into the song with passion and without tone.

"Oh boy," Dale said.

"What the hell is happening here? Is this what they're like when they're drunk?" Laura asked.

At the table across the room, Marlys slapped Evelyn on the shoulder as she laughed, and coughed, at the story she told. Patty and Phyllis's eyes focused on the stage as they sang along with Donna, and Ilona listened intently to the young waitress who was sobbing as she told of her troubles while continuing to balance the tray holding a single lowball glass.

"Pretty much," Dale replied.

Donna had reached the chorus and was belting out the words with full lung capacity. The MC briefly returned to the stage to show Donna how to pull the microphone back from actually touching her mouth. She pulled it back, then put the mic right back up to her lips. The MC scurried away. "He's gotten hit with the mic before," Dale explained. "Not everyone likes his advice."

After the second chorus, Donna returned her microphone to the stand and walked away. She was done. Laura began to laugh, and Dale just shrugged. "I don't like how the song ends," Donna shouted to the crowd as she walked offstage by way of explanation. The MC laughed uncomfortably and called the next singer up to the stage.

Next was Evelyn. Marlys joined their table to watch Evelyn sing.

"Oh, this will be good," Marlys slurred. "I imagine she'll sound just like Eartha Kitt. A sexy purr."

Instead, Evelyn stood awkwardly at the microphone. Laura knew that stance. It was the "crap, the jig is up," stance that she inevitably shrunk into when she had to get up in front of the debate club. God, what a disaster that was. Her dad had been a state debate champion and was almost prouder of that feat than he was of being a successful lawyer. Laura had not inherited his talent. Her attempt to make him proud only brought disappointment.

Evelyn folded her hands together and let them fall below her waist. She took several audible breaths and seemed to recover enough to sing the song she had chosen—"Neutron Dance" by the Pointer Sisters—at a level only slightly above a whisper while moving as if she had been glued to the floor despite the rapid beat of the song.

"Nope. Not Eartha Kitt," Marlys said, and took another swig. "Not even audible, really."

Evelyn continued the song at the same volume, quiet enough that everyone lost interest, which seemed to be her entire plan. Laura smiled. Maybe, when your life seemed to be almost like a performance, a stage was just an inconvenience.

With a little help from the MC, who mercifully cut the last minute from the song, Evelyn ended her performance with a bow. She joined their table and Marlys poked Dale to lavish praise upon her. "Well, you did it, Ev," Dale said without enthusiasm, a sentiment that Evelyn decided to accept as an accolade.

Laura had just finished her diet Pepsi when her mom rushed through the front door, telling the bouncer that he had just seen her leave less than ten minutes earlier and could kindly stand down. He nodded her inside without further comment.

Cherie looked at Dale's red wine and cream soda—no Lambrusco at the VFW—and exhaled deeply. Then, she picked it up and drained the drink in one go. Dale picked up the glass, looked at it, put it down, and shrugged.

"I was just speaking to your dad, Laur."

Laura felt her body tense. "That's nice. How's Dad?"

Two days after Phone Message Monday, Laura had called her dad. Laura was her dad's favorite. She was the easier of his two daughters because he understood what she wanted. She wanted a life like the one he and her mom had built. Jessica, on the other hand, freaked him out a little because he wasn't close to understanding his younger daughter's plans, this extraordinarily talented musician who wasn't using her gift to join a world-class orchestra to perform in venues where people wore suits to sit in velvet seats.

Laura did want to call a lawyer. But she also wanted to hear her dad's voice after she told him the type of lawyer she was looking for. If she heard judgment, sadness, anger when she said the word "divorce," she thought she might turn back. But there was no judgment. There was no sadness or anger. His voice was even. Professional. *My secretary will send you a list of names.*

This kind of thing happens, Laura remembered thinking. *This kind of thing is now happening to me.*

"He's actually a little busy," her mom said, and Laura could see that her cheeks were flushed. "Seeing as he just spent the last half hour at your house negotiating with the police."

"Huh," Laura said, digging her phone out of her purse. She had five missed calls from Justin and four from her dad. There were no missed calls from Melissa.

"You changed all the locks at your house," her mom said.

"I did."

"But why would you do that?"

"Because Justin doesn't live there anymore."

Laura saw a woman about her age sitting near them. She was wearing a Banana Republic blazer and a knee-length skirt, as if she had just come from work. She appeared to be listening in on their conversation while sipping what looked like a Sprite.

"Laura. Pregnancy isn't always an easy time for a marriage. Maybe it was wrong, to ask you to come here. I thought a little time away would be good for you both, but perhaps you should go back home and work it all out. Whatever he did can't be bad enough to end your marriage over. Jesus, Laura, you're having a baby together in less than three months."

"He fucked Melissa, Mom."

"*Melissa*, Melissa?"

"That's the one. Repeatedly."

Laura had to admit that the satisfaction she felt watching her mom put her hand over her mouth in shock was not insignificant.

Marlys sobered up, quickly. "Justin has been cheating on you? But you're pregnant!"

"I am indeed."

It was clear that something interesting was happening and Patty, Phyllis, Donna, and Ilona abandoned their table, and their drinks, to join Laura at hers.

"Laura's husband has been cheating on her. She changed all the locks and he called the cops," Evelyn told the other women, filling them in.

"She can't take care of this baby all by herself," Marlys said. "She hasn't been raised that way. After the baby is a little older, she can figure out what she wants to do."

"How was she not raised that way?" Cherie asked.

"I took care of a baby on my own. Laura is perfectly capable of doing the same," Dale said quickly, before Marlys could explain what she meant.

Marlys snorted. "You took care of a baby on your own. Look how well that worked out. The first excuse you had to flee, you took it."

"Marlys, you're drunk," Dale said, quietly.

"He was sleeping with this woman for how long?" Donna asked, in a teacher tone of voice.

"At least three months. Three admitted months. And she wasn't just a woman. She was my best friend. Her husband was one of my husband's best friends," Laura said, and Donna and Ilona both held up their hands to indicate that they were out. Clearly, Laura had been wronged.

"Laura, make sure you think this all the way through," Marlys said.

"I have. I want Justin out of my life."

"Then that's what should happen," Dale said, matter-of-factly.

Marlys waved her off. "You never liked him, Dale."

"At least Grandma Dale told me she didn't like him. You never liked him, either, Mom, and you didn't say a fucking word."

Cherie opened her mouth as if she were going to comment on Laura's language, and then understood that a few flying fucks were not the biggest issue in front of them. "You said you loved him."

Marlys laughed. "There was your first mistake, Laur. If you married for love, Cherie, you'd be married to Randy. Tom wouldn't have ever been in the picture. But he is and it all turned out wonderfully, didn't it?"

"Randy? You're bringing up Randy?" Cherie said, her anger rising. "Why would you mention him? Why would you even say his name?"

Laura looked at her mom, whose face had turned red. Who the hell was Randy?

She had asked her mom once why she was so old when she had Laura. Giving birth to your first child at thirty years old in the early 1970s was practically geriatric.

Her mother looked away as she said something about how her dad was worth the wait and the best-laid plans of mice and men and John F. Kennedy's legacy with the Peace Corps and the history of French colonialism in western Africa. Laura was so confused by the conversation and her mother's reaction to the question that she walked away and didn't try again.

Instead, she and Jessica decided that there had been a secret child that her mother had given up for adoption when she was in her early twenties when the other women were having babies. It was a boy, because they both wanted a brother, and one day he would show up at their house and ring the doorbell and ask to see his mother and meet his sisters and would take Laura and Jessica to meet his older friends who were all very cute and very interested in them.

Some poor college kid would come to the door to give them a brochure for his painting company or want them to contribute to Greenpeace, and Laura would grab Jessica and run to the top of the stairs in anticipation of meeting the brother they always wanted.

"What did the police do?" Laura asked, giving her mom a save she wasn't sure she deserved.

"What police?"

"The ones who came to break down my door?"

Her mom shook her head, as if to break out of a spell.

"Your dad told them what was going on and they left. Justin left."

As the opening notes to "November Rain" by Guns N' Roses

began to play, Laura turned to see Ilona on the stage, microphone in hand. She turned her body to the left, just slightly, elongating her figure. Had she been on a stage before? Laura saw the younger woman in the Banana Republic blazer write notes on a piece of paper she had with her.

As Ilona began to sing, the women looked at each other. She was feeling this song. This wasn't the delivery of an average Guns N' Roses fan. This was someone who was digging into the words and pushing them back out from the deepest level. This was someone who had felt the rain in November.

"Maybe November was when she was taken to the camp?" Phyllis asked. "Or maybe it was when she was released from the camp? Something definitely happened in November."

"Maybe it was when she lost her husband and child," Evelyn offered.

"Don't forget the mastectomy scar. She had cancer too."

"This isn't a cancer song, Phyllis," Donna said.

"She's a widow, right? Or was it divorce?"

"Her husband died in the camp."

"Not that husband. The second husband. Or was there a third husband?"

"Who the hell knows?"

"Sometimes a song is just a song," Marlys offered, finally.

"There have been a hell of a lot of Novembers," Dale said.

As the song continued, and continued—it was an extremely long song, they all agreed—Ilona losing no steam as it went on, Laura realized what her mother had said.

"You knew that Justin and I were breaking up," Laura said to her mom. "That's why I'm here."

"I thought you just needed time apart. I didn't know why."

"Do you honestly think I should just forgive him?"

"No. I don't think that. But the timing . . . it's just going to be very hard."

"But do you think I can do it?" Laura asked. "Do you think I can raise this kid on my own?"

"You won't be on your own."

Laura looked toward Marlys, who Dale was trying to help off of her stool and into a chair. Phyllis was beside her, holding the other side of Marlys to make sure the landing was soft.

Both mother and daughter needed Cherie Anderson. In both cases, the next step was inevitable. Laura would have a baby. Grandma Marlys would die. Each thing would happen without Cherie's help.

But they would want her help. They needed her help. Laura needed her mom's help. She could admit that. She had admitted that, freely. She looked at her grandmother, drunk and obviously sick, and felt anger for the first time.

She wasn't angry that her grandma was dying. That would have been unfair. But the fact was that Laura needed her mom's attention. She needed to know what she was supposed to do once a baby was placed in her arms. Her Grandma Marlys had moved to Florida not long after Cherie left for college, so Cherie had to figure out how to be a mom on her own, more or less.

Grandma Marlys didn't babysit. Even once Laura and her sister were older, she didn't show up. She didn't come to her mom's big fortieth birthday party or her bigger fiftieth. She didn't come when her mom won an award for being a volunteer of the year or when her dad's law firm had honored her parents for their hospitality and mentorship toward new associates. She didn't come to Laura's wedding.

Laura knew what a good mom was. She had one. When Laura was seven years old, she flew off her bike while chasing the ice cream truck and was knocked unconscious. Her mom was there with her in the ambulance, in the hospital, during all those lost summer days when Laura had to be home in bed. Her mom had been completely present. All the school events and carpools and dance recitals, she was there. She was always there. Where had her grandmother—her grandmothers—been?

Phyllis and Dale continued to hold Marlys, and Laura said nothing as Cherie briefly put her hand on Laura's shoulder, then dropped it to walk over to Marlys. Cherie told the other women that it looked like it was time for them to go home.

At that moment, in the VFW in West Palm Beach, Laura looked from her mother to her own pregnant belly. Both women were there, in that old building, trying to hold it all together and not at all sure that it hadn't already come apart.

CHAPTER 12

10 Days

CHERIE

Cherie watched the busboy clear the table nearest to her. He was methodical in how he placed the dishes in the tub he held, as if he were completing a puzzle. What was the game that Tom had briefly been obsessed with? Tetris. Laura had bought him a handheld device that played only Tetris a few years ago for Father's Day. Cherie would wake up at two or three in the morning and Tom would be sitting up in bed, holding the device so intensely that his knuckles were white, his expression verging on madness. One morning, she opened the trash to throw out the old coffee grounds and found the game within it. "I had to make it go away," Tom said, his jaw set.

She wanted to be the first one at the restaurant. She wanted to choose the table, choose where she sat at the table, to be the first one to greet the waiter so that he would know, even if it was never said, that she was driving this. Even if she wasn't paying for the meal—and Cherie had not yet decided how she wanted to handle that part of the evening—she was the one that he should look to for guidance.

It was crazy, Cherie knew that. To go to the bar where she had met John Blunt with the mustache, to use the information she got (paid for) at that bar to go to his job, to wait at his job until he came back from lunch and then to ask him to dinner, made absolutely no sense.

She just . . . Cherie sighed as she ran her hand through her chlorine-stained hair. It had all gotten away from her. Her mom was dying. Her secondary mom seemed to believe she would slip right into the primary position as soon as it became open. Her daughter, the one daughter who acknowledged her existence, was getting divorced less than three months before she gave birth to her first child. Her husband had stopped calling, which is what Cherie thought she wanted until the calls no longer came. Her dad was dead. Her dad was long dead.

"Cherie," John Blunt said as he approached the table and she stood to meet him. Dammit, she hadn't been paying attention. She had missed him walking toward her. Cherie had wanted to see if he walked tentatively or with confidence. "You look lovely."

She smiled when he said this. When they spoke again, she heard the soft southern drawl that she had missed in the noisy taxidermy bar. It was reflexive, this compliment on her appearance, almost ritualized for men of his age from his area of birth, but he seemed to genuinely mean the words that he had said.

When they sat down again—he didn't pull out her chair, which was both a relief and a disappointment—they put their napkins on their laps and looked at each other intentionally, both determined not to have a moment of awkwardness.

"Have you been here before?" she asked him, and then cringed at the question. Though she was genuinely interested, it sounded like small talk. She did not want to have a dinner of trite conversation until they finally hit on a subject they could happily discuss.

What did she want to talk about? She wanted to tell him that she was sad. That she hadn't been sad like this in years, if not decades. Cherie was usually the person that sad people talked about their sadness with. She wasn't a happy person, but she did give off an aura of evenness, steadiness, that made people come to her. Happiness is too much anyway—what's more excruciating than an evening with a couple newly, blissfully in love?

John Blunt shook his head. "It's relatively new. There's a lot around here that's new. But I guess that's not unusual in a state where there's a lot of turnover."

Turnover. That's what was actually happening, right? The old die, the young take their place. She would soon no longer be a daughter, only a mother. A grandmother. Then, in another twenty to thirty years her granddaughter would become a mother, pushing her daughter to become a grandmother. Again and again and again. This is how it had always been.

"My mom is dying. That's why I'm in Florida." Cherie bit her lip, resisting the urge to cover her mouth. What had she just said?

John looked suitably stricken. "Oh, Cherie, I'm very sorry."

She shook her head. "I didn't say that to make you feel bad. I just . . . I haven't said that out loud yet. Even to my husband. I said that my mom's sick. I might have said 'very sick,' but I didn't say that she was dying. The doctors that I've seen say that she has maybe three months. Possibly less." Cherie had managed to grab her mother's latest pathology report from her mailbox and showed it to a couple of well-regarded consultants that were willing to see her for their standard hourly fee. The meetings hadn't lasted anywhere near an hour. Within minutes, they told her the only thing they could ethically say. There was nothing that could be done to save her. "Three months is the amount of time I have before my daughter gives birth to my first grandchild. My only grandchild, very likely, since she's divorcing her husband. So, either the timing works out—one dying before the other goes into labor—or I'll have to be two places at the same time. Which, honestly, I'm not quite sure I can do."

Cherie realized she was holding her knife in her hand straight up and down and raising and lowering it as she spoke. She put it back down on the table. That large mustache covered the top of his mouth, but she could very clearly see that John's mouth was set in a straight line. What the hell was she doing? She wasn't ready for normal human interaction. *Have you been to this restaurant before?* Boring, but a decent start. *My mom is dying, my pregnant daughter is getting divorced, and everyone wants me to do everything and I'm clearly coming apart?* Bad, wrong, way, way too much. Good God, she realized as she reached in front of her for a glass that wasn't there, they hadn't even put in their drink orders yet.

Cherie cleared her throat and attempted to smile. "So you're in real estate. That's exciting."

"It keeps me busy," he said, relaxing, and Cherie knew this night had been a big mistake. John Blunt was the one person she had met in the last two weeks who had wanted her while everyone else needed her. She wanted a single night of being wanted. She had taken her time getting dressed, choosing a flattering navy sheath dress. She had opened her travel jewelry case and chosen the diamond earrings and sapphire and diamond pendant necklace because it was tasteful but beautiful. She wore the only pair of high heels that she had packed for the trip. She had tried to look good. She thought she did look good. Evelyn had winked as they passed each other on the staircase, intuiting that Cherie had dressed not just for herself.

He was a mere mortal, a man, delighted to have a woman track him down and request his company. This whole night should have been nothing but light conversation. She couldn't have done that?

The waiter, finally, took their drink orders and they discussed the various items on the menu that looked good. When Cherie took those first sips of chilled white wine, she felt the liquid going down her throat. This might do something. This could help.

"Before I was in real estate, I sold cars. Luxury cars."

He emphasized the word "luxury" and Cherie knew that he had noticed her jewelry, assumed her dress was designer. He wasn't trying to flirt with her, he was trying to impress her. Cherie felt herself deflate.

It was actually while she was meeting with the Jackass that she decided to try to find John Blunt. Though the Jackass—Curt, dammit, Curt—was clean-shaven, he had willingly listened to her, and seemed interested in her opinion, just like the mustachioed man in the taxidermy bar. Curt agreed that he thought there was still very much a market for an apartment complex for the Social Security set. The Hawthorne Havens of the world got all the attention, but they were for the few, not the many. Soleil City just wasn't working well. The place needed repairs, he agreed. But that wasn't the reason the apartments weren't being rented. "Soleil City just isn't on anyone's map these days. Retirees are coming to West Palm Beach, but they don't know what they don't know. If the profile was raised, if people knew about it, I could make the repairs to the cement. To the windows. It isn't that people aren't renting because they think the place is getting run-down. They aren't even looking at the place to know that repairs need to be made. The place needs . . . a hook."

Cherie had taken care of this. She had called the *Palm Beach Post,* pitched a young reporter who was handed her call on her uplifting human-interest story and invited Amanda, as the reporter insisted she be called, to the VFW the other night to observe, to see if this was a group of women that she might be interested in profiling. She got more than she bargained for with the public announcement of the dissolution of Laura's marriage and a window into the fissures in her happy two-mom family. But, Amanda said, she was in. She'd like to come to a few practices, do a few interviews. She'd attend the competition at the end. Cherie had taken out the small notebook she kept in her purse and had crossed out the *press?* item on her list of to-dos. She had done her part.

"Italian cars. Ferraris, Lamborghinis, a few Maseratis. Beautiful things. Even went over to Italy a few times to talk to people there, learn what was coming up. You ever been to Italy?"

"No, actually. But it's somewhere I'd like to go."

"Let me know if you do. I can give you the names of places that will make you the most amazing food you've ever had. It's been at least ten years, but nothing changes. It'll all still be the same."

Cherie felt offended by this comment, by the assumption that nothing in the lives of these restaurant owners had changed in ten years, that they were all ready and waiting for John Blunt to return to them and demand perfection. Even in Italy, there was turnover. No place, no matter how fine the pasta, how fast the cars, could escape turnover.

"I got into real estate after Hurricane Andrew. People moved here for the ocean, saw what it could do, got scared, and moved inland. I helped them do it. It's Florida, so it's always a little boom-and-bust here, but it's a boom time right now, I'm happy to report."

That morning, Cherie had found herself back at the ocean, sitting in Dale's Lincoln Continental, watching the waves. Still, she wouldn't get out of the car. About ten years ago she started to have a nightmare about having wet sand in her mouth. In the dream, Cherie was surrounded by the darkness. There was a loud, indistinguishable sound that was oppressive in its weight. Finally, a light would break through, the sound would subside, and as she began to breathe normally again, she realized that her mouth was filled with sand.

The previous week, when Dale had sent her into her bedroom to retrieve a cardigan—though Cherie had bought her a throw for the couch, she deemed it too nice to actually use—Cherie had stared at the painting of Cape Cod again. She felt goose bumps prickle her skin. The same reaction, a different parent. Again, what did her body know that her mind didn't?

In the past few days, Dale had started to pull back from her a little bit. Though Cherie wasn't comfortable with the casual familiarity of the interactions early in her visit, she now found herself wondering what she had done to make Dale retreat. But this is how it had always been between them. Momentum into inertia. Closeness into distance.

Cherie looked around her at the other couples eating their meals. Most of them were older than her, with the women in dresses and the men in sport coats. About half the couples seemed engaged with each other and the other half seemed to be going through the motions.

John was engaged, though not necessarily with Cherie. Even as they ordered their meals—mahi-mahi for her, steak for him—even as they ate their meals, even as she continued to drink her chilled wine and fidget with the napkin on her lap, John continued to talk about himself. If he asked her a question, and he did ask a few, it was always in service to furthering his own story, to show how shallow her knowledge of the subject was and how deep his own.

At first, she thought he was trying to shut her up, to keep away the stories of the dying mom and the birthing daughter. But he was too practiced; it came too naturally. He knew he was interesting. He assumed she wasn't.

John didn't ask her any questions, Cherie decided as she watched him laugh at his own joke as she tried to smile, because he assumed she'd want to hear all about him. Justin, her son-in-law, her banished son-in-law—Cherie had told Tom to make sure to find Laura a vicious lawyer—didn't ask questions because he wasn't curious. His world was small, and he was perfectly fine to keep it that way. Laura hadn't wanted the world. But she had always wanted more than Justin would have been able to give her.

Now, it was over. Cherie knew, and she knew that Laura knew, which didn't necessarily make it any better, that Justin's betrayal with her friend wasn't entirely about Laura. It was also about becoming a father. This was his idea of how to get out of it. There wouldn't be a custody fight because he would hand over the reins to Laura without any battle. Cherie's grandchild wouldn't have a dad. The idea felt like a punch in the gut. At least Dale had made sure she had a replacement before she left her child. With Marlys in place, she felt free to run to Mexico. Laura's child wouldn't have any kind of father at all.

"Well, you just seem a million miles away," John said. Though he smiled as he said it, there was an edge to his voice.

He didn't want her. He wanted an audience, which really meant that he needed her too.

"I guess I've just had a little too much sun," Cherie said, lightly. "I'm still not used to the intensity."

"Too much sun, or too much wine?" he asked. "If you aren't even listening to me, why did you want to go out with me?"

"I wanted a distraction."

"That's what I've been trying to do for you all evening. Look, I can listen to you talk all about your mom and your daughter if you'd like. My mom has been dead for twenty years and I don't have any kids, so I don't know what I could contribute. But if that's what you want . . ."

It wasn't what she wanted, or what she needed. Here, in Florida, she was on duty. She knew how to do this from her years of nursing. When she was on shift, there was nothing else happening in the world except for the patient in front of her at that moment. Once again, she had to focus, to do what needed to be done.

She'd gotten two years. Should she have done more during her break from daughtering and mothering? Sure, of course. But the truth was, at this point in her life, she didn't know how to do anything but be needed. Wasn't that better than the alternative? To not be considered at all, like Evelyn or Ilona? To have so much time to spend on yourself that you didn't know how to think about anyone else, like John?

Cherie looked at John. She had done the right thing by walking away the first time. "Let me tell you about my garden," Cherie said. "Aphids," she said, leaning into the table. "Predator, or prey?"

"Maybe it's best if we call it a night."

CHAPTER 13

8 Days

MARLYS

Marlys and Laura were alone at the Dunkin' Donuts by Marlys's hair salon except for one table, a man with a cup of coffee who looked like he hadn't slept for the last three nights. "Drugs," Marlys had whispered to Laura.

Marlys picked at the plastic lid on her coffee, opening and closing the tab that allowed for drinking until it broke off into her hand. "I hate these things. Can't we just get a mug? I'll wash it myself if I have to. Jeez." As Marlys put her cup down, coffee splashed onto the table through the opening.

Laura took a napkin from the pile that Marlys had grabbed at the counter and began to clean the spill up.

"Let me do it, Laura. I made the mess."

"I'm already doing it, Grandma. It's fine."

"It's not fine. It's my mess."

"Grandma. I got it," Laura said, firmly.

A few days after Laura arrived in Florida, once she began to dig through the box of loose photos that made up Marlys's life, granddaughter and grandmother had begun to talk. Who is this? Where is this? When was this? Marlys would hold the picture that Laura handed her and take a deep breath before telling her whatever she could think to say about the image. When her granddaughter dipped into the box for another take, Marlys knew she had lost Laura's interest and it was time to move on to another moment, another memory.

Since the night at the VFW, Laura hadn't been back to the box of photos once.

Was it wrong for Marlys to ask Laura the next morning if she was making the right decision in leaving Justin? Laura certainly seemed to think it was. "He cheated on me, Grandma. Why the hell should I have to accept that?" Her granddaughter went to her room for the next two hours. Marlys had definitely lost her interest.

"So you had fun yesterday with Dale in Palm Beach?" Marlys asked.

Laura smiled and nodded. "It was great. Dale really is quite . . ." Laura looked at Marlys and stopped herself. Marlys didn't prod her to continue.

"You went window-shopping?"

"Something like that," Laura said and took a moment to chew her bite of doughnut. "We got drinks at a café on Worth Avenue. It was a good vantage point."

"For what?"

"People-watching. We watched the women go by with their shopping bags and guessed how many different cosmetic procedures they had. When the two women at the next table figured out what we were doing, they joined in. They pointed out possibilities that neither of us had even begun to consider and added price tags."

Marlys laughed, then began to cough. Laura didn't watch as she brought her napkin up to her mouth. The half-conscious man at the next table put his hands over his ears.

"The taller woman of the two had had eight procedures and

the shorter woman had just scheduled her sixth," Laura continued, as if nothing had happened. "The first thing they told me
to do when the time came was to do an eyelid lift. The taller
woman said that it made a world of difference. Then, from there,
tighten up the jaw."

"The wisdom of elders," Marlys said.

"Dale said she almost got a face-lift. When she was at Marshall Field's in Chicago. She was older than everyone else but she
didn't want to *look* the oldest."

"Dale didn't need a face-lift. She's aged well."

Laura shrugged. "She didn't do it because she'd have to take
weeks off of work to recover and she was afraid they'd get rid of
her when she was gone. But then they fired her anyway because
they said she was too old. She should have sued them. Age dis-
crimination."

"The shit women have had to put up with in the workplace.
The stories I could tell from my modeling years would make
your toenails curl."

Laura watched the man at the table near them as he stared out
the window but said nothing. Did his mother know what had
happened to her son? He was a perfectly healthy young man,
killing himself.

Laura picked a chunk of glaze from the top of her doughnut.
"The thing I was going to say before about Grandma Dale is that
she's led quite the life," Laura said, flicking the glaze into her
mouth.

"She certainly has," Marlys said, careful not to say more.

"When she was my age, she had already met the man who
would be husband number three."

"I think, Laura, with marriage, it's quality over quantity."

"Well, if you don't have quality, I guess you have to up the
quantity."

Marlys looked at the man at the other table as he put his head back onto the table. How had he gotten into drugs? Marlys drank too much when she was younger, she knew. When Ed was always gone. When she looked around their small apartment and stared in the mirror and knew that it hadn't had to turn out that way. Marlys's mother resented her daughter's beauty because it meant that she wouldn't have to struggle. She'd have it easy. Beautiful girls marry rich men. Except, she hadn't. Marlys had a winter coat with holes in both pockets.

"You're familiar with my situation," Laura said. "Except," she said, wiping her mouth with her napkin, "you were the Melissa. I'm the Dale."

Ah. This is why Laura had suggested doughnuts. She knew more about Marlys than she had let on and now she could confront her judgmental grandmother while indulging a pregnancy craving.

"I took my best friend's husband. That is what happened," Marlys said, matter-of-factly. She brought the coffee to her lips.

Laura frowned, as if getting to the point had been too easy. "Why, though? Why did you do it?"

"Because I had fallen in love with Ed. I had fallen in love with your mom. Ed and Dale were talking about moving away to try to save the marriage—which wouldn't have happened, that marriage was going to fail—so I decided to force the matter so that we could stay together. I loved all of them. The next woman wouldn't."

"Are you saying that you were actually doing Dale a favor by helping her marriage fall apart sooner?" Laura said with a disapproving scoff.

Marlys moved her head back and forth, as if she were shaking water out of her ears. "Basically, yes. In the end, we all got what we wanted. Cherie got a stable life. Ed and I got fifty years of marriage. Dale got someone she knew and cared about to raise her daughter while she explored on her own. Was it clean? No. Was it easy? It was not that. But it's what happened, and then we lived the rest of our lives."

Laura's mouth dropped open a little as she stared past her grandmother. "Right after my big ultrasound, the one that Justin missed, Melissa told me that I was better than him. That I should know that and remember it. I just kind of nodded along at the time because it was a best friend sort of thing to say. I mean, I was *pissed*." Laura touched her doughnut and then pulled her hand away. "Now I know that she was already sleeping with him. What you're saying is that I should think of the whole cheating thing as her doing me a favor. She showed me who I was really married to."

"I never thought I was better than Dale," Marlys said. "I just knew that Dale wanted other things."

Laura's eyes flashed with anger. "But Dale lost her child."

"Dale left her child. That was her decision."

"Was it really, though?"

Marlys nodded. "It was. Dale didn't always make great decisions, you know. She was married to her fourth husband for less than a month. She didn't even tell any of us, including your mother, that she had married her fifth husband. She married her second husband weeks after meeting him and that ended with him dead and her in jail."

Marlys stopped herself from putting her hand over her mouth. This was one of the things they didn't say, but now was said. Laura's face registered the shock of the statement.

"What?"

Marlys didn't know everything, but she knew that Dale had met Bob at the art school in San Miguel de Allende, where she taught painting and he was studying sculpture—was it sculpture?

Marlys only knew it wasn't painting. They got married just a couple of months after meeting. Dale told her that Bob filled up every room he entered and pulled the party with him when he left.

It was only after they were married that Dale understood how fully the war had destroyed him. He had left a small stone building in France where his already depleted unit was taking shelter so he could take a piss and look for any hidden food. He was gone for about an hour. When he returned, the building had been shelled by the Germans and everyone was dead.

After their first anniversary, he started to hit Dale. It started with a few slaps, then moved into punches. She was left with black eyes, a bruised cheek, arm, back. She never tried to hide it, which only made Bob angrier. He wasn't concerned that other people could see what he had done to her; he didn't want to be reminded of it himself.

When he was murdered, Dale had long since kicked him out of their apartment and he had moved in with a friend. She said he had started disappearing for long stretches of time, then reappearing in San Miguel with his own black eyes and bruises. He had added gambling to his list of bad deeds and the luck he had in the war had long since passed.

The police arrested Dale because it was easy. The dead man beat his wife. The wife snapped. Easy, simple, clean. No need to listen to the very loud rumors about the gang boss who sought revenge for unpaid gambling debts. No need to ask questions of people who would never give the correct answer.

Finally, after ten days, the police admitted that they didn't have a real case. Dale's friends told them that. The art school administrators said the same thing. Bob was troubled and trouble. Hadn't Dale already been through enough? The morning after her release, she left Mexico with only a single bag.

"When Bob turned up dead, they arrested Dale because it was easy. They didn't have any actual evidence."

Laura's eyes were still wide. Marlys continued. "She didn't do it, obviously. They put her in jail for a week and a half—"

"A week and a half!"

"But she was never charged with anything. She was released, she got the hell out of San Miguel. It was all a mistake."

"That was a hell of a mistake."

About six months after Dale moved to Florida, she showed up at the hospital cafeteria for her chicken salad lunch date with Marlys holding an obituary clipped from a newspaper. "Bob's brother just died. Bob's sister-in-law—I never met her but I guess she kept track of me—sent me the obituary. I don't plan to respond."

Marlys had told Dale to lie to his family. Marlys had benefited from Dale's first bad decision: to walk away from her family. Dale should benefit from her second bad decision: to marry Bob.

Under Marlys's guidance, Dale told Bob's brother in Michigan that it had all been a horrible case of mistaken identity. Bob was in the wrong place at the wrong time and nothing else. Since no one was ever charged for his murder, why couldn't that be the story? That way, Bob could continue to be their war hero and Dale could continue to be the grieving widow. She got Bob's life insurance money that would let her start over again in Los Angeles. His family could keep that picture of him on the sideboard and talk about him with pride at every Sunday dinner. They didn't have to be broken by a broken man.

"It must have been startling to see the name of anyone connected to Bob again," Marlys told her then.

"It took me a few read-throughs to figure out what the hell I was looking at. 'Preceded in death by brother Robert.' Even that wasn't a clue." Dale shook her head.

Marlys remembered how Dale looked up at her after putting the clipping back into her purse, then practically pushed the next words out of her mouth. "You've never told Cherie that Bob hit me, have you?"

"Of course not. That's not my story to tell."

Dale straightened herself. "If she thinks I was having a ball and wouldn't leave San Miguel to return to her because I was having too much fun, then I'm just selfish. If she knows how bad things were, that before one bruise healed another took its place, then I'm just weak. Stupid. I don't want that."

"She wouldn't think that you're weak, Dale. Dammit, I've told you this for years. Let her know what happened. She'll look at the whole thing differently. She'll forgive you."

"She'll never forgive me, Marlys. She'll just hate herself for not forgiving an abused woman. Which is worse." Dale laughed. "All those fundraisers for women's shelters she's held and she has no idea how close to home it hit. Pardon the pun."

When Dale had shown up at Marlys and Ed's door with almost no warning in the middle of a Minnesota winter after running from Mexico, Marlys felt a weight lift from her shoulders as Dale told her the full story. Marlys now had a way to make sure Dale could never take Cherie. Dale had been in jail. She was never charged. She was released with an apology. But Dale had worn handcuffs, been placed behind bars. That would be enough for any judge to turn against her. Dale had walked away, and now she didn't have a path back.

Marlys was determined, from that point on, to leave some bread crumbs along the way. She told Dale to visit whenever she wanted, to call in the weeks and months in between. Dale took the invitation as an example of Marlys's goodness, of her superior heart. It wasn't that; it was purely self-interest.

"Was the next husband, uh, was he better?" Laura asked.

Marlys laughed. "I think she overcorrected with that one. Apparently, he was boring as hell. He'd been a member of the Communist party before the war—most of the people who joined then were for workers' rights, that kind of thing—but when the blacklisting started happening in Hollywood his name never came up because no one could remember him ever being at a meeting. He was too dull."

"How many of the husbands did you meet?"

"One. Ed."

"You didn't meet any of the others?"

"Your mom met some of them. The fifth one, I believe. And Frank, the sixth one, who Dale would have likely stayed married to if he hadn't died. Cherie really liked him." The man at the other table groaned, and both women turned quickly to look at him. He turned his head the other direction.

"She never got married again after Frank. That's kind of sad."

Marlys shrugged. "It was the seventies. She didn't have to get married again."

"Because she was old?"

Marlys laughed. "She was in her mid-forties. Not much older than you."

"That's like twenty years older than me."

"Honey, you have no idea how quickly those years are going to pass."

Laura looked like she was going to object, then thought better of it. Marlys picked up a packet of sugar, then put it down. "Dale didn't have to be married because things had changed. Before, if you wanted things, you needed a man to get them. Dale said that whenever she wanted to rent an apartment when she was single, she had to have a band on her ring finger and a story about a husband in the Merchant Marines. And that was in New York! Famously live-and-let-live New York. That's just how it was."

Laura took a bite of her doughnut and chewed it for a while, thinking. Finally, she put it down and took a sip of her coffee. Then, she looked directly at Marlys.

"How are you and Dale still friends?"

Was it friendship, or something else entirely? The fact was that Marlys and Dale needed each other. Dale was always going to leave. Marlys was always going to stay. They were their daughter's mothers, two halves making up a whole.

Dale had come to her, now, for the end. But Dale also didn't know that even as she didn't try to pull her husband closer all those years ago, Marlys had done all she could to push Dale and Ed apart.

Nine months after Ed returned from the war, Marlys and Ed hadn't yet slept together. But it was clear that it was only a matter of time and once that happened, there would be no going back. So, Ed tried to stop the inevitable by packing up his family and moving them out of town. As far away from Marlys as he—and Cherie, and Dale—could be.

Ed found out about the job at the Escuela Universitaria de Bellas Artes in San Miguel de Allende, Mexico, from a veterans' fair. The Americans were coming, using the GI Bill to study at the school and live cheaply in the lovely town, and they needed more teachers so they could have more classes. Qualifications were low, as was the pay—Marlys only did the math years later and figured out that Ed would have made more studying on the GI Bill, earning a federal stipend, than he ever could have made in salary—but Ed, with a single year of art school himself, could live the idealistic, artistic life he was convinced he was meant to live. A life that would make him happy, which would make him forget his wife's best friend who had made him happy just months before.

Along with his application, he sent a photographic slide of a painting as a sample of his work. The school was impressed and offered him a position teaching beginner's oil painting, with a request to start in six weeks' time. It was only after he had already bought a linen suit that Dale found the acceptance letter with the mention of the painting, titled, simply, "Cape Cod."

Ed had never been to Cape Cod. He certainly had never painted any pictures of Cape Cod. But Dale had. He had submitted her painting.

Quietly, Dale wrote to the school and told them of their mistake. They had offered a position not to the painting's creator, but to the painting's creator's husband. If they wanted to correct this mistake, she would be available to start on their proposed date. The head of the school wrote two letters almost immediately. A letter to Ed, withdrawing his job offer due to fraud and a letter to Dale, offering her the job. At the bottom of her typed letter, in florid handwriting, was a postscript: Good Luck.

Ed wanted to know how Dale could do that to him. Dale wanted to know how Ed could do that to her. If there was a betrayal, he had betrayed her first. Passing her work off as his own? Was there anything that could hurt her more? Of course there was. As Ed denied he ever tried to claim her work, Dale said out loud the thing they had all been keeping quiet. Ed had fallen in love with Marlys. Dale wasn't positive of her husband's feelings when she made this pronouncement, but his immediate silence confirmed what she thought she knew. What she knew she knew. The inevitable.

Dale packed her bags, walked out of the apartment, returned once more to hug her daughter, and then she was gone. The divorce decree from a Mexican court that arrived in the mail seven weeks later was the only proof any of them had that Dale had made it to Mexico. It was another four months before Dale sent a letter. Teaching was going well. She liked San Miguel. She had met someone, an American student on the GI Bill. A sculptor named Bob. They planned on getting married. Kiss Ceres for me.

By the time the letter was forwarded to Marlys in Minneapolis, another two months had passed. Ceres had become Cherie—"Ceres is the name of a goddess. Cherie is the name of a child," Ed said—Marlys had become Mom and Ed had gotten a job as a traveling salesman. Nothing was the same and would never be the same again.

"I saw that photo of you and Dale and my mom lying on a blanket in the park," Laura said after asking Marlys the question without an answer. "You looked so happy then."

"That's one of my favorites. It was taken in Boston Common in early '44. Dale and I had known each other just a few months." Marlys smiled to herself at the memory. Earlier that morning, a man had crashed his car into a pile of garbage cans on the curb as he watched Marlys walk down the street. She'd had that kind of power, once. "Those were good days. Laying out a blanket in the park, bringing a couple of bottles of beer in brown bags, letting baby Ceres, as she was then, crawl all over us. God, we both loved that child. Still do, of course."

Was Marlys's anger toward Ed since his death really about missing Dale? Ed had come back and messed the whole damn thing up. Marlys knew, now, after having Dale back in her life regularly that in losing her best friend she had lost so much. Maybe too much. She felt her throat grow thick as she remembered those Sundays in the park. The two women and the child they loved. But Cherie only belonged to one of them. She could only belong to one of them, and Marlys was determined that person would be her.

"I'm not going to forgive Melissa," Laura said. "Though it's not like she's asked me to forgive her."

"It wasn't about you. It was about her."

"I know. I guess the question she can ask herself is whether or not it was worth it. To lose me. To get him. To get the life they both think they want."

"It was worth it for me," Marlys said, clearly. "I was Ed's wife. I'm Cherie's mother and your grandmother. I'm about to be a great-grandmother." Marlys watched as Laura lowered her eyes. "It was worth it for me."

"When I told Melissa I was pregnant, she tried, for half a second, to pretend she was happy for me. Just like she pretended with our other friends. But I turned to look at her when she wasn't watching and she was glaring at me with pure anger. With me, the whole issue of kids had gotten too close to her. She told me that she doesn't want to be a parent. Ever. With Justin, she found herself a man who finally said that he didn't, either, even though it was too late. So I guess it was worth it for her, too."

Marlys put her hand on top of Laura's. She looked at her granddaughter and saw the bags under her eyes. She wasn't sleeping well. Marlys would move the air filter farther away from her room, even though she didn't think it was doing much. It had been over a decade since Cherie had given Marlys and Ed the majority of the money to buy the townhouse. The crisp white-painted walls that had greeted Marlys the day she moved in had become stained yellow from all the thousands of cigarettes. What would happen when she was gone and Cherie had to sell the place? Would every square inch need to be repainted?

Laura pulled her hand away. "You slept with your best friend's husband and his child gained a parent," Laura said. "Melissa slept with her best friend's husband and my child lost a parent."

The man at the other table had gotten up and walked out. Marlys didn't see anyone behind the counter. At that moment, in that place, they appeared to be all alone.

CHAPTER 14

8 Days

DALE

One by one, the women of the Hawthorne Haven Synchronized Swim Team dove into the pool. The execution wasn't flawless, but it was orderly, and for the most part, synchronized. Laura had tried the same move with the women of Soleil City, but while it started promising—Donna had a surprisingly beautiful form in her dive, leading Dale to believe that maybe she had missed an athletic opportunity—it ended with a belly flop from Ilona, a particularly harsh belly flop that left Ilona's exposed skin beet red, inflaming her mastectomy and Caesarian scars.

On Cherie's urging, Patty had invited the women of Soleil City over to Hawthorne Haven for "a nice evening visit" which would also happen to include watching Hawthorne's second synchro practice of the day. "Sizing up your competition is very important," Cherie had added, and the women had agreed before she had to throw in a free round at the Hawthorne bar to convince them to come.

The day before, Cherie had pulled Dale aside after watching the last ten minutes of the squad's practice. "I'm concerned," Cherie said, her brow furrowed. "The women don't seem very *synchronized*." As she spoke about how she might be able to convince the judges that "synchronized" simply meant doing things together but not in the same way, Dale looked behind her to make sure that Laura was well out of earshot. They were still a work in progress, but Dale was amazed at how far Laura had brought them.

Now, the women in the Hawthorne Haven pool held hands and formed a star. Patty leaned over to the women of Soleil City and—in a stage whisper that was loud enough to be heard by their entire section—said, "Look at Elaine. Three o'clock. She needs that knee replaced. She's struggling with her kick. They're pretending that it'll heal up by competition, but there's no way. Coach Diane has them going twice a day. It will only get worse. They'll have to cut her from the squad entirely."

Dale noticed that everyone, save Patty, had dressed up for the outing, in their dressed-down Florida way. The women had stopped getting their hair set until after the competition—"That's just throwing good money after bad right now," Evelyn had said—but even under their own direction, they looked very well groomed. Hair in place, lipstick done right, blush under control. Dale hated that these women, her friends, felt they had to prove their worth just to walk the carpeted halls of Hawthorne Haven with a bunch of people who were only different from the women of Soleil City because of a few decisions and a hell of a lot of luck.

"Cut her because of her knee?" Phyllis asked. "Wouldn't they just make some last-minute changes to the routine?"

Patty stared at her. "Phyllis. Honey. If she can't kick one of her legs, she's no good to anyone. In the world of old lady synchronized swimming, that's one of the only moves we've got."

"She wouldn't be on my team," Laura confirmed.

"It's just . . . you know, I've got those concerns with my knee. If I start to struggle . . ."

Laura was silent.

"You'll be fine," Dale said, as Donna patted Phyllis's knee. Dale had heard the two women chatting on Donna's balcony the previous morning. She had walked over to make sure it really was the two of them together. They waved, not acknowledging that just a week earlier, Donna could barely stand the woman sipping coffee beside her.

It was likely that they had bonded over a shared dislike of Laura. She didn't shout more than was necessary or cruelly call out the women's shortcomings. But she was firm. She was certain. She had a whistle and wasn't afraid to use it. If they hadn't executed a move to her satisfaction, the women would be told to do it again. And again. The ice machine at Soleil City had been running nearly nonstop in the last few days. There were certainly evening cocktails made stronger than they had been before Laura arrived. But most of the ice, Dale could attest, had been going to packs that the women could press against their aching muscles. At the same time, the women mentioned how they hadn't slept as well as they were in years.

As the mumbling by the other women in Dale's world grew louder against her granddaughter, Dale found herself becoming even more fond of Laura. She had to admit, she didn't know the girl had it in her.

Laura had never been terribly distinctive. She was the kid who wanted to do everything the way it was supposed to be done. During birthday calls, when Dale was trying to make conversation, she would ask Laura about her favorite song, her favorite movie, her favorite TV show. Without fail, Laura would cite the number one song, movie, and TV show at the time. Laura was like a lighter version of her mother. Cherie may have followed the pack, but only long enough to get to the front of it. As far as Dale could tell, Laura seemed forever satisfied to be firmly in the middle.

It was Jessica who Dale had always enjoyed the most. Jessica seemed headed down a more successful, though strikingly similar, road to her grandmother, much to Cherie's chagrin. "I guess I didn't realize restlessness was genetic," Cherie had said as she described how her daughter had moved into her third apartment in two years after breaking up with yet another boyfriend.

Cherie had also always shown the most interest in Jessica. When her younger daughter was a baby, and a beautiful one at that, Cherie had told Dale that she felt Jessica was something of a miracle. She had bled, the doctor confirmed that she had miscarried, yet Cherie continued to feel pregnant. Tom would nod along, but it was clear he didn't believe her and wanted to give her a little time to work it all out. Weeks passed, and as Cherie continued to believe she was pregnant, Tom, exasperated, went with her back to the doctor. He thought that a full exam would put an end to Cherie's phantom pregnancy, and maybe he could stay back for a moment and ask about the name of a psychologist that Cherie could see.

She got her exam. She was right. Cherie was still pregnant. She was measuring accurately and the heartbeat was strong. She hadn't lost the baby. This kid hung on.

Jessica was special.

And, frankly, she was. Jessica learned to read at four, ran faster than all the other kids in her kindergarten class at five, and was her piano teacher's star pupil by six. Once she found music, her world opened wide. She didn't just love to listen to classical music, she was a prodigy when she played it. First piano, then violin. When she decided to sing, her voice stunned them all. Cherie once joked that Jessica couldn't play the trombone and Jessica responded by teaching herself in three days. She had talent that was rare and exceptional.

Though Cherie doted on her daughter, Jessica didn't return her affection. Where Laura went to her parents with too much, Jessica kept her thoughts to herself. She was talented and obstinate and wanted to do everything her own way. When she was ten, Cherie told Dale, almost as if she were forcing the words out of her mouth, that Jessica had a lot of Dale within her.

When Jessica was a teenager, she would stay on her birthday calls from her grandmother and ask her about all she had seen. Had she seen Billie Holiday play the Mocambo nightclub in Hollywood? Had she heard Bob Dylan at Café Wha? in the Village? Who had she known? What had she seen? She wanted to know it all.

Jessica used Dale's past lives—she hadn't seen Billie Holiday in Hollywood, she had seen Bob Dylan and thought he was awful—against her mom. Cherie, lightly, had reported that Jessica had called Dale "the interesting grandma." After all, Dale had all the stories. The fact that Cherie didn't know that, that she insisted on preferring the mother who had raised her and done the work, was a huge strike against her in her daughter's book.

Yet, Cherie still chased Jessica. Laura chased Cherie. Cherie had shown up for Dale. Dale had grown closer to Laura. Jessica hadn't spoken to any of them in weeks.

The women in the pool at Hawthorne stood up in the water to weave their hands in and out of each other. Laura had nearly perfected this move with the women at Soleil City. It had been maddening getting to that point, but they had done it, accomplished through sheer willpower. Dale looked over at her friends to see the smug expressions on their faces. "We do it better, obviously," Evelyn said. Dale saw a hint of a smile on her granddaughter's face.

Cherie had told Laura she was working on a plan for her. She was talking to her connections to see about apartments and jobs that would be friendly to a new mother. There was talk of the excess furniture that Cherie had in the basement that Laura could use and the legal help that Tom's partners could provide, and Dale found herself looking at her overwhelmed grand-daughter and wishing Cherie would do just one thing. *Hug the girl,* Dale thought. Laura needed a plan, sure. But she also just needed a mother to tell her that everything would be all right. Yet, Cherie held back. Laura was the daughter who had always wanted to be loved. Had that just been too simple for Cherie?

Dale knew that any therapist would hang this reticence on the fact that Cherie's mother had abandoned her as a child. Of course this was the result. Marlys had given her unbridled affec-tion, but it was Dale's that she had wanted. Dale had screwed it up the way that her mother had screwed her up.

But Cherie couldn't screw up with Laura. Jessica had decided long ago that she didn't need her mom. Laura hadn't made that decision. If she needed Cherie, Cherie needed to be there for Laura. Dale hadn't been there as a mother, but she also knew the pain that not having her mother there for her had caused. It was too late for Dale to fix her mistakes, but there was enough time for Cherie to not make this one.

"Look at Gladys," Patty whispered again. "Six o'clock. She's unsteady. This has happened before. She can't get all the water out of her ears and she goes from feeling a little off balance to being paralyzed by vertigo in hours. She'll also be out by the competition."

"She looks completely fine to me," Phyllis said, and once again, was met by Patty's *Are you fucking kidding me?* look. "I mean, they are in water, Patty. Everyone wobbles a little."

"There's a wobble, and there's a sway. Gladys is swaying."

Dale watched for a moment. If Gladys was swaying, they all were.

"Look, you wanted me here for my insight. That's my insight. You won't be seeing Gladys on competition day. Mark my words," Patty said, no longer in a whisper.

As far as the women of Soleil City had come, the women of Hawthorne Haven were still a step ahead. They took direction better. They looked to their coach for instruction and didn't challenge every word she said. They were team players, these women of Hawthorne Haven. The women of Soleil City were better suited to individual competition.

The routine ended and the women paused for applause. They received a smattering, and Laura turned to the team and motioned toward the pool. "That was depressing as hell."

Patty guffawed.

Evelyn puffed up her chest. "Sure, they did a few things better than us. But we've *tried,* Laura. We've tried so damn hard."

Laura leaned forward in her chair. "And they tried too. Harder. But the song they're performing to is just *not right*." Dale felt herself nodding. "I mean, I love Simon and Garfunkel. 'Bridge over Troubled Water' is a good song. A classic. But in this case, it's all wrong."

"Because they're a bunch of rich old women whose waters aren't troubled?" Donna asked, mumbling, more to herself, "Though the tiles around those waters could use some regrouting."

"Oh, honey. They've got problems," Patty said, waving toward the men. "You don't even know what the new Viagra has done to this place. Every man now thinks he's a goddamned stallion. Since that pill came on the market it's like an open-air stud farm around here. Beware of dark corners. A couple of people from the janitorial staff have quit, saying that they aren't paid enough to unsee what they've had to witness."

"Oh, I'm very aware of how that pill has rather dramatically changed the landscape of South Florida," Evelyn said and Dale rolled her eyes. Each Tuesday night, like clockwork, was Evelyn's time to make a new friend who didn't use his inside voice.

"Hoo boy! Has it ever. I was always rather popular with the fellas, being one of a small minority of single women here, but now I've got men—"

Ilona interrupted Patty. "When you say they try harder—"

"I think," Laura said, "I think that our song is wrong too. The tempo is wrong. It's too fast. If we're trying to match the beat, it's just asking too much."

"What did I say?" Patty asked.

"You said, 'She's such a fun gal, the lady that sings this song. If I were thirty years younger, I'd think about her look.'" Laura quoted.

"I said it was moving too fast!" Patty countered.

"You think we haven't tried?" Ilona asked.

Laura turned to her. "You have tried. You've all showed up every day and worked hard and come very far. But right now, they're winning. They've just been at it so much longer. That doesn't mean we're out, it just means we've got to do something to grab attention. A finale of some sort. I'll figure it out tonight and we'll start on it tomorrow."

Laura pulled herself up from the bleacher to standing position. "Music-wise, we need something in between what we've got, and what this was." She gestured toward the pool.

"It wasn't that bad," Phyllis said.

"Did any one of those women look like they were having fun?" Laura asked. "They know that in this context, the song sounds like a dirge. It's all in the body language. They're just try-ing to get through it."

"You remind me of my Ryan," Patty said to Laura. "My grandson. He's got a lot to say too. Wants to be a sportscaster. You're single now. I think he'd be open."

"I'm sort of tied up with commitments the next few months," Laura said, touching her belly.

"Eh. You can always get a sitter."

"Do you really think that Hawthorne is going to beat us?" Evelyn asked.

Laura pressed her hands together. "We just started. They've been at this for years. It's not really a fair fight."

Laura turned to see Evelyn's face fall.

"Listen," Patty said. "Half this team could be incapacitated by next week. So yes, Hawthorne is competition. Just like the teams from Boca and Fort Lauderdale. But do you know the amazing thing about South Florida? A year can be a lifetime. Everything could have changed. People have strokes. They get their hips replaced. They die. They die all the goddamned time."

"Thanks for putting that out there, Patty," Donna said.

"I'm just saying that it's a new scene every year. Just because a team had it together a year ago doesn't mean they'll have it to-gether now."

Dale looked at the women around her, their shoulders slumped, their bodies wearing the softness of defeat. Had they really believed that it would just be this easy? That they'd hop in the pool, learn a three-minute routine, and emerge as winners, all their problems solved? Cherie hadn't promised that, had she? She offered to help. She gave them a plan.

If this failed, if they failed, Dale didn't know what she would do. She wouldn't take anything from Cherie. There wasn't any self-flagellation involved in that belief. It was just the truth. Dale had done nothing for which Cherie should pay her back. She wasn't owed anything. If Dale got any more of Cherie's attention after Marlys was gone, she would welcome it. But that was all she wanted.

Patty was beckoned to the pool level by three of her former teammates. She sat up straight, rolled her eyes, and willingly descended from the upper bleachers where the Sirens sat. Once Patty was in front of the women, they pointed up at the Soleil City gang.

"Have you started attending Bible study?" A blond woman asked Patty.

"What the hell are you talking about?"

"Your friends up there. They're dressed like they've just come from church," an unnatural redhead continued.

"Church? Blow it out of your ass, Pamela," Patty said, looking up at the women from Soleil City. She narrowed her eyes, then turned back to the three women. "These are my new synchro teammates. From Soleil City."

The women all turned and looked up at the squad from Soleil City. Ilona stared them down. Donna moved her hand as if she were making a fist. Evelyn gave them the finger.

"Spies? Are things that desperate that you had to come spy on us?"

"I live here, Pammy," Patty said.

"Pamela."

She made a dismissive motion with her hand. "They're here as my guests. Taking in a show. A *comedy show,*" Patty said, which made Phyllis giggle.

"Holy crap, I think the blonde is going to hit Patty," Donna said, watching as the women got even closer to each other's faces.

"Oh . . . wait. Gladys with the vertigo is Gladys the towel thief," Laura said.

The women watched as Patty stepped closer to Gladys, who got in her face. There were angry words, and then Gladys began to sob on Patty's shoulder. Her son had colon cancer. Stage four. She wasn't sure what she'd do if he died. Patty rubbed her back and began to coo in her ear. After a moment, the two women hugged.

"What the hell was that?" Ilona asked.

Dale saw Laura wipe away a tear.

"What? I'm very pregnant and very emotional," Laura told her grandmother. "And that was just very weird and very moving in a very strange way."

Dale put her hand on Laura's arm.

"I want this." Laura looked around her. "Well, not *this*. But this kind of thing, whatever that is, in forty years. Or now. I want something like this now." Laura put her hands on the bleachers, tried to push herself up in an attempt to find a more comfortable way to sit. "Yesterday, you did that scissor kick three times in a row. It was fine, but not great."

"Thanks, Coach," Dale said, smiling. She thought it had been great.

"Compared to Patty, even compared to Evelyn, it still needs work. But you've been struggling with it and when you got it down, the women congratulated you and told you they were proud of you. Who wouldn't want to be surrounded by that? People who care about you. People who are good. I don't have that at all."

"You'll have that again, Laura," Dale said. "You've got a lot of life ahead of you."

Laura nodded. "Maybe. Evelyn said that I'll live a few different lives and Justin just got a few years of one of them."

Dale laughed. That damn Evelyn. So infuriating, but often so right in so many ways.

"You've done an amazing thing, Laura," Dale said, and together they looked at the women around her, each so different, each coached into doing the same thing.

"Damn. This is all so weird."

"But also so damn good."

CHAPTER 15

6 Days

LAURA

Amanda, the reporter, had called her. Laura had agreed to the interview after she was told that the rest of the synchronized swimming squad had gone before her. She thought, perhaps, it wouldn't be a bad idea to try to clean up her name. She knew what the women called her behind her back.

Laura suggested that they meet at a Pizza Hut near a freeway exit. There wasn't a reason for this choice of location other than the fact that she was seriously craving pizza. In the last week, her cravings—for tomato sauce, for glazed, raised doughnuts, for the usual peanut butter and marshmallow fluff—had come to dominate her thoughts. It was better than thinking of Justin and Melissa and the legal meetings she'd be returning home to in a few short days, or how she would mother an infant, or even the synchro competition. Pizza was better than all that.

After two weeks with senior citizens, Laura was also curious for a taste of the real world again. Amanda was around her age. Laura could still interact with people who had never seen a ration coupon, couldn't she? Or had she walked away from her life so completely that she had erased everything that had come before?

She arrived at the restaurant more than forty-five minutes early. Laura wanted the pizza, but she was also happy to avoid Marlys. Both Laura and her grandmother had been treating each other with exaggerated kindness since their doughnut date. Neither, it seemed, knew where Laura's judgment had landed. All Laura seemed sure of, at that moment, was that in the stories of betrayals and breakups, she wasn't the one coming out on top.

The entire way to Pizza Hut in Marlys's Buick, this is what Laura planned to do: She would only eat half the pizza and save the rest for later. Except, one piece became two and then one glass of diet Pepsi—this town didn't believe in Coke products, not at all—became two and then when half the pizza was gone, it made more sense to just finish it off and pretend she never ordered it before Amanda even walked in.

When she first quit her job, determined to make getting ready for the baby her full-time work, Laura had plans. She would read books about baby's first year—she had already given up on the pregnancy books, having found them more stressful than helpful—including three recommended books about sleep training. She would make sure her diet was balanced and filled with needed nutrients. She would do light exercise and had even heard about a yoga studio that had classes for pregnant women, so she could "bounce back" after delivery. She would do it all.

She had done nothing. People would ask, "What've you been up to?" since she had stopped working and she would start to answer, but then drift off. The hours between Justin leaving for work and coming home from work seemed to pass in minutes. She would clean the kitchen after breakfast, do four or five squats while holding on to the back of a dining-room chair to rein in her rapidly spreading ass, shower, dress, eat lunch, run an errand or two, watch *Oprah* at 4 p.m., and then start dinner. When she went to bed at night, she was exhausted.

In coming to Florida, she had left behind everything that was expected of her as a pregnant woman. Sure, missing doctors' appointments probably wasn't great, but here, no one asked her about her baby registry or her prenatal classes or her hospital tour or her nursery décor. The women of Soleil City had their babies after a traumatic world war and during a housing crisis. Laura was pregnant, then she'd have a baby. That's what they knew— babies today were too good to sleep in an empty drawer?—that's what they expected.

Amanda waved as she walked in the door. *Shit,* Laura thought as Amanda commented on the traffic and sat down at the table. Amanda would ask her about her occupation. She didn't have one. How was she supposed to describe herself? Her dad bought her the plane ticket to Florida. Her mom was paying for the majority of her meals. Once she returned home, her estranged husband would pay for the house they bought together until they sold it. She had nothing of her own. She was no one.

"Do you want to order anything?" Amanda asked, studiously ignoring the greasy napkins under Laura's hand that hadn't been cleared with the pizza tray.

"Maybe just a diet Pepsi?" Laura said.

"I think I'll get a pizza. I'm starving," Amanda said, and Laura moved her hand, pushing the napkins away.

After Amanda promised to look into the players in the West Palm Beach soft drink distribution game that were keeping Coke down, she pulled out a small tape recorder.

Laura answered her initial questions. She got involved because her mom asked her to come to Florida. She had competitive dance experience, though had never been involved in synchronized swimming before. She truly believed the women had it in them to win.

"Donna told me that you thought they couldn't win."

"I don't think I said that. I just said that a win would be difficult."

Amanda made a note on the pad she had in front of her.

"But I don't actually believe that," Laura said.

Amanda looked up from the paper and tilted her head.

"They could win. They could definitely win. I just didn't want them to get too comfortable with the idea. They need to continue to work hard."

"Don't you think that the prospect of losing their apartment building is motivating enough?"

"A loss at the South Florida Senior Synchronized Swimming Competition doesn't mean the loss of their apartment complex. If we win, there would be publicity and prize money, but there's no golden key to the building."

Amanda continued to write.

"Are you only publishing this article if we win?"

"I don't make that decision. But that's the best kind of story, isn't it? Underdogs taking on the establishment and flipping it on its head?"

"That's the expected story. But Soleil City isn't just a team, they're also individuals, and as individuals, they're an extremely interesting bunch."

Amanda flipped through her notebook. "Phyllis Bouchard, age seventy-four. Met her husband at a USO dance during the war. They married four weeks later. After the war, they settled in Providence, Rhode Island, and had a son. They divorced, then remarried two years later. They divorced again, this time remarrying after only six months. They divorced a third time and were discussing getting back together when her husband died of a massive heart attack. This was after the suicide of their only son, who died just over two years after returning home from fighting in Vietnam."

"She worked at a shoe store for years, too."

Amanda smiled and returned to her notebook.

"Donna Howard, age seventy-five. Graduate of the Western Michigan College of Education, class of '46. Spent thirty-six years teaching French in the Detroit school district. Teacher of the Year three times: in '59, '67, and '78. Godparent to four children, great-aunt to six. She is a guest at a former student's Thanksgiving meal each year, an occasion also attended by three other former students and their families."

Laura began to open her mouth to comment, but Amanda continued reading her notes. "Ilona Lowes, age—" Amanda stopped and looked up at Laura. "She won't tell me. I think she's closer to eighty than seventy-five, however. Born in Budapest, Hungary. Moved to New York after the war." She looked at Laura again. "We're missing quite a lot of story there, but she wasn't giving any of it up."

"She doesn't. My grandma doesn't even know it and she's lived beside her for two years."

"She did tell me that she met and married her husband in 1956 in New York—I have to research if there was a death or divorce—and she has a daughter, who lives in Florida."

"Wait, what? Her daughter lives in Florida? But my grandma said that Ilona hasn't had any visitors. Where in Florida does the daughter live?"

"Also unclear. Ilona was a little bit—actually, a lot—of a closed book. Evelyn, on the other hand, was extremely open with me." Amanda returned to her notes. "Evelyn Murphy, age sixty-eight."

Laura guffawed.

"There's a little research to be done on that birth date as well." Amanda cleared her throat and paused as the waitress placed her personal pan pizza in front of her. She picked up a piece of pizza with one hand and continued to read as she chewed. "Born in Atlantic City. Dropped at an orphanage in Camden, New Jersey, when she was seven. Ran away from the orphanage three times before she was sixteen, at which point she married the orphanage's milkman and never went back. Left the milkman after a year and moved to New Orleans during the war. Procured entertainment for departing troops from a house in the French Quarter."

"Procured entertainment?"

"Yeah," Amanda said, looking up, "She clarified that later, in so many words. When we were discussing her Tupperware career, she said she was a great salesperson who always seemed to know what people wanted. During the war, the soldiers wanted sex. So, she found them sex. After the war, their wives and families wanted peace, so she worked as a medium, telling them nice things about their loved one's final moments. During the sixties, she sold Tupperware, and then—"

"So she was a madam?"

"Seems like it."

Laura began to laugh. "Jesus Christ."

Amanda shrugged. "One son, three husbands."

"It's interesting to me, as someone who is about to birth a baby, that these women went through the experience of labor and then all decided, 'Nope, not going to do that again.'"

Amanda smiled. "When are you due?"

"In ten weeks, something like that."

"So, soon."

Laura exhaled. "Soon."

Amanda wiped the last bit of tomato sauce off her mouth and pushed the pan aside. She returned to her notebook.

"Patty Culpepper, age seventy-three. Born and raised on

Long Island, New York. Married her college sweetheart—she went to Smith, he was at Harvard."

"Yeah, she's the fancy one. Lived on the Upper East Side, right?"

"Yep. She went down to Selma, Alabama, after Bloody Sunday."

"What?"

Amanda smiled. "Haven't you seen the scar on her arm? Anyway, rode motorcycles until her sixty-eighth birthday. Is considering getting a tattoo for her seventy-fifth birthday. Or maybe going skydiving. Oh, she has two sons. She said that they make her go to them. They live in Phoenix?" She checked her notes. "Phoenix. And that leaves Dale."

"She talked to you?"

Amanda nodded. "She was more on the Ilona end of the scale than the Evelyn end, but I learned a little bit."

"I won't tell you anything that she didn't. Frankly, I probably don't know any more than what she told you."

"Well, let's see." She flipped the page of her notebook. "Dale Walker, age seventy-five. Born in Boston, went to art school, had a career in fashion that began in the costume department of Paramount Pictures in the early 1950s, continued in New York with her own business and ended up in Chicago as the lead women's buyer at a department store."

"Marshall Field's. It's pretty legendary."

Amanda made a note. *Legendary.* "Six husbands. One child."

Laura ran her hand through her hair. "Of the six there were only two that mattered. The first one and the last one."

"Divorced four times, widowed twice."

Laura held her breath as Amanda put down her pizza and returned to the notebook. This is where Laura would have to fill in her life. Until a month ago, Laura's path had always been straight. Partly because it had been her mom's full-time job to make sure there were no bumps, and partly because Laura had her special plan. She had defined her own idea of success early on.

Over the last week or so, as Laura thought about where it had all gone so wrong, she kept going back to Kyle, her boyfriend during junior year in high school—the first boy she thought she loved.

It was easy to be around Kyle. He was fun. He made her laugh. She would lie on her bedroom floor and speak to him on the phone line she shared with Jessica then feel almost bereft when her mom burst into her bedroom, screamed that it was past eleven on a school night, and tell her to hang up immediately. They had spoken for three or four hours and still had more to say.

What would it have been like to have married a man whose company she *enjoyed*? She and Kyle didn't have some kind of passionate teen romance where they couldn't be near each other without feeling compelled to put their hands or lips on the other person's body. They had some excellent make-out sessions, but those kisses with tongue weren't her brightest memories from their months together. It was talking to him, laughing with him, sharing with him.

Why did they break up? A goddamned rental car. The stupid instinct within her that told her what she thought she should do instead of what she really wanted to do. The same fucking instinct that had gotten her where she was at that moment, pregnant and single in a Pizza Hut in Florida.

Laura had organized a limousine to take herself, Kyle, and three other couples to junior prom. With her first prom, she wanted her fancy night to be *fancy*. A limo was *fancy*. When she told Kyle that his share—their share—of the limo would be over a hundred dollars, he balked.

Kyle had an after-school job. His parents had enough money, but not more. With her requests that he rent the fancy tux and give her a fancy corsage and go to the fancy restaurant and buy the fancy posed pictures at the dance—not to mention the price of the tickets themselves—he was already maxed out. The limo was the breaking point.

"Why the hell would we need a limo? My dad said I can take his car. He'll get it washed."

"Your dad drives a Honda."

"So?"

"It's just . . . it's a special night. That's not special."

"It's our junior prom, Laur. It's hardly the biggest night of our lives."

"What are you talking about? This is a night we'll always remember!" Laura insisted.

She did remember it, because it was the beginning of the end for her and Kyle. They took the limo that Kyle paid for with the last of his savings with the two other couples, who opted to play along. It wasn't fun. They didn't laugh. The driver refused to play the cassette of "Pump Up the Jam" they offered him unless they guaranteed him a large tip, a word that made all the faces in the car contort with anxiety. "We could have played it in my dad's car. We could have played it the entire way there," Kyle mumbled to himself and Laura felt a chill run through her body. She had pushed too hard. Unlike the haircut she talked him into getting or her request that he change his class schedule from one he liked to one that allowed him to have the same study hall as her, he wasn't going to let this go.

A week after prom, they broke up. "I think you just want

the kind of guy that I'm not," Kyle said, and Laura, a year from college, agreed that she probably did. After Kyle, she dated the kind of guys who had gone to their junior proms in rented limousines. After Kyle, she never spoke on the phone to a boy for more than twenty minutes because there wasn't anything more to say.

She had heard that Kyle was back at their high school teaching social studies. He wasn't married and his hairline had receded a bit. But he was still cute. "Still very funny," her high school friend, Angie, who was friends with Kyle's younger sister, told her. "He'd probably like to hear from you," she said, finally, which made Laura believe that he had mentioned her.

What would she say? What would he want to hear her say? They had been kids, and now they were adults. An entire decade had passed; a new century was about to break. Laura crunched the ice from her cup. Weren't ice chips what they gave women when they were in labor? Kyle would be great in a delivery room. He would have joked with her, with the nurses. Doesn't that say it all—a good man is a man who could be useful in a delivery room?

"I was at the VFW the other night. I heard about your divorce. Happening in the middle of everything else." Amanda nodded toward Laura's belly. "Soleil City probably wasn't the worst place for you to land."

Laura nodded, then put her greasy napkin in the middle of her place at the table. "Look, I'm not trying to tell you how to do your job—"

Amanda laughed. "Isn't that what people say immediately before they tell you how to do your job?"

Laura smiled. "Fine. I am trying to tell you how to do your job. Publish this article now. Get people to care about the women of Soleil City. Then, when it's time for the competition, your readers will be invested in their success. Or shattered by their loss. Either way, they'll be primed."

Amanda put her own greasy napkin in the middle of her place. "Okay. I will. I'll try, anyway. They think of me as 'the kid.'"

"Yeah, I definitely know how that goes."

Amanda smiled. "Anyway, I need one more person to tell me their story."

"I don't have a story. Really. I didn't even study abroad in college."

"Everyone has a story, Laura. You have one too."

CHAPTER 16

5 Days

MARLYS

"How long have you known?" Marlys said, as they waited in the emergency room of St. Mary's Hospital. "About my cancer."

"A little while now," Dale said, watching the news on the TV from the corner of her eye. "Do you find him attractive?"

"Who?"

"Bill Clinton."

Marlys smiled, then put her hand on her chest to stop herself from laughing. "No. But hell, I never found Kennedy attractive either."

"Well that's a damn lie. You were all set to marry Joe Junior."

"Joe Junior, of course. But JFK was no Joe Junior."

"Anyway, Kennedy was more attractive than Clinton."

"I guess so. He did have that Boston accent working for him." Marlys smiled. "Ed became Mr. Boston in the end, complete with accent. On a phone call before Ed died, Cherie put him on speakerphone, and in the background I could hear Tom ask Cherie why her father suddenly sounded like Cliff Clavin from *Cheers.*"

Dale laughed.

There were at least ten people waiting to be seen, only one of whom was visibly wounded. One man around Marlys's age was moaning quietly, with the moaning escalating every time one of the nurses appeared to call the next patient back to be treated. He had a pile of reading material with him and a packed lunch. Clearly, he had done this before.

"How long have we been waiting already?" Marlys asked Dale.

"About an hour."

Marlys had called Dale after throwing up blood. It was more than had ever come up before, and though she knew what the doctor would say—you have lung cancer, your body is coming apart—she didn't want to be alone. When Dale suggested they go to the hospital—no, when Dale *demanded* they go to the hospital—Marlys didn't complain. It didn't seem like the right time to get doughnuts.

Dale hadn't asked what type of cancer she had. The lung cancer was that obvious, Marlys imagined. Should she be grateful to her friend for playing along, or upset that Dale had seemed to accept this news and continued on with her own life, swimming with her friends every afternoon and taking their granddaughter to Palm Beach cafés?

The nurse appeared again to call the name of a woman who was holding a badly bandaged arm. The moaning man appeared to give up, dismissing her with a wave. The nurse rolled her eyes at him and tried not to smile.

When Cherie had visited Ed at this hospital, Marlys had asked her what she thought of the nurses. This had been her field, and Marlys assumed that Cherie had been quietly judging them.

"They seem nice, Mom. They certainly like Dad."

They did like Ed, because Ed flirted with them. He knew their children's names. He complimented their scrubs, which they found hilarious. Everyone liked Ed when he wanted them to like him. But that wasn't what Marlys wanted to know. She wanted Cherie to say words that only another nurse would know, to see things that only another nurse could see. Marlys wanted to know this side of her daughter, the one who had her colleagues' respect and her patients' gratitude. She wanted to know what her daughter had been like during the years she had taken on the world on her own. After her parents, before her husband and kids. Back when she only had to think of herself.

"I have a Do Not Resuscitate order. Just so you know," Marlys said.

Dale's face fell. Her body tensed.

"Okay, it's been said. Moving on." Marlys put her hand to her chest. She had watched as Laura had shifted uncomfortably from the weight of the baby against her ribs as she ate breakfast. The two of them, living in the same house, in bodies that they didn't control. Though Laura had something far more miraculous growing within her than Marlys did, neither of them understood what was happening or what would come next.

"Does Cherie know I'm sick?"

"Have you told her you're sick?"

"Dale. Does she know?"

"I believe she has figured it out."

Marlys sighed. "Of course. That's why Laura is staying with me, isn't it? Cherie wants to cram nearly thirty years of a grandmother–granddaughter relationship into three weeks."

"I truly have no room at my place," Dale responded.

They both looked at the TV, at a commercial for a fried chicken chain. "I've never liked biscuits," Dale concluded as it ended.

Marlys looked at her watch. It was ten o'clock. They'd been waiting much longer than an hour. "The thing I don't get is why Cherie didn't stop Laura from marrying this kid in the first place. You don't like him," Marlys said.

"He's a weenie. A six-foot weenie."

Marlys threw up her hands. "It just doesn't make sense. Turning Laura off this guy would have taken Cherie an afternoon. Twenty minutes, tops. Why didn't she?"

"Because it doesn't work that way. Laura said she loved him; Cherie shut her mouth."

"Of course it works that way."

"The kid seemed right, I guess. He fit the mold."

"Still. Cherie should have stopped it." Marlys lowered her voice. "Ed stopped her from marrying a weenie."

"Do I want to know how that happened?"

"Ed paid him off."

"Jesus."

"Hey, Ed didn't make him take the money. He only offered it to him." Marlys looked at the reception desk. The woman behind it was holding a compact and applying lip liner with a remarkably steady hand. "His name was Randy."

"Oh, the one you mentioned at the VFW. His name certainly caused a reaction from Cherie. I wondered if there was more to it." *Typical Dale,* Marlys thought. She wanted to know the story of Randy but didn't think it was her place to ask after the story of Randy. How was Dale going to get closer to Cherie if she kept herself looking in from the outside? Had Marlys's plot to make the two of them knock down a few walls between them by sharing the same roof for a few weeks already failed?

"Yeah, well, apparently they wanted to get married. Ed didn't like the kid. So, he paid him to go away, made up some kind of Peace Corps story for him to tell Cherie—the Kennedy love, he thought it would soften the blow—and the kid took the cash and ran."

"What was Ed's problem with the kid?"

"You know Ed. He said Randy's voice was too high. His walk

was too soft. His laugh was too . . . musical, I think it was." Marlys rolled her eyes.

"That was it? Those were the reasons?"

"Didn't you divorce your fourth husband a month after you got married because he cut his toenails in bed?"

"That was one reason of many. He was as loathsome as he was rich. My only attempt to marry for money was a failure in every way." She shrugged.

Marlys continued. "Randy wanted to be a teacher. Ed didn't agree with that. He had moved us all to that terrible little house in Edina so that Cherie would be surrounded by future lawyers and doctors and investment bankers. He didn't want her to live in a terrible little house. He didn't want her to ever worry about money, the way we had. So, he paid Randy off."

"How much was it?"

"Enough, obviously." Marlys put her purse on her lap. She had never said any of this out loud before. "He won it playing poker, I believe. Anyway, Cherie got over Randy, eventually. She met Tom, had two kids, lived happily ever after in an enormous house on a hill. Fairy tale."

"She has no idea? About the payoff?" Dale asked skeptically.

Marlys shrugged. "She's not an idiot. I'm sure she has an idea. But she never confronted Ed about it, which means she accepted it."

Dale was silent.

"Come on, Dale," Marlys said. "Would Cherie have been happy being a teacher's wife? In Jamaica, she commands an entire household staff. Having money is who she is. It's what Ed wanted her to be. He didn't get what he wanted in life, but Cherie would. She did."

The moaning man near them unwrapped his packed sandwich and began to eat it noisily. He looked at Marlys and Dale and thrust the sandwich at them, offering a bite.

"No, thank you."

He shrugged. "You'll regret it."

A few months after Cherie and Tom bought their gigantic house, Marlys was home alone inside it. Cherie had bought Marlys and Ed tickets to come up to Minneapolis in the spring to show it off. Tom had taken Ed somewhere, and Cherie was off with the girls. As soon as she heard the last of the cars pull out of the driveway, Marlys walked through the house on her own, opening door after door. The kitchen pantry had enough food stored in it to serve a nuclear fallout shelter for at least two months. Cherie had clothes in at least four different closets. Tom had more than fifteen years' worth of *National Geographic* magazines in leather-bound holders kept in one of two closets in his office. There were so many places to put so many things. Coffee tables that opened to hold remote controls. Window seats that opened to hold seasonal pillows. Kitchen drawers that had more drawers inside of them.

In the basement, Marlys opened a small door and found a deep room with a single lightbulb. She pulled the attached string to turn it on and found a lone fake Christmas tree in the corner of the room. Her daughter lived in a house that had a room whose only purpose was to house a Christmas tree, one of four that she put up in her house every holiday season.

When Marlys told Ed the story of the Christmas tree room later, he beamed. "This is what I wanted for her and she got it all. All of it. So, I was right."

Maybe he was right. Right about moving to the rich suburb during high school. Right about giving Cherie his cashmere sweater samples so she could fool everyone that she came from a different kind of family than the one she did. Right about getting rid of Randy so she could hold out for Tom.

Had Ed known that in saying the other people were better, the only conclusion that Cherie could have drawn was that he and Marlys weren't as good?

Cherie was around twelve when she understood that she was different from the other kids. She had two mothers and she called one of them by her name. Her dad was always gone. They lived in a building, not a house, and took the bus.

At her friends' homes, their mothers put three or four different dishes of food on the table for dinner, none of them containing cigarette ash. Their dads came home promptly at 5:45 and did not go directly to the bar cart. At the dinner table, the kids joked with each other and the dads told stories about their days, and their moms got up from their chairs to get more milk out of the refrigerator—milk that they didn't even have to smell to know was fresh. After dinner, the kids played in the streets until it got dark, then Cherie got a ride home. The parent—whether it was the mom or the dad—frowned when they saw where she lived.

When Cherie was in high school, Marlys stood in the window and watched as her daughter pretended to walk up the neighbor's driveway after getting dropped off by a date. Marlys switched off the lamp and hurried into her bedroom so Cherie wouldn't know she'd been caught. Her daughter didn't need to feel Marlys's shame on top of her own.

"It's going pretty well, though," Marlys said. "This whole grandmother-granddaughter cram session. I tried one of those peanut butter and marshmallow fluff sandwiches she loves so much. Not half bad."

"Laura's stronger than I gave her credit for," Dale replied. "You know what they're like, the Soleil City ladies. But she's commanding them. She's keeping them in line. I sure as hell never thought I could have done what I'm doing in that pool every day."

"I heard she has a whistle."

Dale laughed. "She has a whistle." She dug into her own purse and pulled out a tissue to dab at her nose. "I think she'll be fine without this *Justin*. At some point, we all have to stand on our own, don't we? Now it's her turn."

"She's been spoiled. Cherie spoiled her."

Dale shrugged. "Because she could."

"Still, there's providing for your child and there's spoiling them. You don't think Cherie went too far?"

"We spoiled Cherie."

Marlys jerked her head back in confusion.

"Not in terms of things, obviously. I just mean . . . maybe we kept too much from her. Maybe she should have known about some of the shit. She has no idea how my own mother treated me. She doesn't know that I was in jail once."

Marlys didn't tell Dale that Cherie knew that fact now. Laura had told Cherie, with the apology that she could keep some secrets, but that one she just had to tell.

"She doesn't know that Ed could have made more money if he just swallowed a little of his pride. Maybe she should have known, Marlys, that we've meant something to each other all these years. That we've both done things for the other that . . ."

Dale drifted off.

Three weeks after Frank died, Marlys got a call from a woman named Babe in Atlanta. She had found Dale unconscious in her bed the day before. It looked like she had taken a handful or so of tranquilizers before a few long swigs of gin, pulled the bedcovers up to her chin, and tried not to wake up. Babe had gone to look for her when she didn't stop by her apartment for a cup of coffee by nine the next morning. "My own daughter had the same idea a few years ago after a bad breakup," Babe told Marlys. "Unfortunately, she didn't screw it up."

Dale had told the psychiatrist at the hospital who talked to her for a half hour after they had pumped her stomach that she didn't necessarily want to die, she just didn't want to live. When he learned she was a recent widow, he folded her into the desperate woman category and recommended rest before she be let back out into the world.

That afternoon, Marlys got on a bus from Florida and showed up in Dale's hospital room early the next morning. As Dale began to cry, Marlys held her hand. For the next six hours, as Dale felt she could finally try to sleep, Marlys sat next to her and continued to hold her hand. When she was released from the hospital two days later, Marlys had already been to her apartment and, with Babe's help, had cleaned it up and cleared Frank's clothing out. "You would have had to do it sometime," she said, and Dale didn't try to argue. When Dale climbed into bed that night, she found that Marlys had put one of Frank's T-shirts under her pillow. Dale would have to feel her grief—her deep, relentless grief—but now she knew she wasn't alone.

"Maybe Cherie should have known about the hard parts. Instead, she just knows what it's like when things are easy."

Marlys stared at Dale. For all the things that Cherie didn't know about her parents, there was an even longer list of things that Dale didn't know about her daughter.

The story that Dale and Cherie believed is one that said Dale went to Mexico and Marlys became Mom. But that didn't happen immediately. There were the days and hours and at the beginning, the minutes, when Cherie would ask Marlys when her mommy was coming back for her, where her mommy was, why her mommy had left. And then, even more heartbreakingly, there was the day when Cherie stopped asking the question entirely.

There were the calls from Dale to Cherie, calls that sounded cheerful and informative and as natural as could be. Calls which, after they ended, sent a teenaged Cherie into her bedroom where she would close the door, turn out the lights, and lie silently on her bed in the dark room until she would finally put herself to sleep.

There were the questions that Cherie got from her friends about the presents she received from New York. Who was it that sent her that skirt? Where did she get the playbill for the new Paul Newman show on Broadway? "A family friend," Cherie answered, once. "Someone my mom knew during the war."

Those were the things Marlys would never tell Dale. Those were the things Dale already knew without ever being told.

Marlys began to cough. She pulled herself up from her seat and began to walk toward the door, unsure of what might come up with the next heave. Dale followed behind her, uselessly holding a tissue. When she turned around after the coughing stopped, she saw the tears in her friend's eyes.

"This sure as hell isn't easy," Marlys said.

The nurse came out to call another name. The women didn't look up as they found new seats, away from the man with the sandwich.

"What are the doctors going to do for me, Dale? They'll tell me they can 'make me comfortable.' That means morphine, by the way. Just a little at first. Then, enough to slow everything to the point that it doesn't want to keep going."

"Is that how it was with Ed?"

"Ed did everything he could to avoid a natural conclusion, even if it was foregone. All the treatments, the diets. So I don't know if this is how it's supposed to go. I don't know if this means

I'm in the middle or at the end. Maybe they'll tell me. Maybe not. They know, of course, but I can't. But I just need one to break rank. I just need one to tell me what everyone but me gets to know."

The door opened again and a new nurse appeared.

"Marlys Kelly," the nurse said, finally.

Marlys stood up, then steadied herself on the edge of the chair. Dale stood with her until she understood that Marlys wanted to do this alone.

"It will be hard, Mar. But you do need to talk to Cherie," Dale said as Marlys began to walk toward the nurse. "We can't keep this from her too."

Marlys nodded. That was all there was left to do.

CHAPTER 17

3 Days

DALE

"I feel like I'm in the Ice Capades!" Phyllis exclaimed from be-hind the screen. Even without being able to see Dale, she knew to explain herself. "That's a good thing. I took my son, Paul, when he was a kid. He hated it but I absolutely adored it."

Dale had set up her living room to approximate her New York atelier (she had never used that word publicly—she didn't think her Boston accent allowed it—but it was what she had tried to create). Evelyn's boudoir screen—she did use the word, and no one had once attempted to question it—had been set up against the back wall. A hanging rack, which had appeared cour-tesy of Cherie without any explanation of its origin, held the women's swimsuits—tagged and hung in order of appointment. Dale's few chairs had been repositioned into a waiting area. Ilona was providing hand massages to the women at the kitchen table. Laura sat near the screen at a folding table that had been covered by a thrift store scarf next to a pitcher of water filled with lemon slices, holding a clipboard to keep track of any last-minute al-terations or issues. Cherie stood next to Dale with a tape mea-sure around her neck, her role not completely defined. The whole operation, Dale noted with satisfaction, was thoroughly civilized. Even, dare she say, professional.

Dale knew that the women of Soleil City needed a fantastic costume but waited until Cherie came to her with the request before beginning work. Cherie had tried to find something on her own. She had driven the Lincoln around South Florida to boutiques, costume stores, and dance supply outlets, even met with a beauty pageant consultant. Still, despite the miles, she hadn't found anything that was right.

There was contrition in her voice when she came to Dale. She should have thought of her sooner, Cherie said. She just . . . she thought she could do this on her own. She ignored the obvious answer that was in front of her the whole time.

Dale would do it. She knew how to do drama. Before she dressed the women of New York, Dale had worked in the costume department of Paramount. Sure, she had only been an assistant then, but she had picked up a few things. She knew the trade.

Cherie bought the black tank suits that Dale requested and pointed to the sewing machine and strips of sequins that were set beside it. "Water reflects light. Sequins reflect light. Together, we should be able to blind the judges enough to miss our mistakes," Dale had said with a needle already in her mouth.

Now, days later, Phyllis emerged from behind the screen in her swimsuit, the first to do so, and Cherie and Laura gasped in unison. The effect of the sequined waves that Dale had created out of shades of yellow and orange to approximate the sun on the black suit were stunning. As the sun streamed in through the living room window and hit the disks of color, the layers of sparkle were perfect. Dale had devised a way to sew the sequins on with her machine, but it only reduced the need for hand-sewing by about half. Her strained eyesight and numb fingertips were proof of her effort.

As Phyllis stood near the floor-length mirror—Dale had brought the mirror from her bedroom—Dale approached her with the final item of the outfit. She asked Phyllis to step into a pair of tap pants—a flouncy short that Dale had sewn up from black nylon and lined with red nylon, embellished with a line of sequins around the bottom.

"Oooh, coverage," Phyllis said, approvingly. Cherie smiled at Dale and then told Phyllis to reach between her legs.

"Uh, you said that I should—" Phyllis tried to clarify.

"There's a snap near your crotch," Cherie clarified. Phyllis turned away from the women and reached down to find the snap. She pulled at it, and the shorts released downward into a skirt. "For the final formation. You'll all reach under to release the snap and your skirts will float around you. The effect will be stunning," Cherie said, beaming.

That had been Dale's idea. Laura had been working on the finale for the last few days and Patty was in agreement that it was what they had to do. "The judges are old, like us. They can't remember the last team's moves, but they can remember the last team's applause." The women had discussed the move for the last week. Did they try to launch someone, and if they did, who would be thrown into the air? Ilona, who was the smallest? Or Donna, who was the most athletic? Of course, then Phyllis started a discussion about how Ilona was not only smaller than Evelyn, but she also had more muscle, and didn't muscle weigh more than fat, which caused Evelyn to ask who the hell was Phyllis to call Evelyn fat, to which Phyllis responded that Evelyn should know that fat was a natural part of the body and who hadn't put on a little weight after menopause, and Ilona's muscles were kind of scary, if she were to tell the truth.

As Laura worked on the moves, Dale worked on the special effects. She sold it as a costume-based surprise, and after she saw that the women remained unconvinced, Cherie nodded to her to play the Hollywood costumer card.

"It worked for Barbara Stanwyck," Dale said, and the women were silenced. It had never been tried on Barbara Stanwyck, but the clock was ticking. Corners needed to be cut.

Dale and Cherie had assessed the skirt idea only the night before. They had gone down to the pool after most of the complex's balcony lights had been dimmed, and Cherie, wearing the skirt Dale had given her to test, quietly walked herself into the pool from the shallow end. When she got to the middle of the pool, she reached between her legs with one arm while thrusting the other arm into the air—"Everyone will look at the raised arm, so the lowered arm won't look, you know, *questionable*"—and undid the snap. The skirt spread around her, flowing up as she lowered her arm back to the water, creating the exact effect both women had hoped to achieve. Dale decided to add another half inch of fabric onto the skirts to heighten the effect.

The women had sat on the loungers after Cherie removed the skirt and wrapped herself in a towel.

"You haven't slept in two nights," Cherie said to Dale. "The amount of work this must have been for you . . ."

"I've slept. Just not a lot."

"You know, I still have the suit you made for me after graduation when I visited you in New York. I pull it out sometimes when I want to remember how I looked in my youth."

"You still have it?"

"I do. I wish I had kept more things you made me from that trip. They were all so beautiful. Laura still has the bubble skirt you made her when she was, what, twelve, thirteen?"

"Thirteen." Cherie had brought the girls to Chicago as she had for the last two years, during their school's October break. For the first time, the *Seventeen* magazines that Dale had in the apartment for work caught their eye. After their traditional dinner of Chicago deep-dish pizza they paged through the magazines and announced what they loved. When they got to the spread with the bubble skirts, an item that Dale thought was rather clever, they began their chorus. "Can we get one, please, please?"

The second day of the trip was always when they went to Marshall Field's. The visit to the magnificent State Street store was supposedly for the girls. They could buy some Frango chocolates at the basement candy counter and eat lunch at the Walnut Room, receiving an extra bowl of whipped cream with their hot chocolate. The girls never complained, but it was Cherie who loved it the most. The grandeur of the store, the professional saleswomen who always remembered her name and her size (after Dale's prodding a few days earlier) filling her favorite dressing room with items they thought might "suit her," thrilled Cherie. Dale's employee discount was the icing on the cake.

Dale knew that when the girls went to the store the next day, the bubble skirts they would find in the junior section wouldn't fit either of them. Jessica was still in the girls' department and Laura was small for her age, not yet fully in adolescence.

Dale decided to solve the problem that night. She had enough of a small black and white checkered cotton sateen in the apartment to make two skirts. Dale brought her sewing machine into her bedroom—the girls were already asleep in the other bedroom and Cherie had insisted on taking the couch—and placed it on the farthest wall so that the noise wouldn't disturb her sleeping family. She spent the next four hours sewing two bubble skirts. Before she went to bed around three in the morning, she placed the skirts at the foot of the guestroom bed, where the girls slept.

Just after seven, the girls' squeals woke Dale up. She smiled, then pulled on her robe. She had never been with Cherie's family for Christmas morning—she had never been invited—but this was how she thought it would be. On her Christmas mornings, as she sat drinking coffee as if it were just another day, the sun low on the horizon, she imagined the girls squealing as they opened the mountain of gifts they had received from their parents. This, for all future Christmas imaginings, was the soundtrack.

"I know clothing isn't what you thought you would do," Cherie said, straightening her towel. "But you've made a lot of people very happy by doing it."

Dale shifted in her lounge chair. She bit her lip to stop herself from offering some kind of self-deprecating response. Her daughter had just told her that she made people happy. That, perhaps, Dale had even made Cherie happy too. Dale wanted to accept this. She wanted to leave this moment as it was, so there would be nothing to mar the memory when she returned to it in the coming weeks and months.

The last couple of weeks had made Cherie seem different to Dale in a way she wasn't sure she could define. Dale knew that all the afternoons of Cherie borrowing the Lincoln and driving around South Florida to speak to doctors had not given her any new hope to hold on to about Marlys's illness. The red, puffy eyes and the closed bedroom door that followed her return from these appointments said all Dale needed to know. It was as final as they all believed it to be.

But there were signs that the deep humidity had sunk into Cherie's bones and allowed her to relax a little, or at least to let her guard down just a bit. When Cherie had been accidentally splashed by the women in the pool at the end of practice the previous day, Dale had seen Laura tense. Instead, Cherie had leaned down to the pool, made her hand into a cup, and splashed the women back. The splash was returned and five minutes later,

Cherie and her linen separates were drenched, everyone was laughing, and Cherie's arm was around her daughter, holding her close to her in a half-hug. Laura's look of disbelief at the whole situation soon morphed into pleasure. They continued to joke with each other as Cherie kept her daughter close. When Cherie laughed, it was a little bit louder, a little less appropriate. It was a laugh that was of Cherie, but not quite the Cherie she had allowed her family to know.

Now, a radio quietly broadcast the West Palm Beach weather report in Dale's apartment. Sunny, hot, humid. Dale looked at the women who surrounded the costumes she had created in an attempt to keep her life as she thought she had known it. Phyllis held her costume in front of her in the mirror once more before putting it back on the rack and moving into the kitchen for her hand massage. "Dammit, Ilona," Phyllis said between moans, "you could have been doing this for us the entire time?"

When Donna came in for her fitting, then turned to the mirror and saw herself in her full costume, Dale noted that her eyes got a little red. "Look at us," she said, and Dale saw that Cherie had also gotten a little teary.

It was Patty, however, who got the most emotional. "It's just . . . it's almost over. Maybe we'll keep going. Maybe I'll put *Soleil City* on my calendar once a week and just hang out here because you have no security to keep me out. But this has been . . . I'm not going to lie, this has been the best part of my year. I loved doing this with all of you. Whatever happens at the competition," Patty said as she hung her costume on the rack, "we did an amazing thing. Laura, you kicked our asses, but you made a jumble of old ladies work together as an actual team."

Laura put her hand on her stomach and winced. Dale's granddaughter seemed less tolerant of the baby's kicks in the last couple of days. "I can't believe we're almost there," Laura said, finally, and Dale could feel Laura's pride in having been a good coach, but also her trepidation in what would come next. "This isn't the real world to me, Grandma," Laura had said as they left the Palm Beach café after an afternoon of watching women who had spent fortunes on surgery and weeks in shrouded recovery to try to regain the person they once appeared to be to the world.

"Honestly, honey, I don't know if this is the real world to me, either."

As Patty gathered her things together to leave, though made no move to actually do so, Cherie looked at her watch and frowned. Evelyn hadn't yet arrived.

"Have you, uh, have you heard anything about when the article will be published, Cherie?" Patty asked.

"No," Cherie said, tersely.

The other women in the room exchanged a look.

"It's just that . . . we all talked to the reporter—to Amanda—for a while. I gave her some personal information. The publicity would have been good for the team. I'm not sure if I would have bothered inviting her in if there was any question as to whether or not she'd publish the damn thing. I thought it was a done deal."

"She tried." Cherie looked directly at Patty. "Amanda tried. But she's a young woman reporter in a very male newsroom. We—you—aren't news, apparently. Not according to them. We're not a good enough story. She fought for the story and she was shot down. That's where things stand."

Patty mumbled how some things just won't ever change.

Dale felt a pang for Amanda. She knew about being dismissed all too well. Dale still dreamed about the day she was fired from her job at Marshall Field's in Chicago. Men who had treated her as a colleague the day before looked at her as a fragile old crow after her fall. For months after—years—she blamed herself for the loss of the job. Why hadn't she sat at her desk for the fifty seconds it would have taken her to eat a banana? Why hadn't she taken the elevator the two floors she needed to go instead of taking the stairs? It was for the men. It was because she needed them to know that she was busy. She needed them to know that she didn't waste a single moment of her time. She needed them to know that she wasn't just like them, she worked harder than them. She fainted as she took the back staircase, hit her head, and stained the concrete with blood. Now, a decade later, she could feel anger. But for so long, all she felt was shame. Another one of her failures. Another one of the ways she hadn't gotten it right.

"She'll write about the competition. Whether or not that gets published depends on how well you all do, I guess," Cherie said.

"Thanks for nothing, I guess," Patty said.

Dale interrupted. "Patty, no alterations on your costume then? It looks lovely on you. The whole team together will be quite a sight, if I do say so myself."

"I never got the hang of a sewing machine. Always had to ask the maid to help out with the kids' things. She did a great hem. Do you do hems? I've got a couple of pairs of pants that I could bring . . ." Patty turned to see Cherie glare at her. She cleared her throat. "Evelyn is rather late, isn't she?"

Cherie looked at her watch again, shot another warning look at Patty, then walked to the kitchen to grab the ringing phone.

"She's been spending a lot of time with William, a new widower, over at Hawthorne. He seems quite smitten. Wife died of a heart attack. Not many women with heart attacks around our place. Usually it's cancer. A few strokes. I'd take a heart attack."

"Patty," Dale said.

"Well, we all think about it, don't we? Not you, dear," Patty said, looking at Laura. "You shouldn't be thinking about it. Having a baby is so safe these days. Something truly awful rarely happens. Those ankles of yours look a little swollen though. Is that new? You might want to get it checked out."

"I feel fine," Laura said, though Dale noticed that her granddaughter did look paler than normal.

"Are you one of those young women who insist on having a woman doctor? There's part of me that would have loved to have a woman handle everything that happened between my legs—I used to have terribly heavy periods—but then there's another part of me, a horrible, old-fashioned part I'm sure, that thinks that a man just does a better job."

Laura scoffed. "That's why things don't change," she said, firmly, and Cherie looked up as she walked back into the room, then sat down hard on the chair nearest to the changing screen. "You're why things don't change," Laura repeated.

Patty opened her mouth to say something, but no words came out.

"Well," Cherie said, "I know one thing that has changed. That was Evelyn. She quit. She's going to swim with Hawthorne."

CHAPTER 18

2 *Days*

MARLYS

Before Ed died, he insisted that he didn't want a memorial service. His world had gotten very small in his last years, consisting primarily of Marlys and the nurses at the hospital. Cherie only came to visit a few times; his granddaughters hadn't come at all. He had finished paying for his Neptune Society cremation plan years earlier and was proud that his death wouldn't cost his wife a thing. Marlys knew that the thought of a sparsely attended service horrified her husband. It was Ed, which meant that the only two options he deemed acceptable were overflowing venue or nothing at all. The result was nothing at all.

Cherie wasn't pleased. She said that she needed there to be something. *Of course she did,* Marlys thought. For Cherie, her dad was sick and her dad was dead. She had missed the dying part altogether.

When Cherie arrived in West Palm Beach the day after his death, she sat at Marlys's kitchen table and cried as Marlys made her a tuna fish sandwich that she barely ate, listened as Marlys told her that she would have ten photocopies of Ed's death certificate made to send to various agencies, and held her hands out reverentially to receive her share of her dad's ashes. After that,

Cherie got into her blue rental car and returned to her hotel room at The Breakers, Palm Beach's finest.

Cherie later told Marlys that after she returned home, she found her dining room table filled with sympathy bouquets from friends. Cherie put on a black dress to read the cards, imagining the tight smiles and head tilts of condolence from each person who had bothered to call their florist. "How thoughtful," Marlys said, knowing that not a single card addressed Cherie's father—instead, they mentioned her "loss," her "difficult time"—by his name. Edward Kelly, 1925–1997.

Now, Marlys stood at the edge of the ocean, a bag of her dead husband's ashes in her handbag. She balanced the bag against her hip as she watched a seagull fly above her.

She had done this before, come to the ocean with the remains of Ed in tow. Six other times, to be exact. Ed had asked to be scattered in the ocean and more than two years later, Marlys had not fulfilled that request. She could take his paintings out of the house, but the thought of removing him, this part of him, was too much. She had come to the water's edge, held her husband in her hands, and then turned around to bring him home.

If she sent him out to sea, would she release the rest of her anger? He was scared to die. Did she finally understand that? Wasn't she scared too?

The emergency room doctor had told her the blood, that amount of blood, meant that the timeframe had changed. It was moving faster. Marlys was still breathing fine. Not great, but good enough. For now. Each day she would get a little worse, then even worse, and then the pain would come, and finally it would be the end. It meant that she might be gone before Laura's baby was born. Her daughter's grief papered over with baby joy.

Marlys would finally tell Cherie that she was dying. They would send Ed's ashes out to sea, together, and then Marlys would tell her, as simply as she could, that soon she'd be gone too.

"Cherie! Come down to the water!" Marlys called up to her daughter, who was standing two hundred feet back.

Marlys hadn't told Cherie they would be going to the beach. She had asked her if she was available for an outing and her daughter had readily agreed.

When Cherie had come over to Marlys's house for lunch, she'd always directed her mother to the patio table, instead of the dining room with its piles of clutter. Cherie never stopped to look around Marlys's house, the place that was still filled with pieces of her father: his razor in the bathroom drawer, his suits—the handsome uniform of his salesman days—in the closet, his books on the bookshelf while Marlys's romance novels were stacked up in front of the shelves on the floor. A bottle of Ed's tomato juice was still in the fridge, two years past its expiration date.

In all the times Marlys had seen Cherie during this trip to Florida, she had mentioned her dad less than a handful of times. She still missed him, she had told her mom. She still thought about him a lot of the time. But if Marlys had noted grief in her daughter's voice, it was when she spoke about Jessica. Her daughter, gone off to live her own life.

Growing up, Cherie's friends all giggled when they were near Ed. "Your dad is just *gorgeous,*" Marlys heard one of them say after meeting Cherie's parents on the sidelines of a high school football game. Marlys shook her head at the thought of it. God, they had been so young, playing the role of adults. How old would Ed have been then? Thirty-five?

Cherie was equally smitten with her father. Why shouldn't she have been? Ed was easy. She had one man who played the role of father in her life, even if he was gone more than he was around. He told her kind things, sang her little songs about how she was his gal. Then, just as he was starting to feel restless again, he could leave. Who couldn't act good for a single week at a time?

"Did Grandpa ever cheat on you?" Laura had asked after she had returned to the big box of photos one rainy evening and held a picture of Ed smiling at an elegant woman at a cocktail party. "That was, like, kind of common back then, wasn't it?"

"I don't know," Marlys answered, honestly. She didn't know. She had never allowed herself to find out. Marlys refused to check his pockets after he got home from the road. He always gave her time, taking an almost comically long shower after they'd made love when he returned from his sales trips midday—he always timed it so that it was midday—while Cherie was at school.

Marlys imagined what the evidence could be—matchboxes with women's phone numbers, restaurant receipts with dinner for two, lipstick kisses on cocktail napkins. Maybe even a full note, promising Ed her undying devotion if only he would stay.

She didn't look because she didn't want to know. If she found a note, she'd have to know the story. If she knew the story, she'd have to do something. If she did something, said something, she couldn't take it back. Instead, she wouldn't allow herself to find out. He could be the good husband, the fine father. If there was another side of Ed, Marlys and Cherie wouldn't know it.

Cherie moved closer to the water, yet still not all the way to Marlys. "Pretty!" Cherie shouted with forced cheer, pointing to the ocean.

She had frowned when she saw Marlys pull into the parking lot. "The beach? What are we doing here?" Cherie had asked. Marlys assured her that she had a plan. Besides, she wasn't in

Florida much longer and it would be a shame if she left before watching the waves.

It was a clear, sunny day, and it did look lovely. Marlys and Ed hadn't visited the ocean very often. Maybe ten times in all the years they lived in Florida. Possibly less? There was talk about going to Key West for a long weekend, but they never had. Ed sold men's suits at Macy's and Saturday was his biggest day. Why hadn't they gone midweek? Why hadn't she asked?

Marlys motioned for Cherie to join her. Cherie moved up a few more feet.

"Come down to the water!" Marlys shouted when she was ten feet away.

"You know, I . . . I don't love the ocean," Cherie said, finally.

"We're not going swimming, Cher. Just come put your feet in the water. I want to show you something."

Cherie continued to hesitate, looked at the sky above her— perfectly blue—and exhaled, loudly. "Okay," she said, finally.

After watching the seagulls dip into the water for a couple of minutes, Cherie standing two or three feet behind her mother, Marlys decided it was time. She reached into her handbag and pulled out the bag of Ed's ashes.

"Oh my God! Mom! Is that Dad?"

"He wanted to be scattered in the ocean. I think we should."

"Now? You want to do this now? We can't do it now. We should have Laura here. We should have—" Cherie stopped herself. Who else would they invite? "Tom should be here. Maybe Jessica too."

"The two of us were his world, Cherie. It's enough."

Marlys had been surprised by Ed's request to be scattered at sea, told to her just the day before he died. He loved to fish while they were in Minnesota, but that was always done in lakes. If he

230 | SARAH C. JOHNS

had a deep connection to the ocean, he had not shared it with her during their fifty years of marriage. But she promised him that he would be scattered into the sea, and so, finally, he would.

"So that's Dad, in that plastic bag with a produce department twist tie? Is it straight off a bag of tomatoes, or was it a few mushrooms?"

"I think it was from onions."

"Mom! Dad hated onions." Cherie took a deep breath and another step back from the ocean. "I bought you that beautiful urn for your birthday. That beautiful navy enamel urn with inlaid lapis lazuli and malachite. Why wouldn't you keep him in that?"

"Yes. The birthday urn. How could I forget?"

On her first birthday after Ed died, Marlys opened the door to a delivery from Cherie of a very heavy cardboard box that she had to sign for before the delivery man would leave it with her. Marlys had a standing request for any gift-giving holiday: a carton (or more) of cigarettes and a bottle of Tabu by Dana perfume. But here was this heavy box, and inside of this box was yet another box. When she opened it, she found a beautiful, expensive, useless urn. Marlys put it back in the box, lit one of the last cigarettes from her Christmas carton, and pushed the box across the kitchen floor with her foot. Couldn't this day, this one day, be about her instead? Couldn't she go to the door, receive a gift, and open it to find something she really wanted for herself? All day, as she had bills changed to her name and renegotiated with the credit card companies, she told people about her husband's change in status. They gave her their condolences and some of them told her about their own recent loss. The days were long and hard and a goddamned urn, no matter how lovely, no matter how expensive, was the last thing she wanted to see.

A couple of days later, with the urn still in the middle of her kitchen, Marlys did her hair and makeup, put on earrings and a necklace, and slipped on the last outfit she bought when Ed was still working and had his employee discount—a red pencil skirt with a flattering jacket. She drove to a consignment shop in Palm Beach that she found in the phone book and showed them the urn. How much would they give her?

They gave her $500. They knew a guy who knew a guy doing a brisk trade in high-end urns. Big market. She took her cash and bought herself an ice-cream cone with sprinkles.

Cherie slapped her hands on her head, then raised them to the sky. "Oh my God, you sold your dead husband's urn?"

"He wasn't in it at the time, obviously," Marlys said, trying to keep her voice even. "Cigarettes and perfume, Cherie. That's all I wanted."

Her daughter walked away, spun in a circle, looked up at the sky—clearly asking God for the strength to deal with her mother—and returned to Marlys. "I'm not going to do this so informally. There needs to be a ceremony."

"Cherie, I don't know if you know this but," Marlys leaned closer to her daughter and lowered her voice, "this isn't exactly a *sanctioned* activity. Human remains and a public swimming beach aren't really two things that usually go together. But it is the ocean, the surf is up, it's not busy—now is as good of a time as any."

"Oh my God."

"He wanted this! This is your dear dad's request."

"It can't just be here and now. What about . . . what about Walt?"

"Walt? Walt from Minneapolis? Ed hadn't spoken to Walt in at least a decade, and even then, it was to tell him that he had read a magazine profile about him and there was a spelling mistake on page sixty-three. Walt tried to keep the conversation going, but your dad wasn't interested. He hung up."

Cherie looked around her, trying to find another excuse. She turned to her mom. "I'm not dressed for it. You're not dressed for it. Dad would definitely have wanted us to be dressed."

"Cherie, I'm not putting on panty hose and heels to stand in the ocean and scatter my dead husband's ashes."

"Fine, then maybe I'm not ready. Maybe I need a minute to figure this whole thing out."

"He's been dead almost two years."

"I know that!" she exclaimed, then returned to the water and put her hand into it just as a wave came up and slapped her wet. Cherie stood up quickly, coughing out the water that got into her mouth. Marlys moved as quickly as she could and put her hand on her daughter's back, being transported, as she did, back to that spring day in 1944, the day that Marlys knew she would always be in Cherie's life.

It had been a beautiful day in May. The sun provided enough heat to warm Dale, Marlys, and Cherie, and to tempt them into wading into the chilly Atlantic water off the Cape. The drive down to the beach made Marlys realize she had no real idea of where she had been living during those months in Massachusetts. She hadn't been outside of Boston, and even much of Boston itself remained a mystery. The war brought people to faraway places that they'd remember all wrong once they were gone.

The three of them stopped in Hyannis. Their months of collected gas coupons had brought them this far in Dale's father's borrowed car, the car that would become hers after his death, the car she would sell to help her get to Mexico. That day in 1944, Dale didn't have a real plan other than to go toward the ocean, and Marlys wanted to see where Joe Kennedy Jr. spent his sum-mers. "You know, so when we get together, I'll be familiar with the place," Marlys said with a wink just months before the world learned he would never return. When Marlys read the news, she felt numb. All the loss, all the pain.

Cherie—Ceres then, no nickname—was in a fussy stage. She had spent the car ride fidgeting on Marlys's lap while Marlys tried to distract her. When she finally pulled a bobby pin from Marlys's hair and missed poking her in the eye by the length of an eyelash, she was dispatched to the back seat where she promptly fell asleep.

In the trunk of the car was a canvas and Dale's paints. She had told Marlys that she would paint her portrait.

Dale had tried to sketch Marlys the previous summer but was never satisfied with the results. When Marlys had posed for photographers who would tell her how to move and stand and what she should feel, the results were pictures of a woman she barely recognized. A beautiful woman, maybe, but not her. It was how these men that she didn't know and wouldn't meet again saw her. She was who they wanted her to be. What was Dale looking for? Marlys had looked at one of the sketches when Dale jumped up to chase after her daughter and could see that Dale was a very talented artist. But she hadn't drawn Marlys. Why couldn't she get her right? Dale had tried to sketch her as more than a pretty woman. Maybe that's where she had gone wrong.

Ceres woke up when the car stopped. She was refreshed, playful. Marlys chased the blond-haired two-year-old around the beach, both of them barefoot. As Dale began to sketch Marlys, Marlys fed Ceres the sandwiches she had packed. Between bites, she ran to the ocean, touched it with her bare feet, then ran back to Marlys farther up the beach, squealing when she touched the cold water and shouting for more.

After lunch, their perfect day began to turn with storm clouds filling the horizon. Ceres started to cry and Dale picked up her paints. It was going to rain.

Dale continued to paint, quickly, trying to capture the beauty of the storm that would soon be upon them. Marlys shouted after Dale to watch Ceres and ran down the beach to collect the shoes that the little girl had kicked off before stepping into the water.

When Marlys returned, Ceres was gone. Marlys called her name with increasing hysteria and watched as Dale barely looked up from her painting. She ran to the water's edge and shouted Dale's daughter's name into the ocean, the sob growing in her throat with each letter. Finally, over the wind, she heard a cry.

Ceres was in the water. Marlys looked back at Dale only long enough to see her turn her head up at the dark clouds above. As Marlys shouted Ceres's name into the water again, Dale raced away from it, toward the car as the rain began to pound, her painting under her arm.

Marlys sprinted toward the water, watching the blond hair float on top of the dark sea, then get pulled under again. The rising tide and the growing waves had snatched the child from the sand and Ceres didn't have the strength to fight back. The sea would win—it wasn't a fair contest. Marlys ran into the water and splashed toward her, grabbing fistfuls of ocean as she tried to cut through it. Ceres was thrown above the water long enough for Marlys to try to grab the back of her dress. She missed. Ceres was pulled under again. Marlys waded deeper into the water and Ceres broke through the water six feet in front of her, her eyes terrified, her body still too far to reach. Marlys threw herself into the water with all the determination she had, praying while cursing God's name as she reached for the girl one more time. This time, Ceres was saved.

Dale met them at the edge of the water and put her arms out

to accept her shivering, sobbing daughter. Marlys held Ceres even more tightly, ignored Dale and went straight to the car. Still holding Ceres, Marlys swept the toddler's mouth with her finger. She pulled out a mouthful of sand from the sea floor. When Marlys reached the trunk, she grabbed the blanket that Dale had loosely wrapped around her painting and swaddled Ceres. As she held Ceres in one arm and used the other to close the trunk, Marlys looked at Dale's painting only long enough to see the sky. Dale had captured the power and beauty of the sky but hadn't seen the terror of it at all.

They drove back to Boston in silence, Dale looking straight ahead at the road, Marlys continuing to hold Ceres tightly against her. Marlys had been concerned with how Dale might capture her in paint. Instead, Dale revealed herself. She protected her art. Marlys saved her child.

It was then that she decided. Marlys would get Cherie. Dale could have her paintings.

Even in the darkest days, as Marlys watched Dale prepare to walk away from the three people she had loved the most, neither Marlys nor Dale ever mentioned that day at the beach again. But they both knew what might have happened. They knew that without Marlys, Cherie would have drowned. Now, the woman standing near her, the woman who, as a three-year-old, had greeted the father she had never before met at the train station, the woman who had made Marlys a mother, the woman who had saved lives as a nurse, who was a mother herself and would soon be a grandmother, had nearly died on a beach in Cape Cod on a stormy spring day. Marlys saved Cherie, and because of that, she could justify everything that followed.

She could justify letting Ed into her apartment when he came knocking on her door late at night. She could justify giving Dale bad marriage advice when she complained about how things were going with Ed, further pushing him into Marlys's arms. She could justify using the painting—the painting that had almost cost them both the little girl they loved—to get exactly what she wanted.

"I'll come back to Florida. Soon. A couple of weeks. I'll bring Tom. We can do it then."

Marlys didn't respond. The women turned away from the water and walked up the beach before sitting down on the warm sand.

"You didn't come to see your dad when he was dying. You came down here three times. In three years, you came down three times."

"I couldn't do it," Cherie said, so softly Marlys could barely hear her. "I just couldn't see him like that."

"Mortal. You couldn't see him as a mortal."

"No, Mom. You've always gotten that wrong. I always knew he was just a man. A flawed man who could easily lose his temper. It's just . . . his life was different than he thought it would be because of the sacrifices he made for me. How could I not feel guilty about that?"

"His sacrifices? What exactly did your dad sacrifice?"

"His painting. He had a family to support, so he couldn't focus on his painting."

Marlys snorted. "This idea, that your dad was too dedicated to his family to continue to paint, is probably Ed's greatest self-generated fallacy. You remember your dad being on the road all the time. Do you remember that between every two-week stint, he was home for a full week? Seven entire days open for him to paint. When he got the job, he told me that it was perfect, that he had enough time between sales calls to stop and sketch along the back roads and then when he was home, to put those ideas onto canvas in oil. After his first stint on the road, he came home and painted for an hour. After that, there was no consistency. He blamed me, he blamed the weather, he blamed Walt, he blamed being in Minneapolis. He blamed everyone but himself. Your dad lost his courage. It had nothing to do with you. Ever. To be a famous painter, you have to paint. Your dad didn't paint."

"The apartments were so small, he didn't have the room," Cherie tried.

"He and Walt split the cost of the studio for five years. Walt painted. Your dad rarely showed up. We ate soup for dinner with the money we had left, and your dad rarely showed up."

"Maybe being with Walt made it worse. Maybe if he could have just—"

"What? If he could have lived in a world where he was the only artist? Walt's success gave your dad a network. Don't forget the effect your dad had on people. They wanted to be near him, wanted to help him. Walt's representatives set up multiple appointments to meet your dad and see his portfolio. He never showed up. Three different times, he never ever showed up. The world was not against your father, Cherie. Your dad did it to himself."

Cherie put her hands on her own cheeks and looked at Marlys. "If that's all true . . ."

"Cherie."

Cherie stood up and walked toward the car. Marlys watched her. From the back, Cherie was eighteen, walking to get onto the bus for the University of Wisconsin, off to college. Away from her.

Her daughter pivoted, then walked back down the beach, back to Marlys.

"Was it just all a lie? Was everything a lie?"

"What?" Marlys said, the exhaustion she felt deeply in her body heard in her voice.

"All of it." Cherie stood above her mother. "Dale isn't bad. She isn't bad at all."

"Cherie. I never said that Dale was bad," Marlys said, trying to stand up.

"No, Mom. But you never said that Dale was good. Not once."

Like a parent determined to take the high road in the divorce, Marlys pledged to never (rarely) say a bad word about Dale. But had she ever said anything good?

"You know what? I like Dale. I like her a hell of a lot. And that kills me." Cherie laughed bitterly. "I've gone through my life angry with her, keeping her at least an arm's length away, because it made all the time we spent apart manageable. It didn't matter that I hadn't really known this woman, because I didn't want to know her. But that's wrong. It's a goddamned lie. I missed—we missed—so much time together. So many years." Cherie dug her feet in the sand, flicked sand on them both. "And now, what? What?"

Marlys stood, twisted as far as she could manage, and wiped the sand from her bottom. She couldn't look at her daughter.

"And don't tell me there's still time!" Cherie shouted as she walked away from Marlys. After walking a few steps, she turned around to face her mom. "You all lived the way you wanted to live. For yourselves. The smoking. The drinking. The spending. You pawned the urn! An urn! Dad worked until he got sick, and you still had no money because you didn't know how to stop yourselves. If you wanted something, you bought it." Marlys put her finger to the diamond necklace around her neck. Ed had spent their entire month's food budget in April, 1988—in theory, they didn't actually keep a budget—on the piece of jewelry. She went to three local food banks in the next weeks so that they would be able to eat. Still, she loved this necklace. "All I've done is to try to live my life right," Cherie continued, out of breath. "To go to college, to become a nurse, to marry the right man. Not Randy—Tom. Good, solid, dependable Tom. I gave everything to my daughters, and they wanted even more because they somehow believed they deserved it. You know why? Because I told them they were special. I told them they were loved like all the parenting experts told me I should do, even as I gave away even more of myself, my time, my sanity. Now, with everyone all grown up, I get to go around and try to fix the unfixable. I have to try to make it right."

"You think I didn't try to do the right thing?"

"You were a good mother," Cherie said, automatically. "Even when the circumstances didn't set you up to be."

"But I wasn't great."

"I didn't say that." Cherie sighed. "But what could you do? You didn't have the resources."

Marlys smiled. "So that's why you'll always be better, right Cher? Is that what you think? You bought a better kind of motherhood. I had to use butchers' twine and safety pins to hold your childhood together." Marlys put her bag on the sand. "You've always felt this way. You're good. We're bad."

"That's not true."

"Isn't it? How come I've never been a part of your family's life? How come I'm getting to know my twenty-eight-year-old granddaughter now?"

"Because you made it so damn tough." Cherie shook her head. "I had it easier than you and you made sure I never felt good about that."

"What are you talking about?"

Cherie lowered her voice in a decent approximation of Marlys's cigarette-honed timbre. "Oh, *another* closet. *Another* bathroom. *Another* vacation album."

"You have a lot of bathrooms!"

"We have a proportional number of bathrooms to the size of the house!"

A young couple was walking along the beach toward Marlys and Cherie. Once they saw the women's body language, they turned around and began to walk the other way.

"You moved away from me," Cherie said, almost in defeat. "You came here. I stayed there."

Marlys nodded. She had moved to Florida. She had gone with Ed to the place that was supposed to be better. Easier. Sunnier. Because Ed thought they deserved it.

Marlys looked at her feet. They were still nice, after all these years. Dale had large bunions on her feet, limiting the shoes she could wear, usually settling on the same pair of Mexican sandals. They couldn't have been from her years living there, could they? Marlys assumed she bought them in Arizona—close enough, but still a world away.

Dale would never have an argument like this with Cherie. Cherie didn't have decades of grievances against Dale. She had a single complaint that could begin and immediately end any discussion: You left me. You are my mother, and you walked away.

"You always knew where to find me. I moved. I didn't disappear," Marlys said.

"That's true." Cherie moved closer to her mother and put her arm around her mother's shoulders. Marlys pulled them to a child's abandoned sandcastle and stepped on it. Cherie didn't react.

There was one painting of Ed's that Marlys almost kept. He had painted it in a burst immediately after returning from Walt's cabin on a lake in northern Minnesota—his family's cabin, not one that Walt was able to purchase because of his success. It had been a wonderful week away, almost enough time for Marlys,

Ed, and Cherie to believe that life would always be that way. Gentle, lovely, simple.

In the foreground of the painting, nestled in the sand at the lake's edge, was a child's sun hat. Marlys froze when she first saw it. Ed had never seen Dale's Cape Cod painting. Dale wouldn't show it to him, even after the painting exposed everything that had been lying just below the surface. But like Dale and the sun hat in the picture she painted that day at the ocean, Ed had painted their child into his work. Cherie was there, even when she wasn't.

Ed wouldn't hang the picture because he thought that by showing happiness and contentment, the work wasn't good. "It's shlock, Mar," he told her when she insisted it should go on the wall. Instead, it went in the closet. Marlys would pull it out and study it when Ed wasn't home. That had been a good day. Why hadn't they tried for more of them?

"Cher, I have to tell you something."

Marlys saw her daughter freeze. She took a step back, paused, then turned to her mother.

"I'll say you do," she said in a light voice. "Why did I find out from my daughter that Dale spent two weeks in a Mexican jail?"

"It was more like ten days."

"Mom."

"How does that come up in conversation? I make you angry about something, you say that I'm killing you, I say, 'By the way, do you know that Dale was once accused of killing her second husband?'"

"That actually seems relatively natural."

"Well, next time."

Cherie began to tap her foot, as if she were waiting for something.

"What?" Marlys asked.

"What do you mean, what? What are the details?"

"Not mine to give."

"Fine."

"She didn't do it, obviously."

"Yes, Mom. Obviously."

Marlys moved away from her daughter and exhaled, deeply. Cherie moved closer and put her hand on her mom's arm. She looked her in the eyes.

"I'm not sick, Cherie," Marlys said.

Cherie threw up her hands in exasperation. "Jesus. Even now, you won't say it."

"Because it's not entirely true." Marlys paused, only for a beat. "I'm dying."

Cherie sat back down on the sand.

"You're dying," Cherie said, breathless. "I mean, I knew you were. I told the doctors I met with that you were."

"You met with doctors? I knew you would meet with doctors."

"But still, to hear you say it." Cherie began to cry. "Will you let me have a funeral for you? A memorial service, at the very least. Will you let the people who knew you celebrate you?"

"Cherie . . . what did your doctors say?"

She wiped the tears from her cheeks. "That there was nothing to do. I told them that my dad had just died of the same disease and they said that they understood why you opted not to go through chemo. They took your side." Cherie shook her head and bit her lip.

Marlys felt a stupid wash of pride. The decision to not pursue treatment—perhaps the most monumental decision of the last half of her life—had been legitimized by South Florida's finest medical minds. She was right. She made the intelligent choice.

"I didn't tell you because I wanted this time with you without *that* hanging over us."

"By *that* you mean your impending death?"

Marlys shrugged. She looked at the ocean. Was it because of the war? Is that why Ed wanted to be scattered (*and let's be honest,* Marlys thought, *his ashes would be* dumped) into the ocean? He had started to talk about his experiences in the Pacific a little toward the end. The small things he remembered, not the big losses that haunted him throughout his life. His friends were buried in graves on islands in an ocean different from the one in front of her now. Marlys watched as a seagull dove into the water and emerged without anything in his beak. When Ed's ashes were in the ocean, he would be eaten by a fish, which would be eaten by a bird that would fly away. Was that what Ed wanted?

Ed had bought Marlys a Neptune Society plan at the same time that he bought his own. It had been paid off for years. But she had decided that she didn't want to be cremated. She didn't want to sit on a shelf in Cherie's house in a gilded urn. She wanted a tombstone for people to notice and read. She wanted a record that she had lived.

Marlys had written this in the completely informal will that she had created as part of her Living with Dying class, with the instructions to visit a lawyer, or at least to let her next of kin know her wishes. She'd share it with Cherie at some point, but not now.

"Maybe I just wanted to protect you. That's what a mother is supposed to do, right?" Marlys had always protected Cherie, since that day in Cape Cod in 1944. She kept Cherie home almost the entire summer of 1952 during the polio outbreak, terrified that her daughter would be paralyzed. She cooked her daughter's meat almost to the point of no return so she wouldn't get any parasitic illness. She wouldn't let her ride her bike off the sidewalk until she was fourteen and still held her breath every time Cherie got in a car with anyone under the age of twenty-one.

She had protected Cherie from as much unpleasantness as she could in her words and deeds, and as a result, Cherie had grown up to be a woman who fit into the world, who believed she had a special place within it.

"What are you protecting me from? Sadness? Grief?"

"Yes."

Cherie walked over to her mother and pulled her into a hug. Marlys could feel her daughter tense when she put her arms around her diminishing shape. She had put socks in each of her bra cups that morning, trying to fill the space that was gone. Her beautiful breasts, sunken like two deflated souffles.

"How am I supposed to just accept this?" Cherie asked as she pulled away from her mother, a trail of mascara running down her cheeks.

Marlys put her hand on her daughter's cheek. "We get old, we die."

Cherie began to laugh and Marlys joined her. Soon, both women had fallen onto the sand and had begun to roll back and forth as their bodies gave in to the laughter. The tears returned to Cherie's cheeks as she pointed to Marlys's purse. "Dad is in there! In a produce bag!" They roared with laughter. Marlys pointed to Cherie. "You're about to be a grandmother!" The laughter continued. Cherie pointed to her own hand. "I'm old too! Look at my arthritic hand!" Marlys stopped laughing first, as her breath got too short. Cherie stopped a minute later.

"It's been a good run, Cherie. Fifty years of marriage to a man I loved most of the time. An amazing daughter. A couple of granddaughters who know how to ask for what they want. Dale." Just Dale. "I've got a few people to miss me when this whole thing ends."

Cherie stood up again and looked out at the ocean.

"Yesterday Laura asked me if I fell in love with your dad first, or if he fell in love with me first," Marlys said.

"She asked you that?"

"Oh, we've been having some very real conversations."

"What did you say?"

"I told her that I fell in love first. With you."

"Oh, please. Dad had those Paul Newman lips and you're going to try to tell me that—"

"Cherie. It was you from the moment you first smiled at me and called me your 'Mar-Lips.' It's always been you."

Cherie sighed, then put her head on her mom's shoulder. "I love you, Mom."

"I love you too."

Cherie pulled her head up and looked her mother in the eyes. "I'm going to stay here. With you."

"I'm not asking you to do that."

"But I'm telling you that I am." Cherie smiled sadly. "And it's not just my guilt at not having been here for Dad."

Marlys raised her eyebrows.

"Yes, I can make bad decisions. I have made bad decisions." Cherie reached for her mother's hand. "But not this time. You chose me. You always chose me. So now, I'll choose you."

Cherie's phone rang and she reached in her own large purse to grab it. Marlys wondered how the world would change when everyone carried a phone, when everyone could be found at any time. She wouldn't make it to the next century. She wouldn't have to figure out how she'd have to change as the world changed even faster around her.

She watched as Cherie's face transformed, as she dropped the small phone onto the sand and began to run. Marlys reached down, picked it up, and followed behind as quickly as she could.

CHAPTER 19

2 Days

CHERIE

Here it is, Cherie thought as her daughter was wheeled into yet another examination room. The complete helplessness and vulnerability of being a mother. She remembered when Laura was about seven years old and fell off her bike after riding down the hill in front of their old house, chasing the ice-cream truck. The ice-cream truck was there, within view, when Laura flew over the handlebars, hit her head on the ground, and lost consciousness. Cherie could still remember Jessica's four-year-old bloodless face as she ran into the house to tell her mother that Laura was on the ground and wouldn't wake up. She didn't remember running out of the house or pushing over young Cindy Spencer to get to Laura faster. She did remember staring at her unmoving daughter who was bleeding from her head and feeling fear like she had never felt before. Laura had to be okay, she said to herself. *She will be okay,* she repeated out loud. Then, Cherie vomited.

All of her medical training, and when it came to her own child, she was useless. An ambulance came and a couple of underpaid medics took over. Cherie rode to the hospital with her daughter, unable to do anything but remember some of the prayers her Catholic father had tried to teach her before losing interest himself. She held her daughter's hand, and remembered the moment Laura squeezed her hand in return as one of the best of her life. Laura would be okay. Cherie would continue to be her mother.

Now, her daughter had pre-eclampsia. Laura's child would be born within hours, her daughter thrust into motherhood without a single look back. "Does this really have to happen?" Laura had asked, and Cherie could only hold her hand and slowly nod her head. This time, Laura didn't squeeze back.

Tom was on his way to Florida. When Cherie called him and he promised to be on the next flight, she felt the sob in her throat release as he hung up the phone. She'd been away from her husband for three weeks; she'd dragged her heavily pregnant daughter along with her, and what the hell had she accomplished? Dale's apartment building was still standing in obscurity, underfunded and underoccupied, Cherie having done nothing to help either problem. Marlys was dying. Laura was going into premature labor, her soon-to-be ex-husband ignoring all calls and messages, the baby likely unable to be moved for weeks.

She would remain tethered to this place. The tour of duty extended for months, at the very least. How did she know that everything would be fine with her grandchild? God, how did she know that it would be fine with her daughter? She was a goddamned nurse. She knew what pre-eclampsia could do. She knew what it could look like and she had missed all the signs.

Patty had noticed Laura's ankles, and Cherie had blown it off. Dale had commented on Laura's paleness, and Cherie had excused it. Marlys had said that Laura had seemed too short of breath, and Cherie hadn't stopped to listen. Her daughter had been in Florida for weeks, which meant that she had missed at least one, if not two prenatal appointments, and the thought hadn't even occurred to Cherie that this might be a problem. Mother of the goddamned year.

Dale had brought Laura to the hospital after she vomited and fell during their last practice. The practice during which they tried to figure out how to work around Evelyn, who had joined Hawthorne Haven's team—"I'm a hustler, always have been. If we aren't getting in the paper, if we're probably going to lose it all, I have to go find a winner," she rationalized—with Patty working twice as hard and Phyllis all but giving up. Dale was right, of course, to escalate the situation to the emergency room. Wouldn't most people have called it sunstroke and given Laura a glass of lemonade?

Dale sat next to Cherie in one of the four chairs in the small waiting room of the labor ward. She offered her daughter a handkerchief, pressed and embroidered with a small bunch of roses.

"I honestly have no idea where I picked this up from. I'm sure whoever I took it from would have wanted it back."

"Mom told me that I was a colicky baby. That you had to hold me twenty-two hours a day," Cherie said, not looking at Dale.

Dale laughed. "You were a demon until just before you turned five months old. I couldn't put you down or the world would end. Then, just like that, you were perfect."

"But how did you do it? You were a goddamned teenager."

"Sometimes being young and dumb is the best thing," Dale said, and Cherie looked like she was going to object. "Because what other choice was there, Cher?"

"Didn't you ever want to give up?"

Dale pursed her lips. "I haven't ever told anyone this, not even Ed when he returned from the war. I hadn't slept in two months. I had only been eating as much as I could while holding you against me, until you began to cry again and my mother asked me to leave the table. *My nerves,* she would say, until she banned me from the dining room altogether. My best friend at the time, Agnes, would come over only long enough to know that she wanted to leave again. I'd go on walks, putting my coat over my shoulders so I could continue to hold you, and then come back home because all I could see was the emptiness of the city, the sadness. Anytime I saw the color yellow, even on one of your outfits, I would feel my knees go weak because that was the color of the telegram envelopes, coming to tell me that Ed was dead."

"Jesus, Dale."

"I broke. I went to Ed's parents' house, the little place with the crooked porch in Southie. His parents and younger brother were finishing dinner. I called his mother outside and held you out to her."

"To take me?"

Dale nodded her head. "Yes. But she refused. She said, you two did what you did, and this is what you get."

"Oh."

"I told her that I couldn't do it anymore, and she told me that my choice was to push on or to give you to the Sisters."

"She wouldn't even take me for a night?"

"Ed and I had sex before marriage. That was a sin. She stopped speaking to Ed entirely after we got divorced because that was a sin that was unforgivable. Never saw her child or her grandchild—her only grandchild that I'm aware of—again."

Cherie was silent, taking this in.

"The thing is that without the baby, I wouldn't have had Ed. I had one because I had the other. I wouldn't have been a wife unless I was a mother."

"I was all that brought you together?"

"No. But you did speed things up and make them permanent."

Dale told Cherie that when she told Ed that she was pregnant, just four months after they first kissed, he jumped up from the booth they were sharing at Howard Johnson's—ice cream was nearly the only food she could tolerate those first months—and whooped with joy before leaning over to kiss her and then, in the same movement, bending down on a knee to ask her to marry him.

They married and he left and then she had a baby. A baby that didn't act like Dale had been told that babies should act. They should eat and sleep and cry a little when they needed attention. Her baby needed attention every hour of every day. Was it punishment? Was she being punished because she and her boyfriend had sex again and again and again before either of them had even whispered the word "marriage"?

They had done something wrong, something bad, and this was the baby they were given in exchange. No, this was the baby *Dale* was given. The child, for the foreseeable future, was hers and hers alone.

"After I left, after I was surrounded by the hills of San Miguel de Allende instead of the streets of Boston, I knew that I didn't resent you. I had never resented you. I resented Ed. He had escaped all of it. It didn't matter that he was in a war, fighting for his life and taking others' on an island in an ocean I had never seen. All that mattered was that we had done something together, and I was the only one who had to see it through."

Cherie had always seen Dale as an adult in her life who had let her down. But Dale hadn't been an adult then, not really. Her mom was a girl who had fallen in love in the middle of a world that made everyone grow up too damn fast. At eighteen, Cherie was devastated at being turned away from the exclusive sorority on campus, instead relegated to the one filled with the girls whose fathers owned laundromats and corner stores. Then, not long after, her heartbreak over Randy.

Four days earlier, when Cherie went to the library to look up an article in a science magazine that one of the doctors she spoke to had referenced, a useless article that detailed potential treatments for her mother's cancer that were nearly a decade away, she gave up and turned her attention to the piles of phone books that the library kept. Because of the snowbirds in town, the Midwestern selection was robust.

After paging through the phone books of Chicago, Milwaukee, and Des Moines to find Randy's name, she had nothing. She had wanted to find him, and she had wanted to let him go. Instead, he remained out of reach.

Finally, as Cherie decided to leave, she turned back and grabbed the phone book that she knew the best. There was Randy's name, living about eleven miles from her in a suburb south of Minneapolis.

It was as she was distractedly flipping through the Minneapolis yellow pages as she took it all in that she saw Randy's ad. It took a minute of looking at this sixty-year-old man's picture to connect it all, but it was him. He was a realtor selling suburban real estate in the same city where she had lived since after her college graduation. He might have seen Cherie's picture in the social pages of the city's monthly magazine or read her name mentioning an event she chaired, or a cause she championed. He might have seen her across the room at a restaurant in town or at the theater.

He hadn't tried to get in touch with her, just as she hadn't tried to look for him. The Randy she might have wanted wasn't there. The college student who could make her weak in the knees with his kisses was long gone. The idealistic teaching student had since turned to hard commerce. They were both completely different people.

Cherie had Tom now. After nearly a week without any contact between them, Tom had sent her a dozen roses two days earlier. The card simply said that he missed her. He didn't need her. He wanted her. He felt her absence in his life. Isn't that what she had been looking for all along?

"Tom got out of all of those early years because he was more important. It was more important for him to work twelve-hour days because he could charge someone with a lot of money for each and every one of the hours they kept him there. What was I? I was just a boring old nurse."

Dale rolled her eyes.

"The first time that Laura cried out for Daddy after a nightmare in the middle of the night, I almost lost it. Wasn't that supposed to be the tradeoff? I got stuck with the shit, but then they loved me more?"

"It's thankless, motherhood. I could blame my youth for thinking that I could somehow get it all—your love and my dreams—but I think, really, it was ego. I thought I deserved more because I could make a nice painting. I had an art teacher who told me I was special when I was around fourteen. It was a throwaway comment, but I clearly took it to heart."

"You were special. Are special. You were never going to live like the rest of us. You never wanted that."

"I wanted too much, which means I ended up with nothing. No career, no marriage, maybe not even a home," Dale said, avoiding Cherie's eyes as she did. "You remained focused—on your family, on your friends, on your community. You got it all."

Cherie waved her away. "Well, I tried. I do try, whatever that means." She massaged her arthritic fingers. "I ordered warm-up jackets for the squad—did I tell you that?—and the embroiderer spelled "Soleil" wrong. S-O-L-I-L-E. It's too late to get them re-done. Maybe no one will notice."

Dale laughed and repeated the misspelling. "I'll tell you who will notice—"

"Donna," Cherie said.

"Donna," Dale confirmed. "Donna-the-former-French-teacher will have a goddamned fit." Cherie began to laugh too. The women began to laugh harder than they needed to laugh, the release they'd both been looking for.

When they stopped, Dale reached for her daughter's hand. "You take care of people, Cher. That's what you do."

Cherie let her mother hold her hand for a moment until she dropped it. *I manage people,* Cherie thought. But managing wasn't enough. When Laura was settled in her hospital room, Cherie had told her that she loved her. That she was proud of her. That she was special. That whatever was to come, Laura had the strength and courage to face it. The expression on her daughter's face had nearly broken her. Why the hell hadn't she just said all those things before?

"When you think of me," Cherie asked her mother, "do you think of Ceres or Cherie?"

Dale turned to her daughter. "You're Cherie. I'm Dale. Ceres and Mama were all before. Not now."

"You've never pushed me. I appreciate that now. Finally. You knew that we lost something in those years away and you accepted the change. You didn't try to make me come back to you. Marlys was my mother. She is my mother."

Cherie saw Dale flinch with that last statement, then put her hand on her daughter's knee. In the last weeks, the two of them had learned that they were aging and aged women who shared a love of fresh-squeezed orange juice and *Jeopardy!* and had different philosophies on facial moisturizers and dry shampoo. They were just women, like all other women, who had losses and a couple of victories and made the effort to get up and live each day.

Dale stood up and walked to the vending machine at the end of the hall. When she handed Cherie a cup of coffee, she took a sip and put it on the floor.

"I wouldn't have ever told you what happened in Mexico," Dale said, finally. "I know that you know. About the *incarceration*," Dale said, dramatically.

"Laura told you that she told me after Marlys told her."

Dale smiled. "She was plagued with guilt. I should have told you myself years ago. It's just something that happened."

"And you're innocent."

"Of murder, yes. But I wouldn't say that I'm innocent," Dale said. "You thought that I stayed in Mexico for five years because it was so good that I wouldn't even consider leaving for any reason—even to see my child. What kind of story is it that I stayed in Mexico because I didn't make myself leave? Despite the disappointment with teaching. Despite the abusive husband who hit me. It took an accusation of murder to get me to go. No daughter wants to hear that story."

Cherie was quiet and reached for her cup of coffee. She held it without taking a sip. "He hit you?"

"Bob 'had a bad war,' as they said. Would he have been a different man if he had never been given a pair of boots and a gun and put on a ship? Who the hell knows? But the Bob I got fell apart more each week, until finally, he didn't get back up."

"Did he hurt you?"

"He didn't leave any scars. At least that anyone can see."

"But he's the reason you stopped painting? Because it reminded you of that time."

"Probably. Maybe."

Cherie shook her head sadly. "Did any of your other husbands hit you?"

"No. I just didn't love them. I got married because it was hard to be a woman without a husband. Should I have kept trying to live without one? Maybe. But sometimes you just give in to easy. It was easier to be married. It wasn't that hard to let them go."

"I don't know . . . I don't really know what to say, Dale," Cherie said, uncovering her hand. "There are the stories that we tell ourselves. Things we need to believe. I thought I was the reason Dad didn't paint. He couldn't be an artist and have a child. Wasn't that why you had left? To be an artist? But Marlys told me the other day that I was full of shit, essentially. She said Dad had tons of time to paint, he just didn't. His failure was his own."

"And my failure was my own. That's all I can really tell you, Cherie. I'm sorry. I'm sorry if you felt abandoned or unloved. I'm sorry we lost so much time together. Not just then, but ever since."

Cherie nodded. She didn't reach for Dale's hand. Is this what she'd been waiting to hear? Why the hell hadn't they both been able to tell their daughters what they wanted to hear?

"For Laura Wishaw?" a nurse asked. Cherie remembered the coffee as she jumped out of her seat, careful not to flip the cup. Dale jumped up a spritely second behind her.

"I'm her mother," Cherie said, and the nurse nodded. Cherie remembered a night years ago when she was standing at the nurses' station with her friend and fellow nurse, Marge, between seeing patients. They were laughing at some story that Marge was telling and a red-faced man ran up to them, furious. "You're laughing? You're laughing? This is the worst day of my entire life and you're laughing." Cherie apologized but Marge would not. "We're just at work, buddy," Marge mumbled as he stormed off. It was another day in a hospital. A little joy, a little more pain.

"We've induced. She has three hours, otherwise we go into surgery."

Cherie thanked her, and the nurse walked briskly down the hall.

"If anything happens, to either of them . . ." Cherie said, and the tears began again.

"Then we'll deal with it," Dale said, and Cherie turned quickly to look at her. "What else is there to say, Cher? There are things that we can control. But there is a hell of a lot more that we can't. Don't tell yourself that you shouldn't have come to Florida or you shouldn't have asked Laura to come to Florida or you should have done this—"

"I should have noticed that something was wrong. I'm her goddamned mother. Not to mention a goddamned nurse. How many cases of pre-eclampsia did I call in my years working? And I missed seeing it in my own daughter?"

"But she's getting care now, Cherie," Dale said, her voice quiet. "In a few hours, you'll be holding your grandchild. Imagine that. Ten tiny fingers and ten tiny toes. So beat yourself up if you want, but life will keep moving. Your daughter will be a mother."

"Do you think she'll be able to do it?" Cherie asked, barely audible.

Dale laughed. "Did you not hear anything I said? I tried to give you away, for God's sake. If I could be a mother—and I did it, I got you through those first years without any major scars— she'll be able to do it. She'll do it beautifully." Dale looked at the tan on her arms. "Look, what she did over these last three weeks is . . . she made us realize what we could do. We needed to know that we're old, and maybe a little craggy, but we can still fight. We still have it within us. We've been through a Depression and wars and bullshit on every front. Some little pipsqueak with a deed isn't going to be the end of us."

Cherie smiled. "I have absolutely no doubt."

"Except Evelyn," Dale said, her own smile falling from her mouth. "She gets nothing."

CHAPTER 20

1 Day

LAURA

Laura had been pushed in a wheelchair to see her daughter in the NICU. The baby was fine, she would be fine. That's all that Laura could hear. It wouldn't always be like this. Her lungs would get stronger. Her breathing would get better. In a few weeks she could go home, the nurses said. The doctor had smiled, which was apparently how he showed agreement without saying a word.

She was a mother. Laura knew that she was supposed to look at her daughter and be overwhelmed with love, erasing all doubts she ever had about motherhood. Her doubts remained. She was overwhelmed by this small but sweet baby who was hers, who would always be hers. A baby who had her father's chin. A baby who didn't yet have a name. A baby who had been inside of her hours ago and now was just . . . not? Laura looked at her baby and wasn't sure she felt love. She did know, however, that she felt a large amount of confusion.

But she didn't feel fear. That, she knew, was a good thing. A great thing. Fear makes people do stupid things, like sleep with their wife's best friend and tell their father-in-law in a message that they do not want any custody, or "whatever it is that people call it." She felt like she still needed a few hours, maybe a day or two, a week, possibly more, to understand what exactly had just happened, and then she'd be fine. Then, she'd be ready to be someone's mother.

Laura had cried when she saw her father. She was overwhelmed that he had raced to the airport and jumped on the first plane that he could, but after that moment, she registered annoyance. They had this handled. Dale had recognized that Laura needed a hospital. Her mom had spoken to the doctor in that rich-lady voice of hers and told them that she was expecting the best of care. Ilona had called and said things in Hungarian that had apparently scared the doctor into only calling Laura "Ma'am."

But then, when her dad was there with her, bursting into tears at the sight of her baby and hugging Laura with relief, she knew that this wasn't about organizational matters. This was about love. He had come because he loved her.

The nurse left after taking her blood pressure yet again—it was normal, still—and Marlys entered the room.

Laura had seen Marlys every day that she had been in Florida, but it was now, as she cautiously entered Laura's room, that Laura realized what she was looking at. Her grandmother would be gone soon.

"She's gorgeous, Laura. I know I'm not supposed to say this, but I wanted you to have a girl. We don't have boys. We just don't." Her daughter and her grandmother. Young and old, the beginning and the end. And both with a bum set of lungs.

"I knew she was a girl. But also, my friends told me about their sons peeing on them when they changed their diapers and I just . . ." Laura put her hand to her forehead. "I couldn't have dealt with more penis problems than I already have. Had. Justin's mother called me to find out the details. His fucking mother. He hasn't actually called me himself. Which is just as well, really."

Marlys gingerly lowered herself into the chair next to Laura's bed. Laura didn't have to have a Caesarian, but she still felt so utterly fragile. She knew what her body could do—she had just seen the evidence, for God's sake—but she also felt like she might break apart if someone touched her wrong. She felt a delicate power.

"I came to tell you how sorry I am."

Laura looked at her grandmother, then shifted herself in her bed. She could feel the blood seeping from her body, assured more than once that it would, eventually, stop.

"What are you sorry about? We've had a good few weeks together. My mom, once again, knew exactly what she was doing."

Marlys smiled. "It's been a wonderful few weeks, Laur. The best, really." Marlys tucked Laura's hair behind her right ear. "I'm sorry because . . . I'm sorry that I'm dying."

Laura tugged at her sheets. It was out there, now, finally. Grandma Marlys had told them all what they already knew.

"I don't think that's actually something people apologize for."

"I'm sorry that I'm dying at the wrong time. That's the apology."

"Is there a right time to die?"

"I would say that it's a time when the person dying won't need to rely on the same person as the granddaughter that just gave birth."

"Is this about my mom?"

"Yes, it's about your mom. I'll need her, Laura. You need her."

"Yeah. I have thought about that."

"And what do you think?"

"I wish you weren't dying, Grandma. I really do. For every reason."

Laura couldn't yet understand the new life that she had brought into the world, but what would it be like to try to understand that your life was ending? To look in the mirror and to see the life slowly wash from your face as you sorted through the memories you carried? Would Laura ultimately remember this day for the shock of seeing how small her daughter was, or for the first day of the rest of her life with her child? Memories mold to the story you want to tell.

"I also wish that we'd had more time together," Laura continued. "My mom was a great mom. Is a great mom. She always seemed to know what Jessica and I needed before we did. We had the best packed lunches, the best French braids, the best birthday party goodie bags. We never missed any kind of activity or were late to sign up for any sports team—I was a pretty good soccer player once, you know, even in the middle of all that dancing—because my mom had this incredible color-coded calendar that organized all of our lives."

"Oh yes, I remember the calendar. Do you remember when we came to visit you in Minneapolis after you moved into the big house? The calendar was the first stop on the home tour."

Laura rolled her eyes. "But not knowing you better, or Dale, or Grandpa Ed, was wrong," Laura said. "You might even call it"—she lowered her voice into a loud whisper—"a *failure.*"

Marlys put her hand to her chest. "My word. Are you telling me that Ceres Elizabeth Anderson failed at something?"

Laura looked stricken. "I would never. I could never."

The women smiled at each other.

When she first got to the hospital, Laura's mom had told her how proud she was of her. How strong she thought Laura was. She told her how much she loved her. It was then that Laura knew that she could do what needed to be done. She wasn't entirely convinced that her body would know how to have a baby, but she did know that eventually, it would all be figured out. She could figure it all out.

"Look," Laura said, taking a sip from the glass next to her bed, "I was wrong when I told you that you were the Melissa. You aren't like Melissa."

"I did take my best friend's husband."

"Sure. Yes. You did. But you aren't a bad person. You didn't want to hurt Dale."

"But Dale did get hurt. That needs to stay part of the story."

Laura squeezed her eyes closed at the pain of a contraction. No one told her about this part, that the pain of having a baby continues even after the baby is born. Her uterus got large, and now it needed to shrink back down again. Soon, soon-ish, she would look like her old self. Except, of course, she'd be completely different.

"I realized, in those first hours after delivery, that I didn't care that Justin wasn't there. Part of me always knew that he wasn't going to come through. Caring for a baby, hell, caring for me while carrying a baby, was always more than he could do. But I still wanted to call Melissa. I wanted to tell her about the doctor telling me that I had nice feet—"

"Hold on, he said what?"

Laura smiled. "And that I watched an episode of *Who Wants to Be a Millionaire* and got every answer right and that I craved Tang the moment the baby was born. Tang! But I couldn't tell her any of that because she . . . she's out of my life now. She won't know my daughter. She won't know me as a mother."

"I think I'm still figuring out what I lost when I lost my friendship with Dale."

"But you came back to each other."

"Not in the same way, honey. It was never the same again."

"Will I find another friend like Melissa?"

"I'm supposed to say that you will. That you'll find a better friend."

"That bar seems rather low right now."

Marlys laughed and put her hand on her chest. "But I can't promise that you will. A good, true friend is incredibly hard to find. But hey, look at Dale. She's in her seventies and has a whole, wonderful group of friends around her."

"But none of them smile when they're together the way you and Dale smiled in that picture in Boston."

"Of course they aren't smiling when you've got them on their backs trying to get their legs in the air."

"Grandma."

Laura looked out the window. The sky was a brilliant blue. Laura would have to stay in Florida for at least another month until the baby could leave the hospital, and then maybe another month after that so that the baby could be even stronger before flying home. Her mom had rented an apartment at Soleil City for the three of them. Laura felt absolute relief at the news. She didn't want to leave yet. She didn't want to say goodbye to this strange little bubble of women who had continuously called her hospital room to make sure she was okay, who had pooled their money to have a beautiful bouquet of flowers delivered to the room. Who hadn't once mentioned the synchronized swimming championship that Laura would now miss, that would be without her shouts and broad hand movements pushing them on to some kind of a win. A moral victory, at the very least.

"Well," Marlys said, her voice sounding stronger than it had. "Even if you don't find another Melissa, you'll almost definitely find another man better than Justin—"

"That bar is lower than low."

Marlys laughed, then touched Laura's arm. "We all carry losses through our lives. Now you have them too."

Laura nodded. More than once, she had looked at her mom and her mom's moms and wondered how they could all be linked. Physically, there was virtually no resemblance. With Marlys, that was explainable. With Dale, she wondered how that had felt, to have birthed a child in which you could see so little of yourself. But they had the same resolve. The same strength, though they had used it differently. Her mom used it to hold on to the world she had created—one filled with stability and security and solidarity. Dale had used her strength to change her world as soon as she believed there could be something else—someone else—that was better.

Marlys's world had revolved around Cherie. The smiles that Dale and Marlys shared in that photo in Boston during the war were nothing compared to the smile that Marlys had when she looked at Cherie in every picture since. With her daughter, she was positively beaming with love. Marlys adored Cherie. That's how she withstood the loss of Dale. That's how she spent more than fifty years with the same charming but difficult man. She was Cherie's mom.

Laura would love her daughter. But she couldn't live for her. She needed to have her own stories, her own dreams. She would have a little piece of all three of the women above her within her, and she would help her daughter grow into someone that would have all that and a little more.

"Melissa hasn't called me, but my sister did. After I told Jessica she was a piece of shit for ignoring all of us for so long. She told me that she's coming down here next week to meet her niece."

"Oh, Laura. I'm so glad."

"She also wants to, uh—"

"Say goodbye to me. That's good. I don't want people schlepping down here when I'm dead. What do I get out of it once I'm in a box?"

"I'm sorry that you're . . ." Laura swallowed hard, determined to say the word. If her grandma had, then she could too. "Dying.

I'm so sorry that you're dying. But I'm glad that you'll have Mom with you. She made the right choice."

"What are you going to do, Laur?"

"I've had a little interest in baby-holding from the women in Soleil City. Donna taped a sign-up sheet to the laundry room door and apparently it's quite full. I'm not entirely sure if there's a shift left for me."

Laura heard the nurse approach her door before she heard the halfhearted knock. *I'm coming in, either way.*

"I'm glad you got to meet my daughter," Laura said, shifting herself up higher in her bed. "I guess she came early for a good reason."

"Have you decided on a name yet?" Marlys asked.

Laura nodded. "Yes. I think I have."

CHAPTER 21

1 Day

DALE

Dale stretched her legs out on the lounger next to the pool. She had barely slept in the last twenty-four hours and was drinking the Lambrusco and cream soda she had made slowly so it wouldn't go to her head quite as quickly. In the morning, her daughter would wake up as a grandmother, her granddaughter would wake up as a mother, her great-grandchild would wake up another day stronger, and she would be putting on a sparkly swimsuit and getting in a pool.

Ilona cleared her throat and sat down next to Dale. "My daughter is coming to watch us dance in the pool tomorrow."

Dale sat up taller and looked at her friend. "That's wonderful, Ilona. Has she traveled—"

"She lives in Fort Lauderdale," Ilona said, cutting Dale off. "She moved there eight years ago. It's why I am here, close but not next door. To talk to her. Now, finally, it worked."

Dale looked at the calm water of the pool. Isn't that what she had been doing with Cherie all these years? Standing back, looking forward, trying to be just a little patient.

"You made me a dress. At your store in New York. It was green. Formal," Ilona said.

Dale sometimes played a mental slideshow of the dresses she had made to entertain herself when she was stuck somewhere she didn't want to be, to calm herself when she was upset. So many lovely dresses made for so many women, many of whom were distinctly unlovely. Later, when she was done making dresses and was driving around the southeast with Frank as he painted portraits, she heard him make the same complaint. So many lovely pictures of so many unlovely people.

Dale remembered the green dress. Forest green, with a slight sheen. One of three green dresses she had made in her career. She turned to look at the woman next to her. Something unlocked in the back of her mind and she saw a woman with numbers tattooed on her arm, happy and twirling in the mirror before her.

For two years, Ilona sat with Dale at the pool and for two years, she never told her that they had met before, that for a brief moment, they had been a part of each other's lives.

"I . . . I can't believe I made you a dress."

"I still have it."

"What? I didn't know any of them were still out there in the world."

Ilona nodded. "I married in Hungary. Husband and child died. I married in New York and wore your dress. Child didn't die. So, I keep dress."

Dale didn't have a response.

Ilona spit her tobacco into a cup. A few nights earlier, Ilona had gotten Cherie to try a pinch. The other women of Soleil City had held their breaths, waiting to see what came next. Cherie spit in the cup, then removed the pinch into a tissue. "Not for me, but also not at all bad," Cherie had said, and the group erupted into nervous laughter. She had taken a sip of Dale's Lambrusco and cream soda to wash the taste down. "That isn't bad either."

"She'll be fine, your Laura. Her baby will be fine."

"Yes."

"Yes. It is the only answer. Yes."

It was the only answer. Years ago, the second year that Cherie brought the girls to Chicago, Dale took Cherie across the street for a drink after leaving the girls set up with a movie on her newly acquired (and rarely used) VCR. There, into her second glass of wine, Cherie began to talk.

"I love them so much, I do. But God, I wish I could have a real, solid break. Tom works so much. Sure, they're at school all day but as soon as they get home, it's everything at once." Cherie took a long sip and Dale knew to say nothing. "When Laura was a baby and I handed her off to the babysitter for the first time when I went back to work, I felt almost giddy. Grammy K. I mentioned her the other day and Laura has no memory of her. Can you believe it?"

Dale only nodded. Just like her landlord at the boardinghouse all those years ago, the woman who took her child from her every morning and gave her back at the end of the day. Dale would always remember her. Cherie never would.

"Laura was clingy," Cherie continued. "She wanted to be held all the time and when I held her, she would pull at my hair or my necklace or rub her face against my shirt. She had a hard time falling asleep and when I was desperate, I would lay on the floor next to her crib. Having a babysitter five days a week," she sighed. "It felt like I got a little of myself back. And damn if that didn't make me feel guilty as hell."

Dale looked at her daughter, the wine making her speech freer, giving her cheeks a blush. "I know about guilt."

Cherie looked startled. This wasn't the story she believed. In that story, there was no guilt. There were no second-guesses.

Dale had made a decision, and they had all lived with that decision since.

"When I picked her up at the end of the day, I felt this ache to hold her. But by the time we got home and she was fussy and I had to make dinner and Tom was late, again, I counted the hours until I could drop her off. Release, guilt, ache, release, again and again. It became routine. And you just adapt."

When Dale was in Mexico, feeling the guilt of leaving her child, the ache of being without her, there was no release. Painting helped, but not enough. Bob helped, at first. His personality was big and seeped into every corner of every room. She didn't have to talk when he was there. She didn't have to explain. She could watch him, watch how quickly people were also happy to let him talk for them, even if he didn't really have anything to say.

He distracted her, she distracted him. They covered up each other's pain until the newness passed, until they knew each other's excuses, the inching away before a hand could find the other in the night. When they had studied each other, they knew too much and education wasn't what either of them needed, despite the fact that a school was their cover for having run away.

When he began to hit her in the beginning of her second year away from her daughter, the pain on the outside matched the pain on the inside, the result of which was a strange neutrality. A settling of her pH level for hurt. Until, months later, it shifted. The external pain overtook her internal pain. It had gone too far.

Eventually, years later when she had left Mexico for California and California for New York, she began to flit in and out of her daughter's life, confusing and unsettling them both each time she did. Dale had walked out, but not away.

At those early hours at the hospital, watching Cherie when they didn't yet know that Laura would be fine, that the baby would be born alert though with some lung problems, she saw her daughter in pain. The pain of not being able to take away Laura's pain, of having this person who you feel is a part of you have to fight in the world completely on their own. Knowing that you can only do so much, and it's not going to be enough.

But isn't that motherhood? Carrying around a little bit of grief that grows each day as your child becomes a person entirely separate from you? Because soon enough, they exist outside of you. The child can do things that her mother never could. The child will do things that her mother never would.

Dale would do something that her mother never did. She would help with Laura's baby. These next months, as Cherie's attention turned to Marlys, Dale would do all that she could. Nearly sixty years later, the memory of being alone with her baby daughter continued to haunt her. It wouldn't haunt Laura, too.

"Can your daughter join us for lunch after the competition?" Dale asked Ilona. "Cherie offered to buy us all lunch in Fort Lauderdale."

Donna had sat down next to Dale, holding a newspaper. "Why would she buy us lunch? Because even losers are winners?" she asked, unimpressed.

"No, because we need to eat," Dale said.

"Is this place even worth fighting for?" Donna asked. She pointed to the new four-foot crack in the cement wall near the laundry room, which still had a broken window. "That wasn't because of the ghost of Dead Barbara or any other little story that you all want to tell yourselves. That's because this place is a dump, our landlord is guilty of neglect, and I'm almost scared to go out on my balcony for fear of plunging to my death. And if that happens, let me tell you, I will haunt this place. For the rest of time."

"You were out on your balcony this morning," Ilona said.

"I said I'm *almost* scared to go out on my balcony."

"This place is worth fighting for, Donna. I'm not ready to give up," Dale said.

Donna tossed the newspaper onto Dale's lap. Dale took the paper and saw the "Weekend Wanderings" headline. Under Saturday, March 12, she saw the entry:

1999 SOUTH FLORIDA SENIOR SYNCHRONIZED SWIMMING COMPETITION, Fort Lauderdale High School, Fort Lauderdale. *Take a trip down I-95 for the region's premier senior synchronized swimming competition. Watch the battle between defending champions, the Hydras of Hawthorne Haven, of the upscale senior complex in West Palm Beach, against newbies the Sirens of Soleil City, of the decidedly more modest senior apartment units in Hawthorne's shadow down the street. Will experience and a professional coach trump grit and determination? In the clash between the new West Palm Beach of ultra-manicured grounds and full-time activity coordinators and the old West Palm Beach of no-frills affordability that is fast disappearing under a developer's backhoe, who will come out on top?*

"Ha! A class war fought in the swimming pool. That's quite an angle," Phyllis said, holding her own copy of the *Palm Beach Post* and sitting down next to Donna.

"She came through," Dale said. "Our reporter. And with a nice little bias that suits us just fine."

"So what? She gets a few people down to Fort Lauderdale to boo at the rich kids and what will they see?" Donna asked. "They'll see the underdogs take on water. We'll lose, and we'll let them all down."

"She—Amanda—seems to have some confidence in us. She's seen our routine and she's seen Hawthorne's routine."

"She doesn't know that Evelyn left. She doesn't know— hell, we don't know—what that cow stole from us. She doesn't know that our coach is in the hospital. She doesn't know that I've just been diagnosed with cataracts. I need surgery or I'll see less than I do now. She thinks we're some kind of Golden Girls feel-good story. She thinks this little bone she's handed us in the newspaper—the 'Weekend Wanderings' column for God's sake?—is enough to set us all right."

"I'm sorry about your eyes, Donna," Phyllis said, tenderly.

"I'll be fine. I have my affairs in order. I'd like a soft gray coffin and a blues guitarist at my funeral. The instructions are on my dresser in the bedroom. Oh, and just so you know, I have no homemade porn stashed in my kitchen drawers like Barbara did."

Dale shuddered at the memory. Barbara did haunt them.

Ilona chortled. "You are not dying. This is routine surgery. Every day, they do this surgery."

"You think this is the end? This is just the beginning. Cataracts today, congenital heart failure tomorrow. Cancer. Stroke. We're hardly on the up-and-up. Look at Marlys. She had a little cough. And now . . ." Donna put her hand on Dale's arm.

Two days earlier, Dale had taken the Cape Cod painting to Palm Beach's fourth-best auction house. There, she had been greeted warmly, offered a cup of coffee, and told exactly what the painting was worth more than fifty years after it had changed Dale's life.

Dale would use the money—a respectable amount for a painting without a provenance—to bury Marlys. Cherie would offer to pay for all of it—the funeral home, the coffin, the headstone, the cemetery plot—but Dale would insist. This is what she could do for her friend. A final settling. The painting that had held decades of guilt sold to the highest bidder.

Cherie might have wanted the painting. Laura might have

liked it for her new home. But it wasn't a nice piece of art. It was the moment that Dale knew she would never be a good mother. It was the object that allowed Marlys to raise Dale's child right.

Before Marlys had nervously told Dale about it as she drove her home from the hospital that night, Dale had always known that Marlys was the one who had sent the slide of Dale's painting to San Miguel and called it Ed's work. There was no one else it could have been. Dale had never shown her husband the painting, the work that was better than anything that Ed had made then and would make in all the years since. Marlys was the only person who had ever seen it.

Marlys was the only person who knew what had happened on the beach that day, the decision Dale made to save her canvas instead of her daughter. She was the one who saw what Dale had been quietly fearing all those nights she laid awake with her daughter near her in their room in that Boston boardinghouse—*I don't know how to be a good mother. My mother is a bad mother, and I will continue on that legacy. I will hurt my daughter the way my mother hurt me.*

The Cape Cod painting was Dale's best work. She painted again, but never that well. She painted until she realized that painting had caused or come from pain. Painting had caused her to lose everyone she loved.

Now, the painting was gone. Off her wall, out of her life. Their lives. Just in time.

"We will go tomorrow. We will dance-swim. People will watch us," Ilona said, looking at Dale as she did, telling her friend that there was only one person she cared about, and who that was would not be mentioned. "We maybe win. We maybe lose. But we do not give up. We never give up. We have jobs. We lose jobs. We have money. We lose money. Husbands leave. Husbands die. Children . . ." She drifted off, not meeting any of their eyes. *Children love us. Children leave us.* "We do not give up."

"That goddamned Evelyn," Donna mumbled.

"Always that goddamned Evelyn," Phyllis said. "Remember the time she got us three free pints of ice cream by challenging the ice deliveryman to prove that his ice was the coldest in all of Palm Beach County?"

As Phyllis and Donna laughed and complained about Evelyn, Ilona put her head close to Dale's and whispered in her ear. "I will give Laura the green dress. Your green dress. When she is happy again, she will celebrate and wear the dress. Even if we aren't there with her, we can celebrate too."

CHAPTER 22

Competition Day

CHERIE

Cherie knew that she'd step in to become the sixth member of the Sirens the minute she heard that Evelyn had quit. Cherie knew the routine. Cherie knew the team. Cherie knew how to always make everything right.

Even when she couldn't. Even when her granddaughter was struggling to breathe. Even when her daughter was lying in a hospital bed. Even when her mother was facing a final walk through the hospital doors herself.

Synchronized swimming, Cherie could do. She could put on a black swimsuit covered in sequins. She could apply waterproof mascara and eyeliner and bright red lipstick with blue undertones. She could put her head underwater and listen to applause.

She wanted to do this. She wanted to be swallowed by the world of Soleil City for a few precious hours. She wanted to ride in Dale's Lincoln Continental for the fifty miles to Fort Lauderdale, with Fleetwood Mac turned to an audible but unobtrusive level as the women all hummed along. She wanted to hear Phyllis howl when Patty pinched her for taking too much legroom, a cry that broke up the quiet and served as a moment of opinion—

you didn't have to pinch her, Patty; you should know how to ride in a car, Phyllis—so they could all exhale.

The newspaper mention had changed things. The other women might not have believed that it would, but it had. It had brought competition day out of their little world and introduced it to others. People would come. People would care.

The equilibrium they had all managed in the car collapsed into nerves the minute they walked into the high school pool area that had been secured for the event. There was an entrance for the competitors—the team had established themselves as such by the misspelled warm-up jackets they wore—and a ticket booth for spectators. Though Donna had snorted when she first saw the professional nature of it all, declaring it ridiculously wishful thinking, she soon shut up when she looked around to see the rows of people, many mitigating the harshness of the concrete bleachers by sitting on hemorrhoid pillows.

"Are we late?" Dale asked.

"No," a woman in her own warm-up jacket replied, ready to guide them to the locker room. "People just came early."

Cherie asked if they could have a quick look at the pool. The women gathered around to see it, Olympic-sized and lovely, sparkling in the day's sunlight. Set up next to the long side of the pool was a table with seats for the three judges, stocked with notebooks and glasses of water and a banner on the front, scream-ing that they were at the 1999 SOUTH FLORIDA SENIOR SYNCHRONIZED SWIMMING COMPETITION. There was a bundle of red balloons that were haphazardly secured to the table's leg.

The women were led into the locker room, where they put on their swimsuits. They looked each other over, then looked at some of the women from the other teams. "At least we look like the real thing," Phyllis said. "Misspelled, but real."

After they were dressed, their swim caps in place, makeup touched up, towels under arms, they walked back out to the pool area, sitting on the bleachers to the left of the judges. "Just make sure we're out of earshot," Cherie said, motioning toward the judgment table.

As the MC welcomed the crowd and the last of the spectators streamed in, Cherie turned to see her mom in the stands, wearing a large straw hat and glamorous sunglasses. Next to her was Tom. She waved to them. When Cherie had first seen her husband running through the hospital halls to find her after he got to Florida, she had felt her heart flutter. She felt the warmth spread through her when he enveloped her in a hug. Cherie loved him. She had missed him.

This whole competition thing had been her stupid idea and not only had the people she loved gone along with it and even embraced it, they had followed through to the very end. This wasn't just writing a check or making a few phone calls. This was putting a group of women into a position they had never been in before in a very public way. And they had all believed that they could do it. She believed that she could do it.

The opening notes of Bobby Darin's "Beyond the Sea" began to play and the Bathing Beauties of Boca Raton began their routine to polite applause.

"I guess they found the one woman in South Florida over sixty-five who was willing to do backflips in the water," Donna observed, as the crowd enthusiastically showed their appreciation.

"That paramedic hanging out by the judges' table suddenly looks interested," Phyllis said. "He might get something to do."

"The other four women just look like they're hanging around, waiting for their water aerobics class to start. Real teamwork there," Patty said.

Cherie looked at Ilona, who concentrated on the pool. "They think they have a superstar," she said, nodding toward the water. "Look at the plugs in her ears. She isn't even trying to work with music. In fact," she said, pointing to the backflip woman brushing shoulders with the nearest team member. "I don't even think she knows the routine. I think they just brought her in and told her to flip."

"She's probably forty-five and a friend of a friend of a friend who was pretty good at gymnastics once upon a time," Patty said.

"The judges are buying it," Ilona pointed out.

The routine ended and the women watched as the Bathing Beauties were given a score that placed them at the top. The crowd seemed happy with the result.

"It's early," Patty said, brushing it away. "They won't stay there."

Cherie watched the man who was walking through the stands selling hot dogs and hoped that Tom would buy one for Marlys. Tom had gone to visit Marlys the night before after leaving Laura's bedside, before he went to his room at The Breakers. "I'm just . . . I'm so sorry, Cherie," he said with feeling, and Cherie knew that even in the time she had been in Florida, her mother had declined. He saw what she was still trying not to see. Before the sun back in Minneapolis could warm her enough to sit outside like she was doing now, her mother would likely be gone.

Cherie and Dale would be on their own, just like they had been at the beginning. Dale told her that she would pay for Marlys's coffin and gravesite. She insisted on that, and Cherie knew better than to challenge her, to ask any questions about from where the money had suddenly come. Her two mothers, sharing one daughter. Whatever agreement they had, spoken or unsaid, she knew it was a relationship that she would never understand. Where Cherie liked to see things in black and white,

Dale and Marlys, the former and present Mrs. Kellys, existed in a world of gray, a world whose unlisted rules she would never know.

The Hydras of Hawthorne Haven were announced and the women around her became still. The crowd did not appear to be on their side.

"This is it," Phyllis said, and Cherie saw Patty's jaw tense.

Evelyn looked away from her teammates and saw her former squad sitting in the stands. She nodded at them, then turned away.

"What does that mean?" Donna asked. "What has she done?"

The rest of the team were also there—Gladys with the vertigo, Elaine with the bum knee. They had all made it. The red tank suits they had worn for rehearsal were replaced by smooth silver tank suits with a stripe of large silver paillette sequins. It was an elegant look, pretty, but Cherie didn't imagine it would be distinctive once the women were in the water. By the way the women were pulling at the straps and elastic at the legs, it was clear the suits were new and unfamiliar.

As the opening notes began, the women of Soleil City turned to each other.

"Uh, this is not the song it was supposed to be," Phyllis said. "This isn't Simon and Garfunkel."

"Ho-ly shit!" Patty said, clapping her hands as the music continued.

"It's her karaoke song," Ilona said, eyes wide.

"She's sabotaged the whole goddamned thing," Dale said.

"Neutron Dance" by the Pointer Sisters blasted from the rented speakers and the women of Hawthorne—and the crowd—seemed momentarily stunned by the quick tempo.

Despite the significant change in the music, the routine hadn't changed since the women of Soleil City had seen the team perform. The Hydras continued to smile, but they were clearly struggling, missing the beat and getting flustered by their misses. Some of the crowd yelled words of encouragement. Some of the crowd seemed to snicker.

"Evelyn Murphy, what the hell have you done?" Donna asked, incredulous.

Patty clapped her hands and laughed. "She went into enemy territory, and she brought down the goddamned ship."

Cherie sat in awe. Evelyn had joined up with Hawthorne Haven to take them down. She had put her friendships on the line, had risked alienating the women she cared about the most, all to give them the win they needed. Evelyn did what Cherie tried to do by bringing Patty onto the squad, but she did it better. Much, much better.

There was the evidence, flailing wildly in the pool in front of her: Cherie didn't have to figure out everything herself. There was help. There were people who were better at things than she was.

As one of the women of Hawthorne began to cough up the water she had swallowed as she tried to keep up, Evelyn put her arms under the woman's armpits and kept her afloat. The women of Soleil City watched as Diane, the Hawthorne team's coach, desperately screamed at the women of her team, waving her arms around as if she herself were drowning in the middle of a rough sea.

"Poor Coach Diane is not having a good day," Donna observed.

The music finally, mercifully, ended. The grand finale move, whatever that may have been, had been scrapped in favor of basic survival. The women ended their routine by clinging to the edge of the pool, desperately trying to catch their breath. The crowd sat virtually silent, save for a few soft claps.

"The Hydras of Hawthorne Haven," the MC reiterated. "The 1998 South Florida Senior Synchronized Swimming Champions, everyone."

As she climbed out of the pool, Evelyn passed her friends in their incorrectly spelled warm-up jackets. This time, with the nod, came a wink.

"Goddamn," Patty said, beaming, and the other women echoed the sentiment. Then, before the women knew what was happening, before the crowd had refocused their attention on the pool, the Delray Beach Doyennes began their routine.

Performing to "Xanadu" by Olivia Newton-John, wearing bright orange suits trimmed in sequined daisies, and precise to the point of having their credentials as amateurs double-checked, the Doyennes were the synchronized swim team everyone else wished they might someday be.

"What the hell is happening here?"

"Delray Goddamned Beach? I didn't even know it was a real place. I just thought it was an exit off I-95."

"Look," Phyllis said, and the women followed her gaze. There, across the pool, was a woman in a sweatsuit with a large oxygen tank, sitting down and guiding the women with enthusiastic gestures. The women in the pool smiled at the judges, but their gaze kept turning toward their friend. They were doing this for her.

The routine ended to the roar of the audience. The judges couldn't give the Doyennes the top scores of the day fast enough.

The woman in her warm-up jacket beckoned to the women of Soleil City. They would be up next, after a short break. "One of the judges probably needs the bathroom. Bet you $100 it's a prostate issue," Patty announced.

If they had performed after Hawthorne, the crowd would have gone wild. The judges would have made the obvious comparison, and Soleil City would have come out on top. Instead, now, they would be compared to near perfection.

The women shuffled off the bleachers, their steps heavy. Cherie felt a tap on her shoulder as she walked toward the starting point and turned to see Tom holding his mobile phone in his hand.

"Oh God," Cherie said, suddenly panicked. "Is it the hospital?"

"It's from the hospital. Laura."

Tom handed Cherie his phone, and Laura directed Cherie to hold the phone up so the rest of the women could hear.

"That last team was good," Laura shouted through the phone as the women leaned in to hear her. "So what." Cherie looked at her husband. He must have been giving his daughter play-by-play commentary over the phone for the entire competition. "Here's the thing, ladies: Maybe we aren't the most technically accomplished team. Maybe we don't have anyone who will do a backflip. Maybe we don't always work together as well as we could."

"Giving us some real pep in our step here, Coach," Patty said, leaning into the phone.

Laura continued. "But no one else has worked as hard as we have."

"Hawthorne was doing two practices a day," Donna said.

Laura sighed very clearly on the other end of the line. "Fine. You bicker—good God, do you bicker—and you interrupt and you piss each other off, but you're there for each other. Through everything. If you win today, you'll celebrate together, working that ice machine at Soleil City harder than it's ever been worked before. But if you lose—"

Laura stopped and took a deep breath and the women leaned into the phone as far as they could without falling over. "If you lose, well, you won't be losers. Because you have each other. Do you know what that's worth? To have a group of friends like yours? That's worth more than any prize money. That's worth more than a big article in the *Palm Beach Post*. Trust me. I don't have nearly the wisdom of any of you, but I do know what it's like to realize you're surrounded by shitty people. You're not. You're surrounded by goodness. By love."

Laura moaned. "Now go get in that pool and get this over with, because I've got a nurse hovering over me wanting to stick something somewhere, and I'm not missing this."

Tom held his wife's hand as Cherie handed him his phone. "You'll do great," he said, and Cherie looked up at Marlys behind him. There, that's what she always wanted to remember. Marlys holding a hot dog as casually as if it were a cigarette, beaming at her daughter, her large-brimmed hat making her the most dazzling woman in the row.

The Sirens of Soleil City were announced. The women looked at each other and nodded solemnly before dropping their warm-up jackets. Cherie saw Donna squeeze Phyllis's hand before feeling Ilona's hand on her shoulder. Patty turned and raised her eyebrows at Dale. Dale smiled at her daughter. They walked to the edge of the pool, smiled brightly and artificially—the way Laura had made them practice—and waited for the song to begin.

As the opening notes of "We've Only Just Begun," by the Carpenters began to play, the women turned to smile at the spectators. The crowd roared with encouragement. "OG WPB, OG WPB!" a small crowd began to chant.

"What the hell?" Patty whispered and Donna answered, quickly, "Original Gangsters, West Palm Beach." Patty threw up her hands. "It's a good thing," Donna confirmed.

Donna waved, reveling in the moment, until the words of the

song began and they did the elegant, staggered dive they had spent the last week practicing. First Cherie, then Dale, then Phyllis, then Patty, then Ilona, and finally Donna, dove into the pool, emerging seconds later to continue their routine. The real smiles that now covered their faces showed that they felt the victory of the moment. Their hardest move was the first one, and now they could go on.

They gathered in the middle of the pool and swam in a clockwise circle, then switched to counterclockwise. From there, they broke into a star formation. As the music began to build at the one-minute mark of the routine, the crowd began to clap along. Cherie looked over at Dale, who was beaming.

They spun themselves around and then all dipped under the water, only to pop up and down in the Whack-a-Mole move that Laura claimed to have originated. The crowd loved it. The women went back underwater to swim together to the center of the pool, where they emerged from the water together, then fanned out in a circle before they reached down and released the snap on their swim skirts. Cherie craned her head as she moved. Dale had sewn one letter on each of the skirts so that when fanned out, the skirts would spell S-O-L-E-I-L.

Cherie felt the tears come to her eyes. Did Dale know how much Cherie appreciated everything she had done for her? All of it? Now, Dale was in the pool of a Fort Lauderdale high school after getting only a couple of hours of sleep, extending her leg and raising her arm. For a woman who convinced herself she'd be a terrible mother, she certainly knew exactly what was needed and when. Her instincts were just right.

The women spun themselves around and extended their legs, the effect of which was of the rays of the sun. The crowd understood—enough people had taken basic French, apparently—and jumped to their feet. The Sirens beamed as they swam into a line, holding onto each other's hands to make a chain, each giving the women on either side a squeeze, and swam across the pool to complete their routine. As the music wound down, they bowed their heads, then began to slowly sink into the water.

The music ended. The routine was over. As the crowd continued standing for their ovation, Cherie saw Evelyn whooping with glee. As Tom blew her a kiss and Marlys waved her hands over her head in celebration, Cherie realized she was crying. The emotions of the last three weeks swept over her like the ocean waves that wouldn't leave her dreams.

They had done it. They had done it well. The Sirens of Soleil City had become a team. Dale enveloped her daughter in a hug and after pulling her head up from her mother's shoulder, she saw Marlys looking at them both, smiling through her tears.

West Palm Beach, Florida

AUGUST 4, 2005

Epilogue

LAURA

Laura lowered herself into the pool as quietly as she could. The sun had only been up for a half hour and there wasn't yet any movement from the apartments in Soleil City.

Dale had died twelve hours earlier. The heart that had been slowly failing her for the last two years had stopped altogether. After Dale hadn't joined her family by the pool for a cocktail before dinner and after her nap, Laura's mother had found Dale unmoving in her bed.

Laura, her daughters, her husband Kyle, Ilona, Evelyn, and Phyllis were standing by the ice machine, taking turns putting an ice cube down the back of Laura's five-year-old daughter Marlo's shirt at her direct request—"More! More!"—as she screamed in delight. "My Ya-Yas," Marlo called the women, and they doted on her as if she were the greatest child on earth, followed only by Delia, Marlo's two-year-old sister.

Laura had run up the stairs to Dale's apartment when she heard her mother's cries. Her mother sat on the living room floor, crying big gulping sobs of grief. "She's gone. They're all gone now. They've all left me behind," she said, finally, and Laura put her arms around her mother as her own tears soaked her shirt.

Now, Laura closed her eyes to the sun as she floated on her back. Kyle would take the girls for a pancake breakfast. He'd stop by the side of the road to bring Laura and her mother a bag of oranges so they could squeeze the juice, a tradition they had started when they lived in Soleil City that spring of 1999. They were sad, but not surprised.

They had come to Florida now because Ilona had called Cherie to tell her that Dale's legs were swollen and she wasn't breathing as well. "It's like with Donna," she had said, and they knew what that meant. Donna's heart had stopped two years earlier. Cherie hung up the phone and booked them all a flight.

It would be another day until they could pick up Dale's ashes from the cremation society. Another day still until Dale's memorial service would be held right here, by the pool. Then, they would go home. In a couple of weeks, Laura and Kyle would start a new school year at the high school where Laura coached the danceline team and Kyle taught social studies. Marlo would start kindergarten. Delia would be introduced to potty training.

Marlo had cried when Laura told her that G-G Dale had died. "No more Christmas dresses for my dollies?" she had asked, and Laura had to tell her that there would be no more dresses from G-G D, that the next Christmas would be different without her G-G, but then after that, the Christmases would be the same. After that, they would live with the loss.

When Laura and her mother landed in West Palm Beach each March to watch Soleil City compete in the South Florida Senior Synchronized Swimming Competition, they lived with the loss of Marlys. They would drive by her townhouse, now trimmed with flowering bushes. They would leave a dozen croissants for the nurses at the NICU unit at the hospital who had cared for

Marlo, then another dozen croissants for the nurses who had cared for Marlys in her last days. They would pick up chicken salad sandwiches from the cafeteria on their way out, as Marlys would have insisted that they do.

Then they would return to Soleil City, to Dale and the other women who had anticipated their visit for months. They would look at the new cushions that Curt, the landlord, had purchased for the lounge chairs. They would comment on the freshness of the new white paint on the repaired stucco. They would greet the new faces that they hadn't yet met in the hallways.

They would get into the pool and slowly swim in a circle with their friends. They would laugh as they raised their legs at the same time. Sometimes they would just lie on their backs together, floating quietly, staring at the world above.

The previous night around midnight, after the girls were asleep at the hotel and Kyle had allowed anyone who wanted to to cry on his shoulder—and many, many did; he was incredibly popular in Soleil City—Phyllis and Evelyn had tentatively approached Laura.

"You'll still come to visit us, right? Are we going to lose you and Cherie and the girls too?"

"You're the Ya-Yas. Of course we'll still come," Laura said, and the women all wiped the tears from their eyes.

Laura dipped her head into the pool and kept her eyes closed as she pulled herself above water. She could sense the sun as it emerged from behind a cloud.

Three weeks in Florida five years ago had turned into a visit of almost three months. Laura arrived in West Palm Beach as a pregnant woman without a husband or a best friend. When she finally left, she was a mother. She was a granddaughter who had gotten to know one grandma before she got too sick to do much more than offer her hand to hold, and watched as the other grandma picked up her daughter and cared for her as if she had been doing just that all her life. She had found a different, more open version of her mother, one who could laugh when things weren't perfect and remind herself that they didn't need to be.

She had been embraced by a community of women who had their own rules and routines and irregularities. Women who were interesting and funny and maddening. Women who had screwed up and lived with the consequences, or who had chosen a different path and not looked back. Exactly the kind of women she needed to have in her life.

Now, she was married to her high school boyfriend after a simple wedding in her parents' backyard while wearing the green dress that had brought happiness to two important women in her life almost fifty years earlier. She had found true, deep love. She had also found a new best friend in her sister-in-law, and a renewed friendship with her sister. She had another baby. She had an amazing job coaching a team of teenaged girls. She had a life that she appreciated, one that wasn't perfect, but that was exactly right. A life that would keep her in one place or send her in many directions. A life filled with love.

Palm Beach Post

AUGUST 5, 2005

WEST PALM BEACH, FL—Dale Elizabeth Walker of West Palm Beach died Friday, August 3rd, at home with her family by her side. She was seventy-nine.

A native of Boston, MA, Mrs. Walker was the daughter of the late William and Elizabeth Rowen. She was an artist.

Mrs. Walker is survived by a daughter, Ceres Anderson (Tom) of Minneapolis; granddaughters Laura Tremmel (Kyle) and Jessica Anderson of Minneapolis, MN, and New York, NY; and great-granddaughters Marlo and Delia Tremmel.

In addition to her parents, Mrs. Walker was predeceased by husbands Ed Kelly and Frank Walker, and friend Marlys Kelly.

A memorial service will be held at the Soleil City apartment complex in West Palm Beach, FL, on Wednesday. In lieu of flowers, donations may be made to the Donna Howard Literacy Fund, care of the Sirens of Soleil City Synchronized Swimming Team, the 2001 and 2003 South Florida Senior Synchronized Swimming Champions.

ACKNOWLEDGMENTS

Though this book is a work of fiction, it was inspired by my grandmothers, Barbara Davis and Jane Spinney. They had *very* different opinions about marriage and motherhood, but were in total agreement about their love for their daughter, my mom. Of all the things my mom learned during her rather unconventional childhood, the importance of having a deep love for your children was, thankfully for myself and my three siblings, the one that stuck.

I would like to thank Jennifer Pooley for taking the big pile of words I dumped on her and expertly pulling out the threads that I could weave into this story. Her enthusiasm for the book from the very beginning was the boost I needed to keep going. Ivy Pochoda put her own enthusiasm into action by orchestrating one of the best introductions of my life, to my agent, Kim Witherspoon.

Thank you to that agent, Kim, along with Jessica Mileo at Inkwell Management. They knew where this book needed to go and through edits, conversation, and a very considered list of options, made sure it landed in the right hands: my editor at Random House, Andrea Walker.

Thank you to Andrea for loving this book. I felt that affection from our first conversation, which made me know it had all gone the way it was supposed to go. The whole team at Random House, especially Noa Shapiro and Monica White, have been incredible to work with.

Thank you to Ryan Wilson at Anonymous Content, who saw the possibilities for this book and launched a plan to bring it off the page.

Thank you to Joanna Curtis, my best friend since high school, who has happily read everything I have allowed her to see and has always believed that this whole writing thing could go somewhere.

Thank you to my friends for their enthusiasm and encouragement. Though I kept this book pretty close to the vest (fool me once and all that . . .), their responses after I began to share news was amazing. Thanks to Rebecca Frederick, Amy Erickson, Karah Bausch, Dave and Colleen Clements, Amy Gattie and Erik Larson, Lance Mendelow, Ed Feldman, Sara Arnold, George Norman, Lisa Jorgensen, Suzanne McCormack, Pat and Catherine Rouleau, Steve and Amy Misterek, Jeanne and Mark Pakulski, Chris Henkemeyer and Matthew DeLeon, and to Jeff Wheeler.

Thank you also to my parents, Ron and Sheila Johnson, for their encouragement and nudges through the years, and to my siblings, Carrie Chang, Chris Johnson, Aaron Johnson, and their spouses, Jin Chang and Malene Johnson. Thank you, also, to my in-laws, Kit and Jerry Henkemeyer.

Finally, thank you to Scott, my husband. You have always been supportive of the time and space I've needed to keep going. Your love and pride mean the world to me. And to my children, Owen and Willa. You are both the very best things I'll ever bring into this world.

ABOUT THE AUTHOR

SARAH C. JOHNS is a writer and video producer. After studying in South Africa, Hungary, Israel, and Germany, she graduated from McGill University before attending film school in Sydney, Australia. She lives with her family in St. Paul, Minnesota.